STEPHANIE AMEY has wor
as Chemistry Teacher, scientist, ̣   ...g.......... a...u .icaiui a..u
safety adviser. She worked in Yorkshire, Kenya and Guatemala
before settling in Norfolk. She has previously published two
novels, 'Holloway 8632' and 'An honourable Man'.

Born in Widnes, Steph lived in Brampton for several years as
a child, very close to Hadrian's wall and this is where her interest
in Roman Britain began. Her latest novel *The Edge of Empire* is a
thriller set on Hadrian's wall during the Roman occupation. Now
she spends her time horse riding, reading thrillers, volunteering
as a Magistrate and, of course, writing. She is currently working
on the sequel to *The Edge of Empire*.

THE
EDGE OF
EMPIRE

Stephanie Amey

Northodox Press Ltd
Maiden Greve, Malton,
North Yorkshire, YO17 7BE

This edition 2024

1
First published in Great Britain by
Northodox Press Ltd 2024

ISBN: 978-1-915179-29-6

This book is set in Caslon Pro Std

To the memory of my brother Mike George, who bravely fought a long battle against cancer. And to his daughters – Jessica and Emily for whom he kept going.

AD 170 BANNA FORT, HADRIAN'S WALL
SOME OF THE PEOPLE LIVING IN THE FORT
AND IN THE COMMUNITY AROUND IT

Silvius Tatius - Prefect in command of Banna Fort

Julia Prima - Tatius' wife

Julius Maximus - Centurion at Banna

Aurelius Petrus - *Optio* - second-in-command to Maximus

Quirinus – *Tesserarius* – watch commander in Maximus' century

Argentus, Germanus, Flavius, Corvinus - soldiers in Maximus' century

Manius - the librarius or record keeper for Maximus' century

Aquilinus - Centurion at Banna fort

Vester, Celsus, Janus, Justus - soldiers in Aquilinus' century

Fabius Ruga – Centurion at Banna fort

Suasso, Albiso, Luci – local tribesmen, working as irregular forces at the fort

Sylva – owner of the brothel

Cara and Metta – prostitutes at the brothel

Carantii – the local blacksmith

Eburacia – Carantii's sister

Aurora – Petrus' wife

Foslius Septimus – Prefect in command at Camboglanna fort, Hadrian's wall

Fabia – wife of Septimus

Carius – Centurion at Camboglanna fort

Chief Gna - local chief of the Carvetti tribe

TERMS

Vicus – the settlement around the fort

Hastile – wooden staff with metal top

Vinestaff – short stick with metal top – symbol of a centurion

Signifer – the Senior record keeper and treasurer at the fort

Librarius – record keeper

Contubernia – a team of eight men, who shared accommodation

Immune – a skilled tradesman, like a carpenter or mason, who did not have to take part in the daily tasks of regular soldiers

Praetorium – the commanding officer's house

Principia – the headquarters building

Pugio – short dagger carried by soldiers

Pilus prior – the most senior centurion at the fort

Pilus posterior – the second most senior centurion at the fort

Hipposandals – a type of horseshoe

Prologue

Four days before the Nones of Martius…

It was the tenth hour of the day, that moment when the light begins the fight with the approaching darkness. Petrus hurried through the vicus. Aurora had sent for him as their son Titus was ill. Petrus was exhausted. Over the last few days, the troops had been on miles and miles of route marches, over the hills, through cold streams and screed valleys. Every muscle in his body ached. He wanted to lie down and sleep, but he had to go and see Titus. Aurora wouldn't have sent for him if it wasn't urgent.

The icy wind bit at his face and dragged at his clothes, pulling him back towards the fort. The mud beneath his feet was thickening and freezing as ice spread across the ground. The tavern door opened, and two drunk soldiers tumbled into the street. Petrus knew he should have given them the standard speech about upholding the honour of the army and appropriate behaviour in the community, but he didn't have the strength. His son was ill. He pressed on.

The streets were emptying as people made their way home. Darkness came quickly during the winter months. It could be dangerous in the streets at night. The stale odour of rotting food hung around the marketplace. A running man bumped into Petrus, jarring his shoulder, and knocking him forward. He stumbled but managed to stay on his feet. The man did not react to Petrus' shouts and curses as he ran on.

Petrus reached the area close to the army's parade ground,

where Aurora's father had built a home alongside other retired soldiers' houses and merchants' premises. He knocked on the door. The key rattled in the lock, the door opened, and he entered the lamplit warmth of the kitchen. Aurora closed the door and stepped towards him.

'I'm so glad you're here' she whispered, 'I've been so worried. He's fitting. Mincona is with him.'

He pulled her close, gently stroking her auburn hair and kissed the top of her head. Her breathing slowed as she relaxed against his body. Her voice drowned in the folds of his cloak as she told him about his son's fits.

She led him across the part-covered yard and opened the bedroom door. In the candlelight, Mincona, their maid, sat on the edge of the bed with her hand on Titus' shoulder. His eyes were fixed wide open, his body rigid and twitching. Mincona rose as they entered and left the room. Aurora knelt beside Titus and placed a hand on his forehead.

They watched and waited.

Suddenly Titus' body went limp, his eyelids fluttered and closed as he took some deep breaths. They waited for what seemed like an eternity, watching his chest rise and fall. He remained asleep.

'My brave boy,' Petrus bent down and planted a kiss on Titus' cheek. He was the image of his father, with dark hair, startling big blue eyes, and a little dimple on his chin. Petrus covered him with a blanket.

In the kitchen a faint smell of meat stew hung in the air. Mincona was stirring the pot on the fire; she added another log, it crackled and spat as it caught light. She poured three cups of ale from a pitcher and motioned to Petrus to sit at the table. Mincona took her own drink and left them.

'We need to get help; these fits could kill him. People will think he's possessed. I've been to the Temple of Jupiter,' she paused, 'And, I've asked around. A woman has been talked about, someone who can cure people. She lives near the forest.'

Petrus shook his head, 'We're not going to give him treatments recommended by old women. I've spoken with the physician at the Fort's infirmary, a man of medicine. He says we just have to wait, pray to the gods, and hope that Titus grows out of it. I will also go to the Temple of Jupiter and pray for him, I promise.'

Petrus took a deep breath and crossed his fingers as he made the promise. He had lost faith in many of the Gods, including Jupiter. He still went through the rituals, made sacrifices, and intoned the words, but he didn't believe in their power. How could Gods allow the atrocities that he'd seen during his life as a soldier? He made the promise, what else could he do?

He took Aurora's hand. 'I must go back to the barracks. Orders are to be back by the end of the second hour of the night. I'm so tired, they've been driving us so hard.'

She smiled, 'Are you really so tired?' she paused, 'Mincona has gone to her room.' She led him out of the kitchen towards their bedroom.

Petrus had to leave; he'd fallen asleep, it would be light soon. He hugged Aurora, picked up his cloak and stepped outside.

The fetid odour of the sewers rose to meet him. He slipped on the ice and staggered a couple of steps as he tried to regain his footing. Ahead of him, the moonlit fort floated on the wispy fog rising from the ditch, and spreading like smoke in the road ahead of him. Shouts and grunts from a nearby fight reached him in the darkness. He pulled his cloak tighter around him and walked on. It was nothing to do with him.

'I'll kill you!' Petrus recognised Drusus' voice. Damn him. Petrus would have to intervene.

Beneath the flaming torch lighting the brothel's side entrance, two men grappled with each other. Faustus, with his left eye swollen shut and lips bleeding, held Drusus' red hair in one hand and punched him repeatedly in the stomach with the other. Drusus gasped and grunted with each strike.

'Stop!' Petrus yelled as he walked towards them.

The two men did not react. Drusus reached beneath his tunic and pulled out a metal spike. Petrus stepped forward, placed his arm around Drusus' throat and pulled him backwards. He screeched. Faustus stared at the clump of Drusus' hair left in his hand, let it fall to the ground and readied to charge.

'Stop! I am Aurelius Petrus! Stop!'

Faustus looked up, lost his footing, and struggled upright to stand to attention. Petrus felt the other man go limp in his arms. He released his grip and Drusus slid to the muddy ground. He crawled forward and scrambled to his feet, turning to stare wide-eyed at his officer. He tried to wipe his hands clean on his tunic, smearing vomit on his clothes. The stink of piss was all around them.

'What in the name of Jupiter is going on?' Petrus growled.

'Just a fight Sir, over a girl,' mumbled Faustus, wiping his bloody mouth with the back of his hand.

'And bringing the Roman Empire into disrepute! Get back to the fort! See me after parade. Go Now!'

'What about Germanus?' mumbled Faustus.

'Germanus? Where is he?'

'In there, Sir,' Drusus pointed towards the tavern, 'at least, he was.'

'Get back to barracks, I'll deal with him.'

Petrus pushed open the battered oak door. The stench of beer and regurgitated food assaulted him as he entered. One torch remained alight in the room. It dripped wax onto the floor and cast a dim light over the tavern's only remaining customer, who was slumped forward with his head on the table in a pool of part-digested food. He snored and gurgled. With each breath the vomit rippled round his mouth and nostrils. In the shadows of the room, the taverner and his woman gathered cups and emptied jugs. Petrus approached the table and kicked the man's stool. There was no response. He grabbed Germanus by the hair, lifted him upright and slapped him hard across the face.

'Wh-wh-what?' Germanus opened his eyes. He jerked his

head back and brought his fists up ready to fight.

'Don't even think about it Germanus!' Petrus growled, 'It's me, Aurelius Petrus. Get up!'

Petrus dragged Germanus to his feet and pushed him out of the door. Holding him at arms' length, Petrus marched him along the track running by the fort's ditch. Germanus tripped and Petrus struggled to stop him sliding into the ditch.

They reached the gatehouse. Petrus banged on the gate. There was no response.

He banged again and shouted, 'Open up!'

Something stirred inside the fort. 'Approach the gate,' a tired voice said.

Petrus leant Germanus against the wall and waited for them to open the spyhole.

'Password?'

'Tabernum.'

The spyhole closed. There were scraping noises as the gate opened. Petrus grabbed Germanus and pushed him through. He fell forwards onto the ground.

Petrus turned towards the guards and growled, 'You lazy bastards were asleep!' He pointed at Germanus, 'Help him! It's only a short time before you're all due at Parade!'

Without looking back, Petrus walked down the dark street and past the barracks. Snores rumbled from open windows. The soft moans and grunts of couples having sex spread out into the darkness.

He reached the rooms kept separate for the centurions and their junior officers. They smelled of fresh straw and damp clothes. He closed the door to his room behind him and hoped he hadn't disturbed the centurion, Julius Maximus. He lay down on the bed and closed his eyes.

Aurora thought she was pregnant. They were not officially man and wife. Petrus had another ten years to serve, and he worried that he would be transferred elsewhere in Britannia, or to another country, or worse still, be killed. Aurora would then be left alone with their children and few rights as an unmarried mother. He had written a will when Titus was born stating that Aurora was his wife and that she should inherit everything he had, all monies and possessions. There was nothing else he could do for now.

I – Dies Solis

The light sneaked into Petrus' room. He struggled into consciousness, yawned, pulled on his boots and shoved his helmet down over his unruly hair. He grabbed his hastile; his fingers fit neatly into the well-worn marks on the oak stick made by its previous owners. He made his way to the parade area inside the fort, for the daily roll check and to listen to the day's orders. They only went to the much larger parade ground outside the fort on important days to demonstrate their power to the local populace.

Petrus hid a yawn as the rain drizzled down and soaked into his clothes. His breath hovered like fog around his face in the chilled morning air. He read his report from the day before, it included the behaviour of Faustus, Drusus, and Germanus, who were all in Maximus' century. Faustus and Drusus were not present.

'This type of behaviour will not be tolerated!' shouted Maximus across the yard. A short stout man, Maximus made up for his lack of height with a fierce rage. 'Some of you are not even fit to be here!' He pointed his vinestaff at two very scruffy men who shuffled their feet, eyes downcast.

Petrus searched the men's faces and settled on Germanus who swayed slightly, his face red with the effort of standing upright. Petrus whispered to one of the immunes who stood near him and the man moved towards Germanus and tapped him on the shoulder, instructing him to report to the centurion's office. Petrus wondered what Maximus would do to punish the young man, and maybe even Petrus himself for being out so late.

After joining the army as an auxiliary soldier, Petrus had been sent to Britannia and served under Aurora's father, Ramirus, centurion at Fanum Cocidi. Petrus had shown himself to be an able soldier and Ramirus had chosen him as his second-in-command, his optio. When Ramirus had been promoted and moved to Banna fort, Petrus had moved with him. Ramirus had retired and was replaced by Maximus as the most senior centurion at the fort, the princeps. Maximus had kept Petrus as Optio, but Petrus had always felt insecure. Maximus was quick to punish and slow to praise. The prospect of demotion and transfer to another unit hovered over the heads of all the junior officers ,regardless of how many years of good service they'd given.

At the office, Maximus stood right up close to Petrus' face; his hot breath forced its way into Petrus' nostrils. Petrus fought to stand still and not flinch.

Maximus roared 'You didn't check with the gatekeepers that they'd got back?' His thick black hair dripped water from his forehead and ran like blood along the broad scar which ran from his nose across his cheek. Maximus was legendary on the battlefield and his thick body bore the marks of many encounters. Today he had bloodshot eyes and looked like he had not slept in weeks. Germanus knelt before him in the headquarters building, the Principia.

'I assumed they would've got back before us. I was delayed by this poor excuse for a soldier,' Petrus nudged Germanus in the small of the back with his foot, knocking him forward.

Germanus remained lying face down with his arms by his sides. Maximus raised his stick and struck him repeatedly across the back, grunting with the effort. Germanus moaned quietly.

It was Maximus' responsibility to find the missing men. He needed Petrus' help. He pointed at Petrus, 'Find out what Germanus knows and send men to find those drunken bastards.'

'I've already ordered Suasso and his men to check the ditches. It was foggy last night, they could've fallen in, they were so drunk.'

'Not very likely, is it? If they had, they would've crawled back out,' Maximus began moving away.

'They could've died in the cold last night. They didn't have cloaks with them.'

'I want a report before dark,' Maximus waved his hand and did not look back as he walked away.

'Take him to his barracks and clean him up. Then I want to talk to him,' Petrus instructed the two auxillae who had brought Germanus to him and witnessed the beating.

They took Germanus by the shoulders, dragged him upright, and helped him towards the barracks.

Petrus went to wait at the East gate; he wore his red tunic and his helmet and carried his hastile. He wanted the people of the vicus to see him. The tall figure of Suasso approached on a brown and white horse, accompanied by two other men. Suasso's long thick auburn hair straggled down the back of his rough brown shirt. His face had a blue tattoo of an eagle across each cheek. An expert horseman, he rode with only one hand on the reins, the other rested on the scabbard at his belt, ready to grab the boned hilt of his sword at the slightest provocation. Suasso was the son of a great tribal chief. In previous times, he might have been taken to Rome as a hostage, trained as a soldier and sent to fight for the Empire. He'd been allowed to stay near his people and work with other local tribesmen as irregular troops supporting the Roman army. The irregulars provided the Army with additional armed men for fighting and tracking and were also a good source of local information. They were known as numeri, or more often, "barbarians" by the army and its officers. They were under the orders of the Centurion but would respond to the Optio's instructions if they believed he spoke with the centurion's authority.

'There's no sign of 'em in the ditches, no slip marks, no footprints,' said Suasso, 'Mind you, prints would probably've been washed away by the overnight rain. But there was this,' he drew something out from under his shirt and made to pass it to Petrus.

Suasso's horse began to whinny and move backwards. He dropped the object and steadied the animal with both hands on the reins. 'Whoa! Whoa, steady there.'

The horse danced on the spot, its hooves churned the ground and there was a flash of metal which disappeared in the mud.

'Bastard!' Suasso kicked the horse forward, almost mowing Petrus over.

'Get that bloody animal under control!' shouted Petrus as he crouched down. He pressed his hands into the mud and scrabbled around. His fingers closed around a metal object, he pulled it up and wiped it on the grass. It looked like the spike Drusus had had with him the night before.

'It's Drusus'. Show me where you found it.'

Suasso walked his horse across the causeway. Petrus followed at a distance to avoid the spattered mud thrown up by the horse's feet.

'Here, just near the bathhouse,' Suasso pointed. 'He must've dropped it.' The mud was churned up, mixed with leaves, bits of food and animal faeces. 'Could've been a scrap with others involved. They could've run that way,' he pointed down the alley past the bathhouse.

Petrus turned back to look at the fort.

'They were within sight of the gatehouse. The guards should've seen it if something happened. They made no report this morning and nothing was said last night. Bastards were asleep.'

That meant the men had several hours head start.

'Send men to track them,' he said over his shoulder to Suasso, 'I want them found.'

He walked back across the causeway and rapped on the gate.

'Amphorae', he murmured and was allowed to enter.

'You were on duty last night, weren't you?' he asked the man who let him in.

'Yes Sir.' The man stood to attention. He was short and squat with red hair and freckles. 'We're on duty from the fourth hour after sunset 'til the fourth hour after sunrise,'

'So, I've got here just before your change of guard?'

'Yes Sir,'

'During the night, do you remember letting me in, with a very drunk man, Germanus?'

'Yes Sir, I do. He fell to the ground, and you ordered us to help him to his barracks, which we did.'

Petrus nodded, 'And shortly before that – did you let in two other men who were drunk? One with red hair?'

'No Sir, we did not.'

'Before I came through, did you see or hear anything going on over there near the bathhouse?' he pointed.

'No sir. Nothing.'

'And what about your comrade hiding up there?' He pointed to the gatehouse and raised his voice, 'Get down here now!'

The man clambered down, clattering his sword and shield against the stone steps. He straightened his uniform and saluted Petrus, his face red with embarrassment. He had strange green eyes below his dark fringe.

'I didn't see anything either Sir. Really, I didn't,' he said.

'Asleep, were you?' barked Petrus.

'No Sir, not asleep. We didn't see or hear anything before you came. We would've reported it,' the red-headed man said.

'Give me your names!' spat Petrus.

'Rufus,' the red-haired man said, 'and Pius,' he pointed at the other man.

'Well Rufus and Pius,' Petrus emphasised the words, 'The Tesserarius will hear about you two falling asleep. Shit gatekeepers. I hope he beats you and docks your pay. Get back on duty!'

The two men scurried back up into the gatehouse and Petrus made his way to the headquarters. Germanus was waiting outside flanked by the two soldiers. He wore a clean red tunic which clung to his back where the physician had rubbed grease on his skin to soothe it after the beating. He straightened up as Petrus approached, pain crossing his handsome face. Petrus sat at his table and picked up a blank tablet and a stylus. He scratched the date into the wax and then looked up at Germanus.

'Tell me about last night. Did you know Faustus and Drusus were planning to run away?' Petrus spoke quietly.

'No Sir,' Germanus shook his head, 'All I know is, they'd been in the brothel and when they saw me, they asked if I wanted to go for a drink. I-I hadn't had a drink in ages. Been saving my money. It went straight to my head, that's how you came to find me in that state.'

Petrus leaned across the table, he smelt rank stale beer on the man's breath.

'What did you talk about?'

Germanus shrugged and winced in pain, 'Nothing really. There're some new girls at the brothel they said, said I should get down there. They were celebrating their good fortune but didn't explain. I was happy enough to drink the beer they paid for and didn't need to ask anything else.'

'Were the others from your room in the tavern as well?'

'No Sir, just me.'

'What were you doing in the afternoon? Before you met Faustus and Drusus?'

'I, err, I'd been looking for a woman.'

'Looking for a woman? What do you mean? A specific woman, or any woman? Where were you looking?'

'There's a family who keep their animals just beyond the vicus. The daughters are often there gathering food. One of them, well, we… you know… there in the trees.'

'Is this a regular thing?'

'Yeah, kind of.'

'And that took all afternoon?

'Well yes, we had a bit of fun and then I was walking back through the vicus when I met those two.'

Petrus sighed, 'Get out of my sight!'

Petrus pressed the stylus hard into the wax as he made his notes on the tablet and then locked it in the office chest, placing the key in the pouch on his belt. He sent for Quirinus, the Tesserarius, who was in charge of the gatekeepers. Quirinus looked alarmed as he entered Petrus' office.

'Quirinus,' Petrus spoke before the man had a chance to salute him, 'I returned late to the fort last night and the gatekeepers Rufus and Pius didn't hear me banging on the gate. They also didn't see a ruckus near the bathhouse involving the two men who are missing. What were they doing if they didn't see that fight?'

'I, err,' Quirinus brushed his hand through his thick black hair.

'They were asleep, the shits were asleep!' Petrus spoke through gritted teeth.

Quirinus stared straight ahead, in silence.

'Sort them out! That's your job! See that they're doing their bloody duty!' hissed Petrus. 'I'm putting that in my report to Maximus.'

Quirinus saluted and left the room. Petrus rubbed his chin thoughtfully. He liked Quirinus; the young man had only been in post for a couple of months. Petrus thought he deserved a chance, no-one got it right when they were first promoted, but he wasn't sure Maximus would be so forgiving.

Later, Petrus walked towards the brothel. The torch outside the front of the brothel was still alight, meaning that it was open for custom. He'd never known the brothel closed to business. He nodded to the large man just inside the door who acted as doorkeeper and would drag customers out of the building if they caused trouble. Petrus walked into the salon where several men were sipping wine as they lounged against thick red cushions on the couches. They looked alarmed when they saw him, immediately rose to their feet, and went away.

Sylva entered the room in a haze of perfume with a slave girl trailing behind her. Sylva's plaited blonde hair hung in loops on the sides of her head, like a Greek Goddess. She settled on a couch and pulled her robe tighter across her body, accentuating the shape of her large breasts and hard nipples. Noticing the direction of Petrus' gaze, she pulled a shawl around her, obscuring the view. She sat with her knees spread widely apart and her feet planted firmly on the ground, like a man. As a local woman there were some finer points of etiquette which still eluded her. She had been the unofficial wife of an auxiliary soldier. When he died on duty, she had been left with three daughters, no rights, and no income. She'd begun working at this same brothel and become the old madam's favourite. She had helped her run the place and had eventually taken over the business when the old madam became ill. Her three daughters lived in the building but did not work as whores. No matter how much money Sylva was offered, their bodies were not for sale. Business was thriving and Sylva paid rent and a lot of tax to the Roman army.

'Petrus,' she purred, 'Have you need of the comforts of this establishment?'

'I'm looking for information about two men who were here last night, Faustus and Drusus.'

'I don't often ask for names. We had several in from the fort last night. I think you must've all been paid recently.'

Petrus sighed. 'Drusus, short man, red hair. Faustus dark hair, flat nose. He had one of those strange birth markings on his arm. They probably didn't speak in the local languages.'

'Ah yes, most of them are those foreign types. I'll ask the girls, find out who was with them. It might take a while, some of them are working. Why don't you relax and have a drink?' she waved her hand towards an empty couch.

He sat down. The slave stepped forward, opened a chest behind Sylva's couch and took out an engraved cup. She poured wine, handed him the cup and then moved back to stand against the wall. Sylva rose, muttered instructions to the slave and left the room. Two women entered. Their short tunics were cut low at the front, showing the blue tattoos of holly leaves snaking from their cleavages up towards their necks. This was how Sylva had marked them as hers. Petrus gulped down the wine and set his empty cup on a nearby table. The slave stepped forward to pour a refill.

Petrus placed his hand over the cup, shaking his head, 'I could be here for a while.' He leant back against the cushions and closed his eyes. He wondered whether the missing men had stolen some horses or bluffed their way into "commissioning" them from some local farmer, claiming that the army needed them. That would have needed a lot of bravado, as they weren't in uniform.

The sweet smell of incense reached his nostrils from a bowl of smoking liquid in the corner of the room. He opened his eyes when he heard movement as Sylva returned.

'Follow Riacus, he'll take you to Cara and Metta. They're Carvetti. They've no Latin,' Sylva said.

Petrus bowed his head in thanks, she waved him away, 'Next time, come for business.'

He followed Riacus, who was a tall man with a shaved head. He wore a tunic that was open at the front down to his belly and he had a blue holly tattoo across his chest. They moved down a long hallway whose lit candles dripped hot tallow into solidifying puddles on the floor. Their grey smoke snaked up towards the straw ceiling, coating it black. Two young women in long robes approached them, their long dark hair partly hiding their faces. They turned sideways to allow the men to pass in the narrow space. Petrus turned his body away from them as he walked. One of them touched his buttocks and pressed her breasts against his back. He flinched and shrugged her off, but his body reacted, and he felt himself stiffen.

Near the end of the hallway, the candles flickered as they struggled to stay alive. Riacus opened a door and gestured for him to enter the room. He followed Petrus in, closed the door and stood leaning with his back against it and his arms crossed over his chest. Lit torches flanked a large bed, laden with cushions and jumbled bedding. Two young women huddled together on a couch; they clutched huge black cloaks around them; their pale white hands were marked with Sylva's tattoos. Their feet were bare, and the outside ankle of each foot also had the holly tattoo. Petrus winced, ankles have little flesh, tattooing them must have hurt the women a lot. Sylva was a hard woman.

He grabbed a stool, dragged it to sit facing them and smiled. 'I am Aurelius Petrus, from the fort,' he spoke in the local language, trying to put them at ease.

They looked like twins; their round faces and blue eyes mirrored each other. They had their straw-coloured hair tied up in the same way, but one had hers pinned slightly to the left, the other slightly to the right. They stared at him, glanced at each other, and then looked back at him.

'Cara and Metta, isn't it?'

They did not respond.

'You're sisters, aren't you? Don't be afraid. I only want to ask you about last night. About two of the customers you were with,' he paused, looking at each in turn. 'They were soldiers, one with red hair and one with a large purple mark here on his arm,' he rubbed his right forearm, 'Do you remember them?'

The women sat silently, staring at him. He waited.

'Shall I fetch Sylva?' He cringed inside as he said that. He hadn't wanted to frighten the girls, but he needed information.

'Yes,' murmured one of them, 'we remember them. They wanted to be together, with the two of us. They always wanted to be together with us.'

Petrus smiled, 'Are you Cara?'

She shook her head.

'Metta then. You'd been with them several times before last night?'

She nodded, 'They always asked for us.'

'Did you know them well?'

She shrugged.

'Tell me, what did they talk about last night?'

'Men don't talk much when they come here,' answered Cara.

'Were they drinking a lot? How did they seem?'

'Wild. They seemed a bit wild and maybe a bit… a bit…' mumbled Cara, looking at her sister.

'Worried,' Metta finished.

'Why?'

Metta did not respond.

'Where they scared perhaps?' he persisted.

Silence.

'Is there anything else you can tell me?'

They shook their heads, pulled their cloaks tighter around their shoulders and seemed to shrink away from him.

He sighed. 'Thank you, both of you.' He stood up.

Riacus opened the door and stepped into the corridor. Petrus placed some coins on the table and then followed him. They passed a small boy replacing the burnt-out candles in the corridor. They reached the salon and Sylva wafted back towards them. The local men had resumed their seats on the couches.

'Did you get what you were after?' she trilled.

'Can you tell me which other men from the fort have been here recently?' Petrus asked.

'I don't keep a list of clients,' she smiled.

'Of course you don't,' he muttered, thinking he would need to speak to her privately about it; she might be more forthcoming if they were not being overheard by local men.

'It might be easier to have a list of men who don't come here,' Sylva continued, 'after all, there are many soldiers, and also many important men who come here – your prefect and your centurion to name but two.'

Petrus walked back to the fort where he made plans to ride out the next day in case the barbarians returned empty-handed. He wrote his report on tablets, recording all the information he had gained at the brothel and his plan to get a list of the men who'd been there that day if Faustus and Drusus were not found. He detailed the gatekeepers' declaration that nothing happened near the bathhouse the night before. However, he wrote that he believed they had fallen asleep and included his discussion with the Tesserarius, Quirinus. Germanus had given him a list of the names of the other men in his team, or contubernia. They all shared a room and Petrus suggested that they be interviewed if the two men remained missing, in case they knew what the two men had been planning. He gave the report to Maximus.

'We could also find out what their duties had been recently and whether they'd been outside the fort much in the last few days.'

Maximus snapped, 'Do you think you need to tell me how to do my job, Petrus? I'll question the contubernia tomorrow, unless the men have already been found. We'll leave Quirinus for now, hopefully he can sort his men out.'

Petrus was surprised and pleased at Maximus' uncharacteristic response. He'd expected him to fly into a rage about the gatekeepers. Quirinus might be able to prove himself by getting his men in order. Petrus and Maximus left the fort to monitor the repairs to the wall. The raiding tribes from the north had overrun it and also damaged some of the milecastles.

Suasso and his men returned as the sun was moving towards the horizon and the cold had tightened its grip on the afternoon. Petrus rushed to meet them at the gate, hopeful for news.

'A body has been found,' Suasso said.

'Where? Who?' asked Petrus.

'In the Temple of Cocidius. Some local people told us about it. They say he's a soldier. I think that means he's in a tunic and boots.'

'Which people? Where are they?' asked Petrus.

Suasso shrugged, 'We were just coming back, when we met two men hurrying in this direction, they stopped us and said we should go to the Temple of Cocidius, where there was a body. We saw no reason to detain them. We came straight here, as its about to get dark and we thought it best to go out in the morning, to the temple, I mean.'

'You should've detained them. We might've wanted to question them.' Petrus was annoyed.

'We didn't think it was important,' said Suasso, carelessly.

Petrus suppressed a groan. He was sure that if Maximus had sent the barbarians out, they would have kept hold of the local people. He was angry and frustrated; he did not have the authority to send Suasso and his men anywhere or complain about their actions. He could only ever hope that they would cooperate with him. He knew that he would bear the brunt of Maximus' disappointment.

At the principia, Maximus began shouting 'The barbarians are idiots! Letting them go! A Roman soldier has been killed! I'll speak to that useless bastard Suasso!' He hurled a writing tablet at the wall. It cracked and split into pieces and shards of wood littered the floor. 'Stupid fools!'

As Maximus ranted, Petrus scooped up the pieces, trying not to get splinters in his hands. Maximus threw himself into a chair and began scribbling orders. Petrus slipped away to check that the horses would be ready to go to the temple in the morning.

II – Dies Lunae

The light crept forward as the sun emerged into the morning. The thunder of the horses' hooves and creak of the cart's wheels tore through the silence as they cantered up the slope. Water from the sacred spring bubbled up through the earth and trickled between stones, cutting a groove in the scree as it flowed down the hillside towards the river in the valley below. A bird screeched in a nearby woodland. Petrus took a sharp intake of breath and muttered a brief prayer as a white owl, an omen of danger, hovered along the treeline. It swooped to the ground and grabbed a small animal in its claws, then rose upwards into the trees.

Maximus raised his hand, and they slowed their horses to a stop under an oak tree whose branches dripped dew onto them as they dismounted and handed their horses' reins to the cart driver. Petrus followed Maximus along the rough path towards the temple. The engraved metal plaque above the temple doorway showed the mighty God Cocidius with his spear. Maximus ran his fingertips over the engraved figure and drew his sword. Petrus traced the raised marks on the plaque with his thumb and then took out his own weapon. Maximus pulled open the heavy wooden door and paused at the entrance, listening. Above his own breathing, Petrus could hear scratching.

'Ready?' whispered Maximus, 'Go!'

Maximus dived in through the narrow entrance. Petrus was right behind him and collided with the centurion just inside the entrance.

'Cocidius save us!' Petrus cried and stepped backwards, blocking the entrance to prevent the other four soldiers from entering the space.

It smelled of blood and tissue, like a butcher's stall. The only light came from gaps high in the walls. In the gloom a headless body lay spreadeagled on a bed of ivy. Rats crowded around the severed neck, feasting on the bloody flesh. More rats sat on his chest chewing his skin beneath the torn tunic. A skinned human head balanced on the altar; its eyes gouged out. A rat chewed the flesh of the man's cheeks as they hung from the skull. Petrus roared, stepped round the body, and brought his sword down onto the altar knocking the rat to the floor. He kicked the rats away from the body, smashing them against the wall.

'It's Faustus,' Petrus said, his shaky voice echoing round in the silence of the temple, 'I recognise the purple mark.' He struggled to stop his hand from trembling as he pointed to the large stain on the man's skin. 'It's one of those strange markings the gods give some children at birth.'

The four soldiers had entered the temple behind Maximus. They were mumbling prayers. One ran outside and they heard him retching.

Maximus turned to the men and said 'Fetch the cart. Tell the driver to wait outside. Bring in the sheet.'

Maximus frowned and pointed with his sword, 'This looks like the work of druids. It's how they sacrificed people to their Gods before the Romans wiped them out all those years ago. The head would've been removed after he died. Must've been as there's not much blood where it was severed.'

'Could've been killed somewhere else and then brought here,' mumbled Petrus.

Maximus shook his head, 'The druids made ritual human sacrifices at holy places.'

Faustus' tunic was ripped from the neck to the belly, Maximus knelt beside the corpse and lifted the torn fabric. A series of deep cuts had been slashed across his chest. Rat bite marks scarred the skin.

'Probably forced to drink a drug that stopped his heart before the mutilation,' Maximus said.

'It can't be druids, can it? They've not existed for a hundred years. Surely, it's someone trying to make it look like druids' sacrifice.' Petrus spoke slowly and quietly as he fought to keep his voice steady. 'They've stolen his boots. He doesn't have a pouch on his belt either. Perhaps they stole that too.'

'Who knows, with these barbarians, anything is possible.' Maximus looked directly at Petrus. 'I want the killers found. You'll ride out to find them after we've taken the body back to the fort.'

'D'you think they've taken Drusus? Or d'you think he ran away?' Petrus was thinking out loud. 'If he'd run away, it would've been back to the fort.'

Two of the soldiers returned; one of them carried a roll of rough cloth. He reluctantly approached the body, with his lips drawn back in disgust and fear as he laid the cloth flat on the ground. Petrus placed his hands beneath Faustus' arms and Maximus helped him to lift the body onto the sheet. On the floor, beneath where Faustus had lain, was a dark lead slate with markings scratched on it. Petrus picked it up.

'It's a curse tablet,' Maximus peered over his shoulder, 'It looks like mirror writing.'

'Curse tablets weren't used by druids,' mumbled Petrus, 'It's written in Latin.' He wiped the slate with his sleeve and placed it inside his tunic. He walked to the altar and lifted Faustus' bloody head. Bits of torn flesh dripped onto his boots. His arms shook as he stared into the empty eye sockets. The metallic taste of blood forced its way down his throat. He placed the head next to the body and wiped his blood-stained fingers on the cloth. The two soldiers wrapped the body in the rough shroud. Trembling, they carried the body outside, and placed it in the back of the cart. The other soldiers stood silently watching.

Petrus knelt and pushed his hands into the freezing spring

water, so cold it was painful. He rubbed his fingers together and brushed them over his palms and the backs of his hands, rinsing away Faustus' blood. He stood and shook his hands; his fingers were numb. He rubbed them on his tunic and went back inside the temple. He used a broom to sweep the floor, pushing the ivy out of the door and into the grass where he kicked soil over it, half-burying the green leaves. He returned to the temple and approached the altar, where he bowed his head and muttered a prayer to Cocidius, God of hunting and war. This was one of the few gods that Petrus still worshipped with fervour, one that he really believed in.

'Cocidius, oh Great One, help me! Look favourably on our work. Help Maximus the great centurion to find the murderers of this poor soldier, Faustus. He was under my command. I should've taken more care of him yesterday. I was too taken up with my own problems. Forgive me. Help us find Drusus alive.'

Petrus had no offerings. He hoped that this did not weaken his plea for help. He chanted, 'Help me! Help me!'

He went outside and Maximus asked, 'What's the hold up?'

'I was cleaning out the temple. I offered a prayer to Cocidius, asking him to help us find the killers.'

Maximus nodded his approval. They remounted and made their way steadily down the hillside, along the meandering river and slowly up the escarpment with the driver trying to avoid ruts and rocks so as not to jolt the body. They reached the vicus and walked down the main street. A young woman carrying a yoke with pails of water moved quickly to the roadside to get out of their way, spilling some of her precious water.

At the fort gate, Petrus was irritated that they still had to give the password in order to get in. Their approach, soldiers of the Roman army, was clearly visible to the gatekeepers, and Julius Maximus, in full uniform, was one of the most recognised Romans in the area. However, Maximus was unfazed and muttered the password in the ear of the guard. Rules are rules.

Word spread quickly through the fort and soldiers lined the road and stood to attention outside their barracks as a mark of respect. The cart took the body to the infirmary where it would be prepared for the funeral rites.

Men had begun to move around the fort completing their early morning rituals, eating breakfast, checking their weapons. A sharp cry cut through the air; a young boy aged about five ran from the Prefect's house with tears streaming down his face. He wore a tunic, but no shoes. A slave girl with a shaved head chased him down the road towards the stables.

'Gaius, son of Silvius Tatius, come back!' her cries pursued him across the fort, 'Stop him please! Someone, stop him!'

Surprised soldiers stood aside and watched the spectacle, some laughed. The boy was screaming as Maximus stepped into the road. He swerved to try to avoid the centurion, but Maximus reached down and grabbed him. The boy struggled and screamed in his arms, but Maximus just laughed. The slave caught up with them, took the boy by the arm, and tried to drag him back towards the house.

He struggled and in his high-pitched voice squealed, 'I'll have you whipped, you bitch! Wait 'til my father hears!'

Maximus bent down and whispered in Gaius' ear. The boy's struggles grew less, and he began walking calmly with the slave and Maximus at his side. At the Prefect's house, the Praetorium, his mother Prima stood on the top step. She was a beautiful woman with pale skin, raven black hair and grey eyes. She wore a green robe but no cloak and shivered as she grabbed Gaius. She struck him across the cheek. The boy recoiled. His eyes filled with tears.

'You little brat! Don't you dare cry! Get in there!' She pushed him into the house. She smiled and exchanged a few words with Maximus, laughing with her hand on his arm. Maximus smiled. The slave girl scurried inside after the child.

Petrus realised he had been holding his breath as he watched Prima. The Prefect's wife was the subject of many young soldiers' fantasies. She was rarely seen outside the house, only ever as she transferred into and out of her carriage.

Petrus went back to his office where he held a polished copper plate next to the lead slate and read the words in the mirrored surface. 'People who gain money by causing misery are utterly accursed and will die brutal deaths.' He wondered what misery they referred to.

He took the slate with him to the prefect's office and stood to attention while Maximus related their findings. 'This type of ritual killing is the work of druids,' concluded the centurion.

Petrus waited. Maximus said nothing further. 'Beneath the body was this lead slate,' Petrus pushed it across the table towards the Prefect, who peered at it. 'It's mirror writing. I used a copper plate to read it. It says that people who get money by causing misery are cursed and will die horrible deaths. Curse tablets are not druidic. As we all know, Sir, the Roman army wiped out the druids a hundred years ago.'

Tatius brushed the surface of the slate with his fingers and then ran his hand through his fine wavy hair. 'So, if not the druids, then who killed him?'

'History does record the end of the druids, but it would be easy for a small group to exist in this place. The whole of Britannia is plagued by wandering holy men,' said Maximus. 'They may have just used the curse tablets to throw us off the scent. They will have taken Drusus to another holy place.'

The Prefect was silent for a moment. From a senatorial family, this was his first posting as Prefect, and he was anxious not to make any errors. He often relied on Maximus for guidance. 'So what do you suggest, Maximus?'

'The druids will probably have gone to the standing stones near Camboglanna. That was always their holy place.'

Tatius nodded and scribbled on his tablet. 'Are you ready to follow them? How many men will you take?'

Maximus said, 'Aurelius Petrus will go, if you're in agreement.

He's well able to lead a team. Travelling light with eight men and some barbarians, they should make good time. If Drusus is not a victim, but the murderer, the barbarians can track him. I have other duties to attend to and will conduct further investigations.'

Tatius looked a bit surprised but nodded, he scribbled the details into his orders and gave the tablet to Petrus. 'There are introductions to the Prefect at Camboglanna.'

Petrus felt proud that Maximus had recommended him as able to lead the hunt for the killers.

'With your leave, Sir?' Maximus said.

The Prefect nodded. Petrus and Maximus bowed and went to the waiting horses. Petrus quickly checked that the soldiers were properly armed and kitted out. They would be marching for the whole day.

'Make sure you find him,' ordered Maximus as Petrus mounted his horse. 'I've already sent Suasso and his men out. They should be coming back to meet you on the way.'

In the open countryside beyond the vicus, the wind whipped hard against their faces, and above them grey clouds pushed away the sun before letting rain drizzle down. Petrus pulled his cloak tighter round his shoulders. He was miserable and wet. They followed the road down the rocky hillside towards the river below. A man trudged towards them alongside a skinny cow; its big head nodded slowly as it walked, the huge nostrils flared, and it dribbled a trail of snot along the ground. The man occasionally struck the beast with a stick across its bony backside. Behind him trailed a flaxen-haired young woman bent low as she carried a bundle tied with rope on her back. She steadied it with cracked hands rubbed red raw by the cold and wind. They moved onto the grass when they saw the soldiers and stood with heads bowed as they passed. After crossing the bridge, Petrus kicked his horse into trot and then cantered up the next hill so that he could get a good look around at the outlying countryside. In the distance Suasso and his men were speaking to locals and looking for indications of druids in the area. As Petrus waited for his marching men to catch up, he walked his horse in circles to keep it warm.

They passed many cairns alongside the road. These piles of stones were used by the local people to communicate messages. Over the years at the fort, Petrus had learned to read them. The cairns bore the wooden and painted clay symbols denoting holy men in the area, but he had no idea when the symbols had been placed there. Suasso and one of his men rode towards them and reined in their horses, splashing through the puddles.

'No sign of Drusus,' Suasso said, 'same as yesterday. There's no talk among the people of priests following the old druidic traditions. There has been a holy man in the area, but he doesn't follow the druidic teachings. His ways are from overseas, the teachings of one great man he called King, trying to spread a message about loving people and caring for them. Not a man preaching violence.'

'Do you think people are telling the truth?' asked Petrus.

'These are my people. I'm the son of Chief Gna. They would not lie to me,' replied Suasso.

Petrus felt despondent. He had a growing feeling that they were too late to save Drusus. As the rain ceased, he turned his face towards the weak sun, but it was not strong enough to warm him.

The light had begun to creep away as they approached Camboglanna fort, and he urged his men forward.

At the gate, Petrus declared, 'I am Aurelius Petrus, Optio at Banna. We require admittance for the night.'

He handed his written orders to the men on the gate. They did not respond, but he could hear running and shouting inside the fort. After a short time, the gates opened, they passed through, dismounted and led their horses down the road towards the Principia. Outside the building stood a short bald centurion brandishing his vine staff. A tall well-groomed man stood on the top step of the building. He brushed his dark hair away from his face and peered at the tablet, moving it backwards and forwards in front of his face as if trying to find the best position to read it. He looked down at Petrus who bowed to the man, assuming he was the Prefect. The aroma of his perfume tickled Petrus' nostrils.

'Hail, Prefect. I am Aurelius Petrus, Optio at Banna. We are searching for a missing soldier. You've seen my orders?' he said.

The man nodded, 'I'm Foslius Septimus. Where are the rest of your men?' he tapped the tablet.

'There are four numeri who are yet to arrive, Sir. They must've been delayed. We apologise for the inconvenience.'

'The centurion Carius will look after you,' the Prefect waved his hand in the direction of the man holding the vine staff and walked away.

'Your men can sleep in the barracks – there's room there. Your irregulars can doss there or go to their people for all I care, it's up to you,' said Carius, who stank like a horse.

'I'd like the irregulars to stay here so that we can make an early start in the morning,' Petrus said.

Carius nodded and began barking orders at his men. His soldiers led the barbarians and Petrus' men towards the barracks, while others stepped forward to take care of their horses. 'You can come with me,' Carius pointed at Petrus and then strode away.

Petrus quickened his pace to catch up with Carius. He wondered if the centurion ever used the bathhouse. Carius didn't speak as he led Petrus through the fort.

'You dog!' Shouts from the gate caused them to look round.

Suasso's man, Luci, was arguing with the gatekeepers. He leant in towards the young guard who stepped back alarmed at the angry barbarian. With his bald head and neck completely covered in blue tattoos, he was a frightening sight. Luci's three companions lurked ominously behind him.

'Are those your barbarians?' Carius asked.

Petrus nodded.

'Let them through!' Carius shouted.

Luci pushed his way forward. 'We've been told where to find him. Well, where to find a body, I mean. We'd been asking around in the villages and threatening that the Romans would burn and loot homes. A messenger arrived to say that they've found a body.'

Petrus nodded, 'At the stone circle?'

Luci shook his head, 'No, at a shrine, not far from the circle. Our Chief said he'll send a guide to the fort at dawn.'

Petrus was sure it was Drusus' body. 'We'll be ready in the morning. Now go with these men, get some rest. The horses will be seen to.'

Carius led Petrus to his barrack rooms.

'You can sleep here,' Carius led him into an empty room. The horsey smell filled the small space. Petrus moved to open the window shutters and let in a blast of cold air.

'You'll be closing them later if you don't want to freeze your balls off,' Carius muttered and moved off towards his own rooms.

Petrus pulled the shutters closed and breathed in the welcome smell of fresh straw. He put his saddle bag on the bed and sat down. The barracks were warm, he closed his eyes and rubbed his arms; his clothes had dried, but the cold and rain had chilled his body to the core. A polite cough made him look up. A slave stood at the door, holding a bowl of stew and some bread on a tray. He stepped forward, bowed, and gave the tray to Petrus.

'Would you like wine Sir?'

Petrus nodded. He felt despondent. He knew it had been unrealistic to hope that they would find Drusus alive, but the news that a body had been found had still shaken him. Who would want to kill these young soldiers? Why would they bring him this far from Banna? They couldn't be druids, could they?

As he lay back on his bed and closed his eyes, he wondered when he would ever have time to go to the temple to fulfil his promise to Aurora.

III – Dies Martes

Petrus woke with a start as someone shook his shoulder. He grabbed the man's hand and just stopped himself from twisting the terrified slave's arm.

'You startled me,' he grumbled and released his grip.

'I was told to wake you, Sir,' the slave scuttled from the room.

Petrus coughed up phlegm and spat on the floor. He took the bread from the bowl by the bed, slurped some water and wrestled his feet into his boots. He grabbed his helmet and weapons and strode outside. It was a cold grey morning; he was grateful it wasn't raining. At the gate, the soldiers and barbarians were milling around. Petrus threw his saddlebag across the horse's back and mounted.

'Where's the guide?' he asked.

'The guards have spotted him riding towards us,' Suasso grinned, 'Shall we wait outside the gate?'

'Let's go to meet him,' replied Petrus.

They passed quickly through the community living around the fort. The residents were just stirring, window shutters were being opened, dogs barked, chickens pecked at the ground, and rats scurried between buildings. The smells of animals and damp hung in the air as the horses picked their way along the road.

The bleak landscape stretched out before them, stunted trees dotted the hillsides, bent by the constant wind. The guide was fully armed; he had long brown hair wafting about his helmet as he cantered towards them on his grey horse. He stopped as they approached. Petrus let Suasso overtake him.

'Greetings Nini,' Suasso said, clearly recognising the man. He dismounted and approached the rider with palms facing upwards and arms reaching forward.

Nini grinned, he had only three teeth. He was young and had the same tribal tattoos as Suasso on his cheeks. Nini dismounted and the two men embraced, whispering the words of their traditional greetings.

'He has no Latin,' Suasso explained as they both remounted and Nini turned his horse around. 'It's somewhere over there,' Suasso waved his arm in the direction of the garrison town of Caria.

Suasso rode ahead with Nini, talking and laughing. Petrus understood the local language, but the men were speaking in an unfamiliar dialect, and he felt strangely excluded. However, he did not disturb them as they were going at a good pace, and he hoped they could find the body quickly and return to Banna the same day. He didn't want to spend another night at Camboglanna with the foul-smelling centurion.

The sun climbed higher, but its weak rays offered little warmth. A set of huge stones were silhouetted against the skyline on the top of a hill as they rode towards it. Petrus was intrigued. He'd heard a lot about these ancient stone circles.

'We're not going up to the stones,' Suasso interrupted Petrus' thoughts, 'We're going round to that wood over there.' He pointed towards a group of trees in the valley.

Petrus tried to hide his disappointment.

Nini paused at the edge of the wood and whispered to Suasso.

'He says the shrine is in here. Are all your men ready to go in?' Suasso translated.

Petrus ordered the soldiers to follow Nini into the wood. The barbarians lingered in the open.

'They're not coming in,' Suasso explained, 'they wish to visit the circle.'

Petrus waited, but Suasso offered no explanation, so he nodded and Suasso released the men, leaving him and Nini to lead the Romans into the wood.

The trees' gnarled branches closed over the path, blocking the light as the horses picked their way carefully across their roots. The men grumbled as they followed. The smell of damp earth and wet bark rose around them. They moved into a clearing where the sun's rays lit a low red stone building with no roof standing next to a pool of water.

'Over there, in the temple of Mercury,' Suasso said.

Nini had stopped. Petrus dismounted, handed him the horse's reins, and strode across the clearing. His boots made tracks across the wet grass. He passed between the building's columns. In front of an altar, a skeletally thin wolf raised its blood-stained face, drew back its lips and snarled. Suasso cried out, brushed past Petrus and drew his bow. The wolf stood its ground and howled. Suasso released an arrow. The wolf fell to the ground, quivering. He ran forward and kicked the dying animal aside. Behind them, the soldiers ran towards the temple, their weapons drawn. The headless body of a naked man lay on the stone floor with its arms by its sides. The neck was a mash of bone and tattered flesh where the wolf had been feeding. The letters SPQR had been carved into his chest. The tattered flesh of the cuts were bloodless. The body's hands and feet bore the teeth marks from numerous animals. The face of Drusus stared at them from the altar; his mouth was a scream, the lips pegged back with small wooden stakes. The hard metallic odour of blood and decay assaulted Petrus' nostrils as he stared at the head. The man's tunic and boots were piled at the foot of the altar.

'We'll bury him here in the glade,' Petrus's voice shook.

The watching soldiers' faces were drained of colour as they stared at the mutilated body; some of them whispered prayers.

The soldiers scraped the earth with their tools and dug a shallow grave at the pool's edge. They trembled as they used their cloaks to carry the body and place him gently inside the hole. Petrus lifted the head releasing its rotting stink. He concentrated on keeping his hands steady as he knew the men were watching him. Bits of flesh oozed out of the head and onto his boots as he walked to the pool and placed it with the body. Suasso carried the clothes and boots and placed them in the grave. The soldiers covered the grave with earth and then pulled branches of leaves across it to prevent scavengers from digging it up.

Petrus plunged his hands into the sacred pool and whispered some words. He knew the men were watching him and so he pretended to pray. The cold water pulled away the flesh and stink of the dead man. He went back to the temple. A lead slate lay on the ground where the body had lain. He picked it up, wiped it with some leaves and peered at the words scratched onto the curse tablet. More mirror writing, he guessed, slipping it inside his tunic. Conscious that his men were watching, he knew he should say a prayer to Mercury, another God whose power and existence he doubted. He approached the altar, bowed his head and wordlessly moved his lips, as if praying. The men needed to see him observing the rituals.

They walked in silence back through the trees towards the welcome sunlight. The barbarians were waiting, all looking towards the stone circle as a group of local men rode down the hillside towards them. The leader of the group wore a bearskin cloak. The bear's head was an elaborate headdress, its legs and claws hung down the leader's chest; he was clearly a chief.

'Let me,' muttered Suasso, dismounting from his horse, he took a few steps forward, held his arms wide and his head bowed in greeting as the riders stopped.

'Greetings Chief Gna,' he looked up and smiled.

The chief dismounted, stepped forward and pulled Suasso into a warm embrace. He whispered in his son's ear and then released him. The two men shared the same auburn hair, green eyes and slightly misshapen noses; their cheeks were identically tattooed. Petrus dismounted and approached the chief.

'You have what you came for?' Gna asked.

'Yes. We buried him. We're grateful for your help. How did you know where to find him?' said Petrus.

Gna pointed to the large black birds circling above the trees, 'It's the sign of death. One of my hunting parties saw them yesterday and went to look. Thinking it was a Roman soldier, we sent you a message.'

'Why are the birds still there, when we've buried the body?' asked Petrus.

Gna smiled. 'You can't hide death. These birds are the omen. Did you see how he died?'

'Ritual sacrifice, a druid's ritual. Have you seen holy men like that?'

Gna shook his head. 'There are holy men now and then, but not those who follow druids' ways. They were stamped out by you Romans many years ago.'

'Tell me, who uses this place?'

'The whole community, even the Romans.' Gna paused, 'You are welcome to come back to our home,' he remounted his horse.

'Thank you,' Petrus didn't want to get too friendly with the chief, 'I've orders to report back as soon as possible. However, Suasso and his men can come with you. I expect they've missed being with their people. They can re-join us at the fort first light tomorrow. I just need one man to show us the way back to the fort. Luci can do that. I thank you again for the use of your guide.'

Gna nodded, turned his horse and rode slowly away.

Suasso turned back to Petrus, 'Until tomorrow.'

'Wait! What was he whispering to you?' asked Petrus.

'Oh that! He asked, "have you got used to the bad smell of the Romans yet?"' Suasso laughed and spurred his horse into a canter to catch up with the others.

Luci rode some way ahead and led the soldiers back towards Camboglanna fort. Petrus hailed the guards at the gate. Behind them the people of the vicus watched, nervously. Word had clearly spread about them finding a soldier's body, and they were afraid of retribution. Petrus released his men and made his way to the Centurion's accommodation.

Carius muttered 'I take it your men are settled in the barracks? You can have the same room; my slave will bring you food. Is there anything else you need?'

Petrus shook his head. Carius still stank.

'Don't you want to hear about what we found?'

'Save it for the Prefect tomorrow morning, I'll hear about it then, before you depart. Or do you need to stay longer?'

Petrus shook his head, 'We'll return to Banna tomorrow morning.'

Carius had already started walking away as Petrus spoke. He was a short stocky man, with huge hands and a big head. He'd been a centurion for more than twenty years and gave the impression that he didn't like people, but his fighting skills and loyalty to his men were well known and he was respected even if he was difficult to get on with. Petrus knew that he had been a Princeps Posterior for ten years, longer than was usual for centurions, and wondered whether being so belligerent had hindered his promotion.

Petrus finished his meal, put the plate aside and drew the lead slate out from his tunic. He cleaned the surface and then reached for the polished bronze plate which the slave had provided for him. He read the scratched words in the mirrored metal, 'The man who took my money is utterly cursed. I take his money and give him to the temple of Sulis Mercury. He who is accursed has spilled his own blood on the earth.' He lay back on his bed and wondered what the words meant. Whose money had Drusus stolen?

IV – Dies Mercurii

'Get off me!' Petrus snarled, fighting off the slave who shook his shoulder.

He rubbed his face and tapped his cheeks with his fingers, pushing away sleep. He grabbed his belongings, stepped into the street and strode towards the Principia building. Tiny water droplets settled on his cloak as fog surrounded him. The clatter of weapons and grunts of men preparing for work reached out to him through the thickened white air.

As he entered the building Petrus was surprised to see a woman talking to Carius. Her long copper-coloured hair was plaited with interwoven green leaves and hung down the back of her hooded blue cloak. She wore thick boots over her trousers. Her big emerald-green eyes settled on Petrus, and her gaze travelled up and down his body, before resting on his face. She made him feel uncomfortable as she licked her lips provocatively.

'You must be Aurelius Petrus. I'm Fabia, wife of Prefect Foslius Septimus. I'll be coming with you to Banna fort today. I'm going to visit my friend Julia Prima, the wife of your Prefect,' she waved her arm, indicating the direction of the Prefect's house, the praetorium. 'My carriage will be waiting.' She nodded to Carius and walked away.

Petrus spoke quickly as he updated the Prefect who sat at his table and nodded absently, murmuring acknowledgement at intervals. Carius stood at Petrus' shoulder and listened in silence. The Prefect touched a perfumed cloth to his nose occasionally, 'to mask Carius' stink' thought Petrus as the smell of horses hung heavily about them.

'Both bodies had curse tablets beneath them. They are not druidic traditions. I'll carry out further inquiries on my return to Banna where Maximus may have more information.'

The Prefect waved his hand dismissively, clearly not interested in the deaths of soldiers from a different fort.

'Here are my wife's travel documents,' he handed the tablet to Petrus who placed it inside his tunic. 'She may stay for several days if she wishes and it suits your Prefect. Go well, Aurelius Petrus.'

At the gate Petrus mounted his horse. Fabia sat looking out of the window of her carriage. Behind her a slave girl had squeezed into the corner amongst the baggage. Another slave was riding a mule. Petrus scowled. Mules were obstinate when they had riders on their backs, he hoped it wouldn't cause difficulties on the journey and delay them.

'I'm afraid you must travel with the curtain drawn Ma'am,' he said and reached a hand towards the black curtain; she tried to snatch it away. 'It's for safety reasons,' he persisted and pulled the curtain across the window.

Petrus was annoyed, she'd been at Camboglanna for several years and ought to know the protocols for travelling. He positioned his men around the carriage and told the slave on the mule to ride behind it.

'Suasso has not returned.' Petrus said.

'He sent a message last night saying they would catch us up,' Luci replied, 'We'll probably see them all this afternoon.'

Petrus took a deep breath. Suasso was an arrogant sod sometimes, bending the rules because he was the Chief's son. Petrus thought he needed reminding of who paid his wages and how lucky he was to remain in Britannia and not be taken to Rome. Barbarians working for the Romans were normally given Roman names, like the auxillae who joined up. For some reason, Suasso and his men had been allowed to keep their tribal names. That didn't help, it marked them out as special.

He signalled to the men, and they set off with Luci walking his horse briskly beside Petrus. The fog was lifting, and the people of the vicus were moving around. The bathhouse opened its sluice gate and water rushed into the open sewer that ran along the edge of the track by the fort's defensive ditch. The waste bubbled along the channel where it would be joined by the main sewer running from the fort down towards the river. Petrus wondered why the Prefect hadn't ordered that the waste channel should be covered with stone. It would have lessened the stale smell which fought its way into his body. A blacksmith pumped his mighty bellows to liven up the fire in his forge and smoke snaked into the morning air. A young child ran into the street ahead of them, shrieking with laughter. He skidded to a halt and stared at the soldiers approaching him, eyes wide as he whimpered in fear. His mother rushed out and grabbed him, dragging him back into a dark doorway.

Glancing back, Petrus saw that Fabia had drawn the curtain aside, he slowed his horse to allow the carriage to pull alongside him.

'Madam, you will just encourage ne'er do wells if they see a fine lady in a carriage. I really must insist that you close the curtains throughout the journey.'

He pulled the curtain closed and signalled to Luci to go ahead and check the route as he continued to ride alongside the carriage.

'They know it's someone important, the ne'er do wells, I mean. The number of guards I have signals it,' Fabia's voice floated towards him.

He did not reply.

'Did you hear what I said, Aurelius Petrus? They know.' She had raised her voice.

'Sorry ma'am, I was distracted,' he lied, 'It's true they'll know an important person is within the carriage, but they won't know it's you.'

'I don't usually travel with the curtain closed,' she whined.

'Nevertheless, I must insist,' he snapped, trying to hide his irritation.

'But I feel unwell, what if I am sick?'

'If you feel unwell, then we can stop the carriage. Shout out, I will hear you. I'll not be far away,' Petrus was annoyed; he was having to treat her like a child, not a woman.

They passed into open countryside in silence. The breeze pushed the clouds across the sky, occasionally blotting out the weak winter sun. The smell of dew on grass teased his nostrils. Luci rode in large sweeping circles. Petrus was nervous, wishing he had more barbarians and soldiers with him. They had to pause frequently for the slave to catch up as the mule was reluctant to travel alongside the soldiers.

They stopped near a meandering stream to give Fabia a break from being rocked in the carriage. The slave helped her out of the carriage and brought out a stool for her to sit on.

'No. Over there,' she pointed, 'I wish to sit near the water. It's so calming,' she looked towards Petrus as she spoke.

He positioned the men in a large circle around her as she lowered herself onto the stool and the slave girl fussed about her.

'Won't you stand near me?' she raised one eyebrow and smiled coquettishly at Petrus.

'I'm sorry, no. I have to stay alert,' he looked around and searched the horizon.

'I only want to talk,' she played with the rings on her fingers, 'a woman such as I has few people to talk to,' she looked at him and fluttered her eyelids.

'A soldier such as me does not have much talk to share with a lady like you,' he muttered, irritated with her flirtation.

He strode away and began haranguing one of the soldiers who was watching Fabia instead of looking out into the countryside around him. Fabia did not take the food offered to her by the slave. She drank wine from her flask, letting it dribble from her mouth. The red wine ran like blood down her pale chin. She made no attempt to wipe it away and stared defiantly at Petrus.

Fabia rose and walked back towards the carriage. Suddenly she leant forward and started vomiting red liquid onto her boots. She groaned. Her slave girl ran to help, offering her some water from a flask. Fabia gulped it down, gasped for air, then pushed the girl aside and walked slowly to the carriage. She climbed in, and drew the curtain closed. Petrus could hear her sobbing as the slave girl clambered in.

'Do you wish to continue on to Banna Ma'am, or would you like to return to Camboglanna if you're unwell?' Petrus pulled aside the curtain. He was anxious not to take an infectious sickness back to Banna. However, none of his men were ill, so he hoped that she had merely eaten something that didn't agree with her.

Fabia was clutching her belly. She was pale, and a thin sheen of sweat coated her face, 'So concerned Petrus?' she smiled weakly, 'I will continue. I wish to see my dear friend at Banna.'

He drew the curtain back across the window.

'Riders!!' yelled one of the men, drawing his sword.

All the soldiers readied their weapons as a small group of men galloped towards them.

'It's Suasso!' yelled Luci rushing forward, 'It's Suasso!'

'Stand down!' ordered Petrus.

'Scared you, did we?' laughed Suasso as he dismounted and approached Petrus. 'Said we'd catch you up. Did I miss anything? Who's in the carriage?'

Fabia drew the curtain aside and leant towards the window. She did not smile.

'Fabia, the wife of the prefect at Camboglanna,' replied Petrus, 'How was the evening at your father's?'

'Good,' Suasso smiled.

'Ma'am,' Suasso bowed his head towards Fabia. 'It's wise to travel with the curtain drawn at all times.'

He stepped forward and pulled the curtain closed. Fabia did not respond.

'Let's go!' Petrus climbed into the saddle.

Suasso rode alongside Petrus for the remainder of the journey chattering about the feast he'd had at his father's compound. Petrus was grateful that there were no further histrionics from Fabia.

The sun was beginning to move towards the horizon as they approached Banna fort. The guards on the gate were alert and clearly expecting them as they were quick with the identification procedures. Petrus led the carriage up to the steps of the praetorium. The door to the house burst open, and Prima raced forward, her loose hair streaming behind her as she grabbed the carriage door and pulled her friend into a tight embrace, kissing her cheeks and lips and crying with laughter. Fabia seemed to have made a full recovery as she clasped hands with Prima and raced into the house, brushing aside Gaius who watched bewildered as his mother shrieked in delight. Fabia's slaves reached into the carriage to remove the bundles of her belongings and then scurried up the steps. A tall skeletally thin slave in a faded tunic barred their way into the house.

'Use the back entrance,' he declared, placing a hand on the slave's arm.

'But we have my mistress' things,' Fabia's man protested.

'Round the back I said. Or do I have to fetch my master to beat you both?' snarled the slave.

The slave exhaled loudly and nodded to the girl. They walked down the steps and round the corner of the house as Tatius' slave smirked and went inside.

Petrus made his way to the principia. Maximus was punishing Rufus and Pius, the two gatekeepers. Both men stood bare to the waist, their hands gripped the table and their taught muscles twitched as they struggled to remain upright against the strokes of his whip. Red weals had risen on their skin. Their eyes were closed, and their lips moved but they did not make a sound.

Maximus was breathing hard, 'Don't fall asleep on duty again! Now get out of my sight!'

The two men gathered up their tunics and walked stiffly out of the building. Maximus threw himself into his seat and began recording the punishments on a tablet.

'Quirinus' men were asleep again on duty,' grumbled Maximus, 'You caught them sleeping on the early morning of Solis, didn't you? It could've been significant; it was when Faustus and Drusus were taken.'

Petrus nodded. He had wanted to give Quirinus a chance to improve things, but now that Maximus had been punishing the gatekeepers, that didn't seem very likely.

'They're not on duty again for four days. Hopefully they'll improve. It's a security risk to the fort. If it happens again, their pay will be docked.' Maximus scribbled some notes.

Petrus nodded and took a deep breath, 'We've returned from Camboglanna with the Prefect's wife, Fabia. She's visiting Julia Prima. I was given these orders,' he handed the tablet to Maximus who read it with a frown and tapped it as he spoke.

'Says here that she's to stay here as long as she wishes – it may be three or four days, or even a week. She's to be guarded at all times if she leaves the fort,' Maximus placed the tablet in a pile earmarked for re-use. 'If she leaves the fort! Does he expect her to go out shopping?'

Petrus hid a smile, 'Her slaves had a bit of trouble at the Prefect's house. That skinny slave, Felix, wouldn't let them in through the front door.'

'Fabia's slaves should've known better. Let's go and tell Silvius Tatius what you found.'

'Don't you want to hear it first?'

Maximus shook his head and stood up.

'Did you get any useful information from the men in Faustus' and Drusus' contubernia, the ones sharing his barracks?' Petrus' question caused Maximus to pause with his hand on the door. 'Or anything from the duty rosters?'

Maximus grunted 'Nothing at all,' and left the room.

They entered the prefect's austere office. The Prefect did not allow any softness in the room – no cushions or drapes, apart from the one red curtain covering the entrance to his robing room. 'I'm here to work, not relax,' he'd said when asked about furnishings. The room was empty. A woman's cry and a man's deep-throated groan made the two soldiers look at the red curtain. Maximus coughed loudly. After a pause, Tatius emerged from behind the curtain, dragging a young slave girl behind him. Her tunic was pulled down to the waist and her small round breasts bore the red imprints of his long fingers. Tears ran down her cheeks as she quickly pulled up the tunic and left the room. Tatius stared defiantly at the two soldiers who moved aside to let him pass.

'Petrus is here to give his report,' Maximus waved his arm in Petrus' direction.

'I can see that,' Tatius sat in this chair and rearranged his clothing, clearly excited by the slave girl. Petrus told them about the message from Chief Gna and how the guide had taken them to a temple in the woods.

'Drusus' naked headless body lay spreadeagled in the temple of Mercury. His body had the letters SPQR carved into his chest. A wolf was feeding on him. His head had the lips pegged back like he was screaming.'

Tatius interrupted, 'SPQR? That is only significant to Romans.'

Petrus looked at Maximus, 'Perhaps.'

'Or someone scoffing at Romans.'

'Continue, Petrus, we'll come back to this,' said Tatius quietly.

'We buried Drusus in the wood. This curse tablet was beneath his body.' He handed it over to Tatius. 'I read the writing in a mirror, it says that he took money from someone and so they have taken his money and curse him. Money seems to be the reason for both soldiers' deaths, which would not be a holy man's motivation. They don't worry about money; they are supported by their communities.'

Tatius nodded.

'I agree with Maximus, the body was arranged in that way to shock us and show disdain for the Roman army, and so was the mutilation, the carving of the letters SPQR into his chest. With Faustus' death, I think the rats were brought there, to shock us. The temple of Cocidius is kept very clean by worshippers and the door is usually closed. I've never seen rats there before, despite the offerings of food sometimes left there by worshippers.' Continued Petrus.

'There were hundreds of 'em!' exclaimed Maximus, 'I was there! No one could carry so many. And why would they? It had to be the work of magic!'

'There've not been any reports in the area of druids or holy men following druidic practices. Chief Gna confirmed that when I asked him, and the barbarians were told the same when they rode through the villages. The only holy man in the area has been preaching about love. Curse tablets are not druidic practices. So, someone has mixed up several belief systems to cause confusion. Perhaps the murderers were recovering money that had been stolen from them.' Petrus persisted.

'Who?' Tatius asked.

'I'm not sure,' Petrus mumbled and looked from Tatius to Maximus.

Maximus grunted, 'I agree robbery could be the motivation. Some other person pretending to be a holy man, mixing up druidic and other local practices, while mocking Rome. That's pretty complicated. I don't believe it. Murder normally has simple causes, jealousy, lust, hatred, money.' He paused, 'How did Gna's men know where to find Drusus' body?'

'They saw huge black birds circling above the temple. They're an omen of death. I saw them myself,' Petrus replied.

Maximus sighed 'Let me take some men and go back to Gna - threaten to have some of his people's farms burned. We should go into the area around here doing the same. That will loosen some tongues. Let's get the spies out, find the 'pretend druids', or whoever they are.'

Petrus tried to sound firm, 'The only holy man they speak of in these parts is one who comes from overseas. He preaches the teachings of just one man whom he calls The King, his teachings are all about loving your fellow beings.'

Tatius pressed his palms together and tapped his fingers on his cheeks.

'I think Maximus is probably right. He can organise the barbarians to search for this holy man or men.' He paused. 'Your idea has some merit Petrus. As these men were in your century, you can both pursue your ideas and report directly to me.'

Maximus opened his mouth to protest, but Tatius raised a hand, 'You, Maximus, must concentrate on the search. These deaths are a threat to the position of the Army. We must find the culprits and make it known when they are punished. As you can see, I'm covering every option. I don't want the Governor to complain that we weren't thorough.'

Petrus smiled to himself. Tatius was always concerned with how things might appear to more powerful men. He was relieved that the prefect was at least considering his ideas about the killers. Maximus clenched his fists and took some deep breaths.

Petrus realised Tatius was still speaking to him, 'What will you do?'

'I'll go back to the temple of Cocidius – that's where it all started.' The truth was he had no idea where to start, he needed time to think the whole thing through.

'You can have Suasso to help you,' offered Maximus through clenched teeth, 'I can manage without him.'

'I don't need him, not at the moment. As the chief's son, he is of more use to you than he would be here. There are informants in the vicus who will help me.'

There were a couple of local men living near the fort who passed information to the Romans in return for money and other goods.

He paused. 'On second thoughts, leave me three of Suasso's men, just in case.'

'Send some searchers into the area around here today and tomorrow. I'll give you orders to take to Camboglanna if needed Maximus. Head off towards the West tomorrow morning. You'll be gone several days.' Tatius began writing on a tablet. 'Centurion Fabius Ruga will be in charge while you are away, he's pilus posterior.'

'I'll brief him,' said Maximus.

'Petrus, you'll report to me every morning after parade, starting tomorrow,' Tatius waved him away.

'Er, Honourable Prefect?' Petrus said.

Tatius put down his stylus.

'Yes?'

'Some of the men who came with me to find the bodies of Drusus and Faustus were greatly affected by seeing the mutilated bodies of their friends and comrades. Perhaps some words of encouragement might help them,' Petrus said.

'Good point Petrus. Keep an eye on them while Maximus is away. I'll try to catch them first thing tomorrow, after parade. Remind me if I forget.' He rose from his chair, 'I'd better go and greet my wife's visitor.' He left the room.

Petrus took a fresh horse from the stables and rode thoughtfully through the vicus. He emerged into the countryside and began to canter. When he reached the escarpment, he allowed the horse to choose its own path down the valley and leaned back slightly with long reins to let the horse balance itself as it slid on the stony ground. As he crossed the valley bottom, he saw two young boys walking together beside the river. They looked like brothers with the same round faces and curly brown hair. The taller one had two dead rabbits slung over his shoulder.

Petrus shouted, 'Hey you, come over here.'

The boys froze and stared wide-eyed at him as he approached. He reached into his tunic and withdrew two coins.

'Give me those rabbits,' he held out the coins.

The boys didn't move.

'Give me the rabbits,' Petrus repeated.

'These are from my traps; I check them every day. They're for our supper, Sir. If I give them to you, we'll have nothing to eat at home.' The taller one's voice shook as he spoke.

'The Roman army needs them. Hand them over!' Petrus raised his voice slightly.

The boy remained motionless. Petrus dismounted from his horse.

Petrus leant down and put his face close to the taller boy who recoiled in fear. 'I'll give you these two coins. If you don't give the rabbits to me, I'll come to your home and kill your parents. The Roman army doesn't ask twice.' He cringed inside as he said these words.

The colour drained from the boy's face, and he handed over the rabbits. Petrus pushed the coins into the boy's hand, remounted his horse and placed the rabbit carcasses across the horse's neck. He rode away, ashamed of his behaviour, knowing that the boys' family would go hungry that night. If Petrus failed to find the murderers, then he risked being replaced as Optio and possibly being sent away from Banna.

In Cocidius' temple there was a strong smell of freshly cut ivy. Ivy covered the altar and cascaded onto the floor. At the base of the altar were some vegetables and a hunk of dry bread. Petrus knelt before the altar. He began skinning and gutting the rabbits. He ripped off the soft fur and smelled the tang of bloody flesh.

He muttered prayers to Cocidius, 'Forgive me. I am leaving these rabbits not to honour you, but to find out whether the rats come to disgrace this place. I must find who murdered the soldiers in order to be able to care for my family.'

He laid the rabbits on the ivy nearest the altar. The bloody carcasses' smell masked the faint earthy smell of the vegetables lying alongside them. Petrus bowed and left the temple, leaving the door open. He knew that rats could enter through the air gaps at the base of the walls, but he wanted to give them every opportunity to get in. Petrus knelt and pushed his hands into the spring water; he washed the blood from his fingers. He mounted his horse and walked down the hillside and along the valley bottom.

Near the vicus, he made his way to the Temple of Jupiter which loomed menacingly over the huge parade ground. He tied his horse outside, pushed open the heavy oak door and entered. Two lit torches hung high on the walls, casting light across the dusty stone floor. The odour of animal fat and smoke hung in the air where dust motes danced in the light. The sound of his feet slapping on the stones rang in his ears as he crossed the floor towards the three stone altars stood against the wall. Petrus knelt awkwardly in front of them, bowed his head and prayed.

'Jupiter! The Best, the Greatest God of Gods. Help my son, Titus. Whatever it is that ails him, please take it away. He's so young and precious to us. We don't want him to be an outcast or for people to say he's possessed. Aurora thinks she's pregnant. Please, if she is, then let that child go to full term and be healthy. We have already lost three babies just after they were born. We can't face anymore.'

He remained kneeling, picturing his wife and son in his head and chanted 'Jupiter help me!' repeatedly, willing himself to believe in the God. He wanted to believe, but he just couldn't. He'd seen so much death, destruction and suffering of innocent people like mothers who died in childbirth and children suffering just like his Titus; he couldn't believe. He prayed because Aurora wanted him to.

He pushed himself to his feet and walked back to the door. Embedded in the wall an offerings box had a metal door with a gap at the top, just wide enough to push money through. He reached into the pouch on his belt, pulled out one denarius and pushed it into the box. There was a satisfying clink as it landed amongst the other offerings. He flicked the dust from his trousers and left the temple.

The darkness was racing forward as he rode towards his home.

The owners of all the houses and businesses in the vicus paid ground rent to the Romans. Businesses also paid tax and for licenses on an annual basis. The ground rent for Petrus' and Aurora's house was low as the ground area was small, just a kitchen, a salon, three bedrooms and a washroom, round a central courtyard. Petrus had plans to connect it to the main sewer which ran down the street, but he needed to save for the cost of it and to get permission from the fort to make the connection. That would also incur an additional annual charge. He tied the horse up near the house and rattled the latch to the door. Unusually for the daytime, it was locked, so he waited. Aurora looked out nervously. Seeing him, she flung the door wide open.

'Petrus! I wasn't expecting you,' she pulled him inside and pushed the door closed. She hugged him tightly and kissed him deeply.

Petrus breathed 'I should call round unexpectedly more often.'

'Are you looking into the murder of the man found in the temple of Cocidius?'

'I am, and also into the murder of another man, his body was found near Camboglanna fort. Someone, a holy man perhaps, is making it look like the work of the ancient druids. Maximus is riding out tomorrow to find them. He'll burn down farms, until someone gives them up.'

'But what if there is no-one to give up? There is no talk of holy men in this area,' Aurora said.

Petrus sighed, 'I think the murders were staged, made to look like druids' work. Maximus is determined to prove otherwise. I've been given time to investigate by the Prefect, while Maximus is away.'

'People are scared Petrus. Many local people worship at that temple. They're worried they might be next. I'm frightened.'

'You've nothing to worry about,' he tried to sound reassuring, but Aurora moved away to the fire. 'What is it?'

'I'm worried about you looking into the murders. That man in the temple was a soldier. He'd been tortured. And the rats ate his body. You could be in danger,' she replied.

Petrus put out a hand to touch his wife's shoulder. She turned towards him and stepped into his outstretched arms. He held her tight, unsure what to say. A soldier's life was all about danger.

He pressed his face against the side of her head and spoke softly with his lips brushing her hair. 'He was mutilated after his death. We know that because there was so little blood at the site. I think it was done to humiliate the army, and the rats were put there by the killers for the same reason. There was a curse tablet under his body talking about money and causing misery. It was personal. A message about him.' He put his hands round her face and looked into her beautiful eyes. 'Don't tell anyone else those details. I'm sure you are not in danger. If ever you need me, then just get a message to the fort. I may not come immediately, but I will come. Everyone will assume that Titus is unwell.' He pulled away from her, 'How is he?'

'He's well. He's out in the yard playing with Mincona's son.'

Their maid, Mincona, had been made pregnant by her previous employer who had then sacked her to placate his wife. She had been desperate for employment in order to feed and clothe her son and so was grateful and loyal to Petrus and Aurora for giving them a home.

'I've been to the Temple today,' Petrus said as Aurora looked up, 'I prayed for Titus, and for you and any baby you may have.'

She placed her hand on her belly. 'Let's hope your prayers are answered. Now, will you stay to eat? I've stew in the pot.'

'I will,' he smiled.

Petrus savoured every mouthful of the meal as he watched Titus gobbling down his food. Mincona and her son ate with them. Mincona's boy was quieter than Titus and ate very little. Petrus thought the boy was frightened of him, too afraid to eat.

The night had settled a blanket of darkness onto the streets as Petrus kissed his wife and she closed the door behind him. A piece of ivy had been tied around the door's outer latch. His informant, Carantii, the blacksmith had some news. His forge was not far from Petrus' home, they were almost neighbours. Carantii's father had built the forge. The Romans had insisted that it be completely separate from any other buildings, so that there was a firebreak in case the forge caught light, as they often did. Petrus had recruited the smith as an informant some years previously. He'd been a good choice; he knew lots of businessmen, was well-liked in the area and he knew about everything that went on locally. Petrus untied the ivy, collected his horse and led it slowly back towards the fort. The horse tripped in the darkness and Petrus cursed it pulling the reins sharply which made it jerk its head up and whinny in protest. He handed the horse to one of the guards, instructing him to take it back to the stables and then he walked back to the tavern.

The tavern was busy, full of loud sweaty men. Petrus sat at an empty table and beckoned over the taverner who poured him a cup of ale. He gulped it down and banged his fist on the table for another. The room had its usual smell of unwashed bodies, ale, and vomit. Petrus leant back against the wall, sipped his drink, and surveyed the other drinkers. Some tables had men drinking quietly. There were a couple of sober-looking men from the fort whose names he didn't know. An old man sat alone at a table weeping and clutching his drink to his chest. In one corner three local men, with bundles at their feet, were arguing. Two of them wore the hoods of their cloaks up, as if not wanting to be seen. The third man ran a scarred hand through his straggly brown hair as he argued.

He grew louder and shouted 'I did! I'm telling you! A stag, alone, drinking at the sacred pool. It's an omen. I'm going to be strong and wealthy.'

He looked across the room and straight at Petrus, then looked back at his companions.

'Are you strong enough to buy us another drink?' laughed one of the men.

'Not this time, I need to get home.' He stood, picked up his bundle and left the room; the door creaked shut behind him.

'Another drink?' the taverner asked, holding the jug towards Petrus who nodded.

'One more,' he raised his voice, 'then I'd better get back to the fort.'

The soldiers turned to stare at him.

'Let's get going,' one of them said, eyeing Petrus nervously and standing up. 'We don't want to be late back.'

The two men left. Petrus gulped down the last of the ale, placed some coins on the table and walked out. He turned in the direction of the forge whose furnace released a thin tail of smoke into the night. A shadow moved. Petrus' fingers closed around his pugio as a man emerged from the darkness; his face covered by a hood.

'Hail, Roman,' he said, pulling the hood down and shaking his tangled hair.

'Greetings Carantii. I saw your sign; do you have something to tell me?' he followed the man back into the shadows.

'The Romans are looking in the wrong place,' said Carantii.

'How so?'

'Your centurion has scouts going out looking for holy men who they say are copying the old ways of druids. The murder in the temple was not the work of holy men. It wasn't priests who fought with the two men near the bathhouse. A man saw four attackers, disciplined men, like soldiers he said; they used a strange language. He said they knocked the drunks unconscious and dragged them away.'

Petrus felt his heart beat faster, 'Who saw them?'

Carantii shook his head, 'The man said one attacker was big,' he spread his hands to indicate a man of bulk, 'and he gave orders to the others.'

'Did he see their faces? Can you tell me who the man was? I need to talk to him.' Said Petrus.

'He's scared. Doesn't want to end up like that dead soldier.'

'Can you get a better description of the attackers from him?' Petrus said, pressing coins into the man's hand, 'Ask him if he'll speak with me. I can guarantee his safety.'

Carantii laughed, 'Of course you can, you can guarantee a trip to that temple! If I have more information, I'll be in the tavern tomorrow night.' He pushed the coins into his bundle and walked into the darkness.

Petrus trudged back to the fort deep in thought. Could the attackers have been soldiers? How could he persuade the witness to come forward and give evidence? Tired, he gave the password at the gate, slipped inside and padded down the street to the barracks. A child's shriek rent the air and a small toddler in a torn shirt raced towards him in the dark street. She cannoned into his legs and threw her head back screaming with laughter. Petrus bent to stroke her hair as she pressed her face into his legs and dribbled snot onto his trousers.

'Come on you, let's find your mother,' he murmured taking her hand.

The door to one of the blocks opened and a woman ran towards them.

'Maaa!' cried the girl.

The woman grabbed her, hugging her tight. 'I am sorry Aurelius Petrus,' she said, 'She slipped away when my back was turned.'

'No harm done on this occasion. Another time you might not be able to find her,' he forced a smile and walked quietly to his room.

'Shall I bring you some food, Sir?' Boga asked. He was Maximus' slave, a slight, bald man whose arms were scarred where his previous owner had burned him with a torch.

'Just some wine tonight,' murmured Petrus sitting down on his bed.

Sipping wine, Petrus reviewed the day. Maximus had not shared the outcome from the interviews he'd done. He had just said that he'd learned nothing important. Petrus wondered whether he should speak to the men himself. He heard the centurion crashing about in his room as he prepared to leave first thing in the morning.

V – Dies Iovis

The Prefect strode into his office dragging the same slave girl who had been with him the day before. He shoved her behind the red curtain. Petrus frowned as the sound of the girl crying reached into the office. The smell of Tatius' perfume filled the room.

'Hail Silvius Tatius,' Petrus said.

Tatius threw himself into his chair. 'Petrus, I've been speaking to the men who found the bodies in the temples. Told them they need to toughen up a bit. Soldiers see death all the time in battle, they must be prepared for it.'

Petrus was disappointed with the Prefect's words. The men's comrades had not died honourably in battle. Their bodies had been horribly mutilated. Some of the soldiers were young and inexperienced, they needed a bit of understanding. Tatius had never been too concerned about the men under his command. All he wanted was for them to make him look good to the Governor and other Prefects.

'What've you got to tell me?' asked Tatius.

'I've put the carcasses of two skinned rabbits in Cocidius' temple. I'll return in a day or so to see if there are rats there,' replied Petrus.

'Why is that important? How will that help us find the killer?'

'It might help to show whether the murders were staged. That would rule out holy men. As I've said, I think the motive of money is a strong one which would not apply to them.'

'I'll let you carry on with this,' Tatius said, 'however, I'm confident that Maximus will return with the holy men and the evidence to prove they are the murderers. We need to make an example of them, to show the people of the vicus and the surrounding local tribes that Rome will not allow its men to be killed without avenging their deaths.'

'Word in the vicus is that there are no priests in the area,' said Petrus, 'A witness saw four men fighting with the two drunks. They were knocked unconscious and dragged away. He thought the attackers were disciplined men, like soldiers.'

Tatius sat up in his chair and frowned. 'Soldiers? Why would soldiers kill each other?'

'If the dead men had got a lot of money from somewhere, or if they had robbed or cheated someone, then that might be a motive,' responded Petrus.

'If it was soldiers, I want them found,' Tatius paused, 'Are you up to this?'

Petrus knew Tatius was worried that if there were murderous soldiers inside his fort, then that would reflect badly on him as their commander. 'I'm trying to speak to the witness directly, but it seems he's afraid to come forward. Inducements may need to be offered.'

'Money? You must get a written statement from him.'

Petrus bit back his immediate retort and said, 'The man probably doesn't speak Latin and even if he does, he's unlikely to be able to read it or want to make a statement.'

'We need hard evidence!' Tatius banged his fist on the table, then seemed to check himself and asked, 'What other enquiries are you going to make?'

'I'm going to go back to the brothel and speak again to the two girls who were with the dead men earlier that evening. I need to check the duty rosters for the last few weeks in case the two men did or saw something that meant they could have created enemies. Maximus spoke with the men in their contubernia, but he said they had nothing of interest to say.'

Tatius frowned, 'What makes you think the girls have more to tell you?'

'I'm not sure. I just want to check it out and to talk to them without Sylva's minder there. They might be more willing to talk to me if we are alone. I also need a list of all the other visitors to the brothel that night, in case they noticed something.'

'You'll probably have to pay Sylva for that information as well,' grumbled Tatius, 'I'm not paying for you to get laid.'

'I have no need of prostitutes Sir.'

'One has no need of them,' Tatius smiled and waved his hand, 'However, they are diverting when one's wife is busy, or entertaining her friend. Do not neglect your other duties Petrus. The wall repairs are falling behind; weapons training and workshops all need supervising. Come to the house this afternoon for the money. I don't want to go through the Signifer. The results of these enquiries are to be kept between us. Report only to me.'

He waved Petrus away, rose from his chair and moved towards the curtain covering his robing area. Petrus was annoyed. Tatius didn't want anyone to know about his enquiries in case they came to nothing. Tatius was, as always, concerned about his image. He didn't realise that looking at other causes for the deaths showed diligence, and this ought to be looked on favourably by the prefect's superiors.

Thick grey clouds leaked rain onto the fort. One of the workshops was making tiles to repair the roof of the barrack's buildings and mixing the mortar for the wall builders. The men were being adequately supervised by the immunes. In the next room soldiers were repairing leatherwork on horses' bridles and saddles. Work appeared to be going well, so Petrus walked quickly through the building and went to the drill hall where one of the newly promoted optios was putting soldiers through their training. All the men were obviously relieved to be inside somewhere dry. Two brothers strongly favoured using their left hands to draw their swords, even when it was explained that their left hand was for holding their shield, their natural instincts went against that. Petrus saw that his fellow optio was trying not to lose his temper. Petrus nodded encouragement and left them.

He had some watered-down wine in his room and then went to look at the repairs on the wall near the northern gatehouse. Work was going well there, so he headed back towards the Praetorium. He walked slowly up the steps. The guard on duty stood aside to let him pass and he knocked on the door. It was opened by Felix.

'I have orders from the Prefect to collect something from here,' Petrus said.

Felix stepped aside; a smile was fixed to his thin face as he let Petrus enter the building.

'The Prefect left it with his wife. The mistress is in the salon, with her friend.'

He led Petrus through the house, past a bust of the emperor, sculptures of birds and animals on pedestals. The walls were painted with rich coloured frescoes showing men struggling against fantastical beasts and the floor tiles depicted heroic events in Roman history. Petrus was amazed that the Prefect had gone to such lengths to decorate a house inside a fort complex. Slaves moved quietly round the building cleaning and tidying.

'They've just come out of the baths,' whispered Felix.

He stood to one side indicating that Petrus should walk through the door into the main salon. The window shutters were closed to keep out the cold winter air, so the room was brightly lit by torches. The walls were richly decorated, there were plush couches and incense burners filled the air with thick scent. The two women, both dressed in flowing robes, lay facing each other on a couch with their arms around each other, whispering animatedly. Petrus felt embarrassed, even though he knew such behaviour was not unusual amongst women of high social class.

Felix coughed loudly, 'Aurelius Petrus is here.'

Prima looked at Petrus over her shoulder, then rolled over to face him. Fabia curled her arm round Prima's waist and pulled her closer as she pressed herself into Prima's back.

'Ah Petrus, I hope you've been admiring our decorations,' Prima purred, 'I had it all done when I arrived here. Army residences can be so dreary, and our children need to see beauty in contrast to the austere conditions of army life. My husband said you would call to collect some money. It's there,' she pointed to a small coin pouch resting on a tablet on a side table, 'There's a receipt there for you to sign as well.'

The pouch jangled as he attached it to his belt; he quickly read the tablet and scribbled his signature. Fabia whispered in Prima's ear and giggled. Prima's face was flushed as she pushed Fabia's hand away.

Petrus said 'Thank you.'

'What will you be doing with my husband's money Petrus? Must my children starve so that you can have his money?'

Petrus felt awkward. 'There are some private matters which I'm looking into on your husband's behalf. I'm sure he wouldn't let your children suffer.'

Fabia moved, making Prima gasp, and with an effort she whispered, 'We will not suffer from the lack of a few coins. Go well Petrus.'

Petrus felt himself redden. She lifted her torso off the couch, turning so that she faced Fabia again. Petrus left the room. Felix was hovering in the hallway. He smothered a grin as he saw Petrus' reaction to the women and led him back out of the house.

Petrus strode through the vicus. The streets were busy as people rushed to get their purchases before the stalls closed. Belligedo, Aurora's favoured butcher, was closing his shop early. Business must have been good. He pulled fragments of meat from where they clung to hooks and ran the cloth over the stained metal. He swabbed the bloodstained shelves and rinsed the cloth in a bucket of water. Petrus nodded to him as he passed. Two well-dressed men adjusted their clothes as they emerged from the brothel laughing and whispering to each other as they turned towards the tavern. He guessed they were probably merchants as they wore thick green shirts and very fine leather boots.

Petrus opened the door to the brothel, stepped into its darkened interior and walked along the corridor into the salon. There were no other customers. A young girl rose from her seat and took his hand.

'Welcome Sir,' she murmured.

He allowed her to lead him across the room.

'If you would sit here,' she gestured to a couch.

He lowered himself down and relaxed against the plump cushions.

'Would you like some wine? I can send for the mistress; she'll find you a girl, or, or a boy, if you prefer?'

Petrus smiled, 'Some wine and your mistress.'

A slave poured him some wine and set the jug on a table at his side. He took a long drink and thought about what he would say to Cara and Metta.

'Petrus,' Sylva's smooth tones brought him back into the room. 'Is it business or pleasure?' She sat beside him on the couch.

'Both, Sylva. Some information from you and then I would like to spend some time with Metta and Cara.'

'Why those two? I have some much more experienced women to pleasure you.'

'I liked the look of those two when I was last here. They have a good reputation back at the fort. They're the ones I want.'

'Very well, I can make them available in the same room as before,' she began to turn away.

'Hold on,' he grasped her arm.

Her eyes widened in shock, and he released his grip.

'I need a list of men who visited here on Solis.'

'All the men? I don't keep…'

'Of course you do!' he snapped, 'Don't make me threaten you.'

She hesitated, 'Very well. I'll make the list while you are,' she paused, 'enjoying your leisure time with the two sisters,' she got up to leave, 'you know where they are. Leave your payment with the girl before you go to their room. Come and see me on your way out.'

He dropped some coins into the girl's outstretched hand and made his way down the dimly lit corridor. Cara was sitting on the bed with Metta kneeling behind her running a brush through her hair. They looked up as he entered. Metta put the brush on a side table. Cara grasped his hand; a smile fixed to her face. She drew him to the bed, and he sat down. She moved closer, placed her hand on his leg.

'How can we please you?' she whispered as she pulled her gown down over her shoulders, exposing her small breasts.

He took a sharp intake of breath. Metta knelt behind him and placed her hands on his shoulders. Aroused, he shook his head.

'Stop. I'm just here to talk with you. Put on your gown,' he grasped the fine material and drew it up to cover Cara's body.

He rose and pulled a stool over to sit facing the two women. Their eyes widened in fear.

'Don't be afraid, I just want to talk to you about the men you were with on the night of Saturni, the ones I was asking about when I was last here. Tell me about their visit with you.'

They looked at him but said nothing.

'Two men have been killed and I am trying to find who did it and why. Please tell me more about them. What did they talk about?'

He took two denarii from inside his tunic and held them towards the women in the palm of his hand. 'This is for you. Your own money, not Sylva's.'

Metta reached for the coins, but he closed his fingers around them. 'Talk first, then you can have the money.'

Cara took a deep breath, 'They spoke in Latin. We… we don't speak much Latin,' she looked at Metta as if for reassurance, 'I only recognised a few words.'

'Which were?' he asked.

'Money, they talked about money and the man.'

'The man, was the man here on Saturni?'

Cara looked away, 'Not enough Latin,' she mumbled, not looking at him.

He did not believe her, 'Anything else?'

She shook her head.

He turned to look at Metta, 'Did you understand anything more.'

Metta replied, 'I did not.'

'It's really important that I find whoever killed these men. Anything you can tell me might help.' He looked from one to the other and waited.

In the silence he could hear them breathing. He waited. Disappointed, and realising he would not get anything more from them, he gave them one denarius each. They both smiled shyly. Cara stroked the coin as it lay in her palm and then curled her fingers tightly round it. He hoped they had somewhere to keep the money, somewhere that Sylva wouldn't know about.

He returned to the salon and lowered himself onto a couch. He'd had two cups of wine and was just beginning to relax when Sylva entered and collapsed down next to him with a sigh, handing him two tablets listing men's names. Her rich perfume smelled of spices.

He glanced down briefly at them and was surprised, 'Centurion Julius Maximus was here?'

'That's what it says. Actually, he didn't really come in, he stopped in the salon, when he saw how busy we were, he turned on his heel and left. Doesn't like to be kept waiting, your centurion. I'm not comfortable giving you the list. Please be discrete.'

'Two men have been murdered, Sylva. I'll do whatever I need to in order to find the killers.'

'I trust you were pleased with the girls. You were very quick,' she smirked, 'I expect you have a lot of things on your mind and are no doubt very tired.'

She was trying to insult him. He wasn't bothered by her words, so she would be disappointed.

'Go well, Petrus.'

He was in a hurry to get back to the fort, but he had to visit the tavern first, in case Carantii had some news. It was dark outside. He put his hand on the door to the tavern, but it flew open, and he heard jeering coming from inside. A man with a hood pulled over his head forced his way out.

'Hail Petrus,' Carantii whispered as he passed.

Petrus continued into the tavern whose welcoming warmth drew him inside. He sat at the table nearest the door.

'Are you here to sort out that lot?' the taverner asked as he inclined his head towards a nearby table where four men sat drinking and arguing.

Petrus didn't know the men. They shouted in Latin and used bad grammar, obviously new recruits. Their arrogance annoyed him. They wanted to appear different and superior to the locals.

'Are they causing trouble?' he asked.

'Not much, but they were abusive to the man who you passed coming in. Carantii, the blacksmith,' replied the taverner.

'In what way?' Petrus was immediately concerned in case they'd realised Carantii was his spy.

'Kept asking him if he was selling rats and squirrels instead of proper meat,' said the taverner.

'Does the blacksmith sell meat?'

'Sometimes. He has his own traps and sells any excess. Hasn't for a while though, too busy making things for the fort I expect. He'll be a rich man soon at this rate,' said the taverner.

'And does he? Carantii I mean, does he sell rats and squirrels, making out they're something different?' asked Petrus.

'He sold rats during one really harsh winter a few years ago. There was nothing else to trap. He made no secret of it, and some people were glad of it.'

Petrus put down his drink and walked over to the soldiers,

'Right lads, I think you've had enough now. Time to get back to the fort,' he said.

'Who the fu…ooof!' the man's words were cut off when his mate elbowed him in the ribs.

'Aurelius Petrus! We're just having a bit of fun,' said the man who'd elbowed his companion.

'And upsetting the locals. Now finish your drinks, pay up and get back to the fort before I put you on report!' snapped Petrus.

He returned to his seat and nodded towards the taverner who poured him another drink. The soldiers continued their banter for a few more minutes and then left.

Petrus took his time over the ale and read down the list of names on the tablets which Sylva had given him. Many were soldiers from the fort, names he knew, including the centurion, Julius Maximus. Carantii, the blacksmith, had been there and so had some other local men whose names were not familiar to him, probably traders from the vicus. He wondered why Maximus hadn't mentioned his own visit to the brothel. Petrus could interview all the soldiers, but speaking with the traders would be more difficult, if not impossible; he'd see what else Carantii could find out. He decided he needed to speak to the rest of Faustus' and Drusus' contubernia at the barracks. He got up to leave, placing some coins on the table.

'So soon?' asked the taverner.

Petrus nodded.

Outside he turned towards the forge, but Carantii stepped out of an alleyway, 'Hail Petrus,' he whispered.

'Hail Carantii,' Petrus pushed him back into the darkness, 'What news?'

'The man, the witness, will not come forward to give evidence, even for money. I cannot question him more without revealing…' his voice trailed off. He meant without revealing that he spied for the Roman army.

'Do you know his name?' Petrus snapped.

Carantii shook his head. Petrus thought he was lying but decided not to press him. If Carantii asked too many questions and was unveiled as an army informant, he might be in danger or forced to leave the vicus, and that would make it much more difficult for Petrus to find out what was going on. He handed over some coins and Carantii melted away into the darkness. Petrus made his way back to the fort. He squinted in the candlelight in his room as he recorded his notes for the day, placed the wooden tablets under his mattress and tried to sleep.

VI – Dies Veneris

Petrus cantered his horse up the hillside towards the Temple of Cocidius. The early morning dew lay thick on the ground and the horse's hooves left a dark trail across the grass. The horse snorted in the silence of the morning and Petrus stroked its neck as he slowed to a walk near the sacred spring. He dismounted and tied the horse to a tree. He touched the engraved plaque over the open door with his fingers and muttered a prayer.

A flaming torch on the wall dripped stinking animal fat onto the floor and cast shadows across the rotting entrails, rabbit carcasses, and shrivelled vegetables alongside them. On fresh ivy leaves were another offering of vegetables. As he moved forward, the rank odour of rotting flesh smothered the smell of the burning torch. He examined the rabbits' bodies. The flesh had dried and blackened in places. However, there were no bite marks or rat droppings on any of the offerings. The putrid smell of decay turned his stomach as he scooped up the rabbits' remains, dropped them outside and kicked dirt over them. The stink did not leave him. He took some deep breaths, pulling fresh freezing air into his lungs and picked up the broom near the temple door. He swept the floor, clearing the ivy and dried blood into a pile. He pushed it out of the door onto the grass, feeling satisfied that he'd been right about the rats on Faustus' body being placed there by the killers. He hoped he could convince the Prefect and Maximus.

He re-entered the temple, rearranged the other offerings and took an apple from his trouser pocket. Its skin was greasy with age, and he wiped it on his tunic. The sweet smell of it teased his nostrils and tingled his tongue. He placed the apple in front of the altar, closed his eyes and muttered his prayers.

'Cocidius, oh Great God of hunting. Bring me success in the hunt for the killers of these soldiers who were in my care. Give me the strength to persevere with my enquiries and stand up to my centurion and Prefect.' He stayed in front of the altar, his head bowed, 'Help me!' Petrus chanted fervently, 'Help me!'

He shivered as he mounted his horse. They walked slowly down the hillside and along the valley bottom. The horse slipped on the wet stones as they climbed up the escarpment and Petrus whispered words of encouragement. Walking through the vicus, Petrus thought about how he might convince Tatius that he was right about the killers when the Prefect's natural instinct was always to go with Maximus' ideas.

He met with Tatius in his office. The Prefect drummed his fingers on the table as Petrus spoke.

'The skinned rabbits had lain in the temple for two days. There were other food offerings there too, left by other worshippers. I deliberately left the temple door open to allow any scavengers easy access. The carcasses stank with decay, but there were no signs of rats eating them, no teeth marks from any animal and the flesh was intact. This proves that the rats on Faustus' body were placed there by the killers.' He was pleased with his conclusions.

Tatius scowled, 'I agree it appears that way. But I don't see how it's significant.'

'It proves it wasn't druids who killed Faustus,' stated Petrus, 'That's not the way druids used to worship or make sacrifices. It's also not the way of any holy men I've ever heard of.'

'That's true. But what about this holy man from overseas?' asked Tatius.

'As I've said, his teachings appear to be all about love.'

'That's what you've heard.' Tatius emphasised the words, 'What else?'

'The witness who saw the drunk soldiers being attacked will not come forward. The only thing we know is that he saw four men; one, a big man who was clearly in charge, giving orders in a strange language,' Petrus threw out his arms to show a stocky man, 'That could've been any language, maybe Latin or maybe a tribal one. Although why four men from another tribe would be here killing soldiers, I can't imagine. The witness saw the four men knock the two drunk men unconscious and drag them through the back alleys of the vicus. I need someone to help me, to find out what duties the two men were doing in the weeks leading up to this and how they got hold of the money mentioned in the curse tablets.'

'No!' Tatius slammed his fist down on the table, 'I won't allow that. I'm looking to you and Maximus to solve the murders. The investigation must be kept between us, confidential. This is your idea, your investigation. I want it done quietly. I don't want to cause further alarm to the men in the fort or the people in the community.' He raised a hand to silence Petrus' protests, 'I've spoken with Optio Salvus Septimus, who will cover all your normal duties, so that you can focus on this. The barbarians in this area haven't been able to find any holy men, nor any talk of them, despite our threats.'

'I've heard as much. There will be resentment building against the army in the community,' mumbled Petrus.

Tatius waved his hand, unconcerned.

'I have a list of men who were at the brothel on that day, they all need to be spoken to,' he showed Tatius the list. 'One name surprised me, Julius Maximus.'

'It's no secret that he frequents the brothel.'

Petrus wanted to yell, 'Yes, but he could have mentioned it.' He said, 'Sylva said he entered the brothel but left straight away. She said it was too busy for him. I may have to speak to the contubernia of the dead men again. Maximus didn't make a written report about his discussion with them, he just told me that there was nothing to learn. I should like to know exactly what was said as there may be something he has missed.' He felt awkward criticising Maximus.

'Are you suggesting Maximus isn't a competent interrogator?' Tatius raised an eyebrow, 'It's a dangerous thing to speak badly of your centurion. Do you suspect him?' he paused, 'Tread carefully, Petrus. You'd better have proof if you're making accusations.'

'I'm not suggesting... I'll ask him about it when he returns.'

'You will not!' Tatius roared. He ran a trembling hand through his hair. 'If, and only if it is necessary, I will speak to him. I won't have you challenging your superior officer like that. It may not be necessary anyway if he returns with the culprits.'

'Very well,' frustrated, Petrus bowed his head.

'Wait, Petrus! Tomorrow morning, you're to come with us on a hunting trip.'

Petrus hid his surprise and waited for Tatius to elaborate.

'Prima and Fabia wish to go hunting together. That is if they ever stop lounging about giggling and spending all their time in the baths. Prima is a good shot with a bow. Good for a woman, I mean. Learned to hunt with her father who was a Senator in Rome and wanted a strong independent daughter who could match any man. That's her story anyway. More likely her wayward brother taught her, just to upset the old man. Maximus usually accompanies us with some barbarians. Prima favours Maximus, her family are from the same clan. He's known her since childhood, so comes hunting with us as her protector, even though it's beneath a centurion to do so. I indulge them in that,' Tatius shrugged his shoulders, 'Not that I need to explain myself to you.'

'I am at your command.' Petrus bowed.

'It'll be straight after parade, or thereabouts,' Tatius waved him away.

Petrus made his way to the records building at the back of the Principia. Its windows were wide open, as the librarii, who were the record keepers, claimed circulating air prolonged the storage life of the records, which were stacked on shelves from floor to roof. They may have been correct, but he thought the real reason for the open windows was that the librarii preferred to work in natural light. They were afraid that flaming torches might set alight the wooden tablets and their precious records would be lost. They had good reason to be afraid, fire was an ever-present danger inside the fort.

Manius, their century's librarius, was busy sorting his reports when Petrus entered the Records office. Seeing Petrus, he flicked his dark fringe away from his eyes with a fine-boned hand and nodded a greeting. Petrus noted his scrupulously clean fingernails. The librarii from the other centuries were also busy and did not look up. The room smelt strongly of the men's perfume.

'Hail Manius. I want to know where these men are right now,' he pointed to his list of men in Drusus' contubernia. He also handed over a copy of the list which Sylva had given him. 'I also need to know where I can find these other men working today.'

Manius looked at Sylva's list and nodded. 'It may take some time with this list, as they are not all in our century. I'll have to talk to the others,' he nodded in the direction of the other record keepers. 'As to the men in Drusus' contubernia, I imagine they've already spoken to Centurion Julius Maximus, he asked for the same thing,' he pushed Petrus' tablet away. 'Where are they working today? Err, ah, yes. They're beyond the parade ground, felling trees and collecting firewood.'

'I'll go to see Drusus' team. When I get back, I hope the other list will be ready. This,' Petrus tapped the tablet with his forefinger. 'This takes priority, those are the Prefect's orders.'

Petrus had not spoken with the Signifer, Ecdicius, who managed the librarii, and he outranked Petrus. He hoped the mention of the Prefect would make Manius comply with his request without referring it back to Ecdicius. Petrus walked out of the East gate. Ahead of him six soldiers armed with shields and swords walked down the street. They looked left and right as they walked, their hands resting on their swords, ever vigilant. Petrus quickened his pace. As he caught them up, he saw Fabia and Prima, walking just in front of the soldiers. They wore trousers with boots and had short cloaks across their shoulders which did not cover their tunics completely. A slave girl carrying a covered basket scurried alongside them, her smock trailed on the ground as she walked, and mud clung to it. Fabia and Prima had their arms linked and their heads bent close together as they whispered and giggled, totally unaware of their effect on the local people who stared at the fine ladies as they walked by with their guard of soldiers.

'Who's in charge?' Petrus muttered to the man at his side.

The man brought himself more upright. 'The Tesserarius,' he said, indicating the man to his left.

'Where are they going?' asked Petrus.

'To the temple of Jupiter,' replied the Tesserarius, a man who Petrus vaguely recognised, 'They wish to make some sacrifices. We've been ordered by Centurion Fabius Ruga to accompany them at all times, to ensure their safety.'

The slave girl had turned her head when she heard Petrus speak, but the two women were too engrossed in their conversation to notice him. He nodded at the slave and sped up, passing them.

'Aurelius Petrus!' Prima's voice made him stop, 'Are you accompanying us to the temple?'

They came alongside him, and he walked with them for a few paces. 'Regrettably Ma'am, I've other matters to attend to in the woods beyond the parade ground. I see you've got plenty of protection.'

Prima nodded and Fabia fluttered her eyelids in the way that annoyed him so much. 'They're sending a carriage to bring us back from the temple in a little while. My husband doesn't think we can walk too far. He thinks we'll grow tired and need to be carried back by one of these brave soldiers,' she sighed theatrically, 'Fabia has been unwell these last few days, so he may be correct. We're going to the temple to pray for her wellbeing.'

Petrus nodded. Fabia ran her tongue slowly across her lips and looked him up and down, exactly the way she had done previously. He felt awkward and annoyed as she was trying to unsettle him. He saluted them and strode away; their giggles pursued him down the street.

The creak and groan of falling trees reached out to him as he approached a copse. Sounds of sawing wood and the blows of axes mingled with the men's shouts. Two horses harnessed to a cart stood with their noses in the food bags attached to their bridles, they munched contentedly as the men filled the cart with chopped wood. Two groups of men were being supervised by immunes.

Petrus spoke to one of the immunes, 'I need to speak with some of these men.'

The man scowled and then realising who Petrus was rearranged his face and saluted him, 'Which men did you need, Sir?'

'I need to speak with the men from the dead soldiers' contubernia,' Petrus explained, holding the list out for the immune to read. The man did not look at the tablet.

'I think they've already spoken with Maximus about that,' he said.

'This is on the Prefect's orders!' snapped Petrus, deciding that he could pretend he'd misunderstood what Tatius had said.

'Yes, Sir,' he called the six men forward, one of whom was the immune supervising the other group. 'Go with Aurelius Petrus, he needs some information about Drusus and Faustus.'

Petrus surveyed the men. They were smartly dressed in clean tunics.

'Let's go back to your barracks. I want to see where the two men slept,' he said and turned towards the fort.

The men began marching behind him.

'At ease, relaxed walk back, no need to march,' he said and noted the relief on their faces. 'Have you spoken with Maximus about the dead soldiers?' he casually asked Argentus, the immune.

'Yes, Sir,' muttered Argentus, 'he asked if we knew where they got their money from.'

'And do you?'

'No Sir, no idea,'

'Is that all he asked you?'

'Yes Sir.'

Petrus was dismayed that Maximus had asked so few questions.

At the fort, they made their way to the men's room. It was clean and tidy; each bed had a folded blanket on it. Their belongings were folded away under the beds. Their weapons were stacked in the second room, along with their cooking utensils.

'Show me where the two of them slept,' said Petrus.

Argentus pointed to two bottom bunks.

Petrus lifted the mattresses, there was nothing underneath, no trinkets, no weapons, or clothes. 'And where are their belongings?'

'In their chests.' Argentus replied and pulled two chests out from under the beds. The locks were damaged where they'd been forced open.

'Did you open their chests?' asked Petrus.

Argentus looked embarrassed, 'They'd already been forced.'

'Why didn't you report it?'

He shrugged, 'We weren't sure when it was done. It's possible they lost their keys and forced the locks themselves.'

Petrus had no authority over the immune, who wasn't intimidated.

Petrus sighed, 'Tell me what you know about the two men,' he sat down on one the beds. 'Sit down if you feel more comfortable,' he pointed to the bed opposite him.

Argentus sat down; the rest of the men remained standing.

'Are you all from the same area back home?' Petrus softened his tone.

They all nodded.

'It's difficult when you lose friends like this,' Petrus said.

'They weren't our friends,' muttered Crispus, a short man with scars on his arms, 'not at the end anyway.'

'Why not?' asked Petrus.

Crispus spat, 'They were arrogant. Said they wouldn't be here much longer, claimed they were going to buy their way out of the army. They flashed their money about and went out drinking at every opportunity. They were careless with our belongings. Faustus broke my bowl. When I complained he just laughed and threw me a couple of sestertii saying, 'Get another, get several.' What was I supposed to eat out of while I waited to get another bowl?'

'There's plenty of bowls in the fort, it wouldn't be difficult to get one,' replied Petrus.

'Yes, but not the night when he did it.' Crispus said, clearly still aggrieved.

'Did any of you take anything from their chests?' Petrus asked, looking round at each man.

They all shook their heads. Petrus was not sure he believed them. 'It would've been normal to share out their belongings.'

'I made them all wait, until we're told by Maximus to clear up their stuff,' Argentus said.

'Whose is this?' Petrus asked pointing to one of the chests.

'That's Faustus',' replied Argentus.

Petrus opened the chest. A crumpled clean tunic had been folded on top of the contents. He placed it on the bed; it had been carefully patched in a few places. In the bottom of the chest were some metal jewellery and trinkets. Lying inside a blue pottery bowl were two bronze-coloured metal armbands with intricate patterns carved on them, two metal finger rings in the shape of serpents and two dice. A roughly carved wooden horse, a toy, suitable for a child, lay next to eight coins, he picked them up. Denarii, a month's pay.

'Did Faustus have any children? Maybe in the vicus?' he

looked at each man in turn.

They all shook their heads.

'None that we're aware of,' muttered Germanus.

Petrus picked up the toy. 'A strange thing to have then, don't you think? Did he have a woman?'

The men shrugged. Petrus placed the items back in the chest with the tunic on top and closed the lid. He pulled the other chest towards him. Beneath an empty sack was a handful of sestertii and a belt whose buckle was studded with glass beads. A green plate, so well-used that the glaze was worn off in parts, lay next to a matching bowl and goblet. He placed the sack back over them and closed the lid.

'Can you tell me about their money?' Petrus asked.

'They boasted about their money all the time,' declared Germanus, who was clearly keen to avoid another beating. 'Said they were carrying aurei in their pouches, ten at least they said. Had them tied to their chests they said, in here,' he placed a hand inside his tunic, the palm flat on his chest.

'When did this start? Them having lots of money, I mean.' Asked Petrus.

'About a month ago. They didn't say how they'd got it.' Germanus replied.

'What had been happening around that time?'

The men were quiet.

'Well?' Petrus persisted.

'Nothing Sir,' Crispus said.

'We'd just been living our normal lives inside the fort and then they started acting like they were so much better than us, treating us like shit,' said Germanus.

'When we were off duty for any length of time, they went into the vicus to drink and visit the brothel. Made no secret of it. Always came back drunk,' said Argentus.

'What duties did you have in the last few weeks? Anything different?' asked Petrus.

'No Sir. We were just on normal rotation. Training, wall building, stores, workshops, gathering firewood, and guarding the Prefect's house,' said Argentus.

'One thing we did do differently,' Crispus said, 'One day we went with the Prefect and his wife on a hunting trip. The centurion, Maximus was also there. That'd never happened to us before.'

'All of you?'

They all nodded except Argentus. As an immune he was excused normal duties.

'And what happened then, anything unusual?'

'I'm not sure Sir, I've never done it before, don't know what's usual. The Prefect's wife was there which was strange. Not sure how many women go hunting. She's a bloody good shot, for a woman that is. Bit loose, the way she swings her loaded bow about I mean, but a bloody good shot,' Crispus replied.

'I'd give her a shot,' sniggered Germanus.

Petrus glared at him.

'She shot a young buck,' continued Crispus, 'and wanted to gut it herself. Julius Maximus persuaded her to let him do it. She's a good rider too.'

Petrus nodded, 'Who else knew that the dead men had a lot of money?'

'They made no secret of it. They boasted about it. I imagine lots of the men in the barracks knew,' replied Germanus.

'Did they gamble at all?'

'No more than usual. Anyway, how could they have won that much money gambling?' Germanus said.

Petrus nodded. That was a good point. A sudden thought struck him.

'I know where Germanus was the night they were attacked. Where were the rest of you?'

'We were here,' replied Argentus.

'All of you?

'Yes. I'd been out earlier in the day, to see my woman. But I was back just after dark and the rest were just here, lounging about,' Argentus said.

'I can check the gate's records,' Petrus looked at each one in turn. 'Were you out in the vicus, lying in wait for them to come back drunk? Waiting to rob them?'

'No, Sir,' they chorused.

'Leave their belongings in the chests until I've checked whether they'd made wills. If they didn't, then you can share them out. Wait 'til you get permission from me or someone more senior. Return their weapons and armour to the weaponry.' Petrus told them.

At the records building, Manius looked pleased with himself as he picked at his teeth with a stylus.

'I hope that has everything you need,' he pushed the tablet across the table.

'It does, but I realise I need another list,' Petrus picked up the tablet. 'All of those who went out on the evening of Saturni and didn't come back 'til the early hours of Solis.'

Manius grunted and pointed to the stack of tablets on the shelf behind him, 'It may take time.'

'I'll wait over here,' Petrus pointed to an empty table and stool, 'I'll be looking at this list. I also need to know whether the two dead men Faustus and Drusus had made wills. You'd have those if they had, wouldn't you? Stored somewhere in here,' he waved his hand around the room.

Manius nodded and started searching the records. Petrus sat down and looked at the tablet. In his immaculate handwriting, Manius had written the name of each man from Petrus' list, stated which century he belonged to and where he was working that day and for the following two days.

'You've put where they'll be for the next couple of days. That was good thinking, as I may not get round to them all today. Thank you.' Petrus said.

Manius smiled. Petrus studied the list, there were about twenty men from various centuries in the fort. It would take a long time to talk to them all individually. He was vaguely aware of Manius moving around nearby.

'Err,' coughed Manius politely, 'I have it,' he slid another tablet across the table. Petrus walked over to him. 'I've put their workplaces over the next two days there for you. As to wills, Faustus didn't have one, so his money will be retained by the army. Drusus, on the other hand,' he tapped at the tablet in front of him, 'he left his money and property to the two whores at Sylva's, Cara and Metta.'

Petrus drew in his breath, 'Really?'

Manius pushed a tablet towards Petrus. Alongside Drusus' name was the number fifty-six and the names Cara and Metta along with the words 'Brothel'.

'What's this?' Petrus asked, pointing at the numbers.

'The balance of Drusus' salary accounts. Fifty-six denarii. Not a small sum.' Replied Manius.

'Almost six months' pay,' Petrus was surprised he had managed to save so much money. Soldiers generally had so many deductions to their pay that it took a long time to build up any savings.

Petrus took the tablets from Manius, glancing quickly at them. There were eleven men who'd been outside the fort during that night, including the two dead men, Germanus, himself, and Maximus. Quickly he cross-checked it with the list of men who'd been at the brothel. There were three names on both lists, one of them was the centurion, Maximus.

'Thank you Manius.'

He went back to his office and sipped some watered-down wine. He looked at the list; four of the men who'd been out overnight were roommates in the barracks, they were under Centurion Ignatius Aquilinus. They did not return to the fort until the last hour of the night according to the records. Petrus wondered if they had seen the two drunk men. They were currently working at a nearby milecastle, some three miles away. He scribbled a quick order for them to return to the fort and come to his office immediately and instructed a messenger to ride out to them. The remaining two men should be with their group guarding the prefect's house, armoury and treasury.

He went into Aquilinus' office and told the centurion that he'd sent for his men.

Aquilinus looked at him and frowned, 'Overstepping your authority, aren't you? Sending for my men.'

'I've been given authority by the Prefect to investigate the deaths of two soldiers from my century. I think we all want to know who killed them, don't we?' He realised this was a bit rude, but he didn't have time to stroke the centurion's ego.

'You can question them, but I want to be there. Some of my men are not very bright, they might incriminate themselves,' said Aquilinus.

Petrus scowled. 'Very well, I'll come and get you when they arrive.'

Petrus went outside and approached the praetorium where two men were loitering on the steps. Seeing him, they stood to attention and saluted.

'I'm looking for the brothers Octavius and Nonus, where are they?' he asked.

'We are Octavius and Nonus,' replied one of the men.

Petrus studied them closely. They had the same oval-shaped

faces, light brown curly hair, brown eyes and eyebrows that joined in a continuous line across their brows. They were short and thin, not having yet built up any bulk during their training.

'Which is which?' he asked.

'I am Nonus,' said one.

'Where were you during the night of Saturni and early part of Solis?' asked Petrus.

The men gave no response.

'Did you have permission to be out of the fort for all that time? Were you together?' Petrus continued.

The two men looked at each other.

'I can check. You know that don't you?' Petrus moved towards them, standing so close he could feel their breath on his face.

'We, we had permission to be out until the sun went down,' mumbled Nonus. 'We went to the brothel and had some fun, with two girls, and the two of us in one room. They gave us wine; we drank a fair bit. Must've fallen asleep. The next thing we know, a girl was shaking us both awake and saying we had to leave. Then that big slave, the one with the holly tattoo on his chest, got quite aggressive. It was starting to grow light as we ran across the ditch and into the fort. We'd just got back to our room when the others were getting up and didn't have time to change our clothes. We were criticised by the Centurion for our appearance at parade as we were in such a mess. Will we be in trouble?'

Petrus remembered them looking bedraggled on the parade ground. 'You've heard about the two dead men? Did you know them?'

They shook their heads.

'One had red hair and the other had a large purple mark on his right forearm, here,' Petrus rubbed his right forearm with this left hand. 'Did you see them at the brothel?'

The two men shook their heads.

'I don't remember seeing anyone like that, not with a mark on his arm. But once we'd chosen our girls, we were just in their room, so we wouldn't have seen them,' Nonus said.

'After leaving the brothel the two men went to the tavern and got drunk. Did you come across them as you ran back in the morning?'

The two men shook their heads.

'Did you know they'd come into a lot of money?'

'We'd heard that someone in your century had money, but we didn't know who,' mumbled Octavius.

Petrus didn't believe them. 'You weren't curious to know how much they had and whether you could get some of it? You didn't come across them and attack them?'

'No, no Sir,' they said in unison.

'What are you supposed to be doing right now?'

'Guarding the prefect's house,' replied Nonus.

'Does that involve lounging on the steps?'

'No Sir,' replied Octavius, 'we're meant to walk around the outside.'

'Then hadn't you better do that?' snapped Petrus. He watched them for a moment as they hurried away. The sound of music and Prima's laughter reached him through an open window in the prefect's house and he wondered if the two brothers had been eavesdropping.

Back in his office Petrus pulled over a new tablet and began writing down all that he'd learned from the interviews with Faustus' roommates and the two brothers. He didn't think that Cara and Metta, the beneficiaries of Drusus' will, could have been involved in his death, as they probably didn't know they would inherit money and they were unlikely to be able to organise and stage the deaths. Even if they could, why kill Faustus as well? He listed all those who were outside the fort in the early hours of the morning and his intention to interview the remaining four men, stating that both he and Maximus were also outside and that both should be questioned about their movements. He thought the two brothers Octavius and Nonus might have had time to beat up the two soldiers, but not to take them out of the vicus. They would have had to work with two other people, as the witness had seen four men attacking the drunks. They would also have needed help to move the bodies. He was disturbed by a knock at the door.

'Enter,' he said looking up.

A young man with hair as white as snow entered the room. He had sky blue eyes and skin so pale that Petrus thought he could see right inside his body; there were blue lines running just below the surface of his skin.

'Vester, Sir. You sent orders for four of us to come back to the fort. Is it about the dead men?' said the man.

'Yes, it is. Are the others outside?' asked Petrus.

Vester nodded.

'Wait here.' Petrus strode into Aquilinus' office. The centurion was already on his feet and moving towards the door.

'I heard them coming,' he said, 'Let's get this over with.'

In Petrus' office Vester saluted his centurion who moved to the corner of the room where he leant against the wall. Vester's eyes flicked to look at Aquilinus and then back at Petrus.

Petrus stood behind the table. 'You and your comrades were still outside the fort in the early part of Solis, weren't you?'

Vester did not reply.

'The records show it. You might as well admit it,' he snapped.

Vester stood silently, staring at a point on the wall above Petrus' head.

'Answer the man!' Aquilinus roared and moved to stand at Petrus' shoulder.

'Yes Sir, we went to the vicus in the afternoon.' Vester's voice trembled, as he watched Aquilinus out of the corner of his eye.

'And what did you do there?' Petrus asked.

'We went to the tavern and had a few drinks.'

'Were you there when the two dead men were drinking with Germanus?' he saw Vester hesitate. 'I can check with Germanus, so don't think about lying to me.'

'Yes Sir, we did see them. We asked if we could sit with them and the one with the purple mark said, 'Get your own drinks, you lazy bastards. You're not having our money.' So, we sat at a different table.'

'You knew they had a lot of money then?'

He did not hesitate and looked Petrus in the eye. 'There were rumours.'

'Did you want some of it?' asked Petrus.

'Who doesn't want money, Sir? But I wouldn't kill a man for money.'

'That's what soldiering is man, being paid to kill people,' spat Petrus.

'That's different Sir. It's noble service to the Emperor. I meant I wouldn't kill a man to steal his money.'

'Did you four have a lot to drink?' asked Petrus.

'Yes Sir, I think so. I sort of lost count.'

'And when you left, was it dark?'

'Yes Sir, almost.'

'Then what did you do?'

Again, there was a hesitation.

'Well?' Petrus felt Aquilinus tense behind him.

'We, we went into the street, it was just growing dark. There were two girls hurrying down the street, carrying baskets. They obviously wanted to get home. We were a bit leery with them.' Vester glanced at his centurion, then back at Petrus.

'And?'

'They tried to ignore us, but we carried on,' he paused, 'and then we started chasing them. They dropped their baskets and ran.'

'And you carried on chasing them?' Petrus grimaced, clenching his fists. He knew where this was going.

'Yes sir, we were very drunk.'

Petrus lowered himself into his chair. He pulled a tablet towards him and began making notes. Without looking up he said, 'I'm writing a statement for you to sign. Go on, you chased the girls, and then?'

'Well, we chased them through the street. They were fast runners,' he grinned, then seeing Aquilinus' face, became serious again.

'You caught them?' Petrus asked.

'Yes, on the edge of the vicus.'

Petrus waited.

'We, we took them to a copse, just beyond the vicus.'

'And?'

'Well, we had some fun.'

'Fun? All of you? You took it in turns? You raped them, repeatedly?' Images of Aurora walking home in the early evening flashed through Petrus' mind. He pushed them away. She was safe at home. He was filled with shame and sadness, shame at being a man and a soldier, and sadness for the two young girls whose lives had been ruined.

'We were just having fun,' murmured Vester. 'They, the girls were out late.'

'So, you think they deserved it?'

Vester remained silent.

'And afterwards?' Petrus asked.

'It was nearly the end of the night. We brought them back to the vicus. Well, I had one and we…'

'I get the picture,' snarled Petrus, 'You brought them back and left them somewhere?'

'Yes, near the forge. Then we came back to the fort.'

The girls had been left close to Petrus' own house. He might have seen them, but he'd been concentrating on getting back to the fort. Maybe he could've helped them. The realisation hit him, like a blow to the chest. He took a deep breath.

'On your way back, did you find the two soldiers drunk? You would've been out at about the same time. Did you rob them? Kill them?'

'No Sir, no. I swear before all the Gods, we just came straight back here. The gatekeepers let us in,' Vester's voice trembled.

'Do you know the girls' names?'

'W… what?'

'The two girls, do you know their names? Their father will no doubt come to the fort for compensation. It would help if you knew their names,' sighed Petrus.

Vester shook his head, 'I… we… we didn't ask.'

Petrus finished writing. 'You're a disgrace to the army! Sign your name, or make a mark, on this report here,' Petrus jabbed his finger on the tablet.

'If their father turns up, the compensation will come out of your wages!' Aquilinus spat.

The young man's hand shook as he signed his name on the tablet. Petrus flung his office door open so hard it banged against the wall. The three waiting soldiers jumped to attention.

'Wait over there,' he instructed Vester, pointing to a place across the yard, 'Don't speak to these men. Don't make a sound!'

Petrus jabbed his forefinger into the chest of one of the other men who was large, broad chested, and had a round pockmarked face.

'Inside!' Petrus walked past the man and resumed his seat. 'Name?'

'Er, Celsus,' the man replied.

Petrus wrote it onto the tablet. 'Tell me what you did when you were outside the fort in the evening of Saturni.'

'We'd been drinking in the tavern in the afternoon,' the man replied.

'Did you see the two soldiers who were killed?'

'Yes, in the tavern. They were still there when we left.'

'And then?'

Aquilinus moved to stand right next to Celsus who tried not to look at him.

'We…er…we had some fun with some girls,' mumbled Celsus.

'Girls? From where?' asked Petrus.

'They were in the street.'

Petrus waited.

'We…er…we found them and well, sort of chased them and

then had some fun.'

'You mean you chased them and forced yourselves on them?' Petrus spoke quietly and slowly.

'Well, yes, sort of, I guess.'

'Sort of? You raped them!' Petrus banged his fist on the table. Celsus did not respond.

'Talk! Damn you!' shouted Aquilinus. His mouth was up against Celsus' ear. Celsus winced.

'Yes. Yes. We did and then we came back to the f…f…fort,' stammered Celsus.

'Did you see the two drunk soldiers, Faustus and Drusus on your way back?' asked Petrus.

'No Sir.'

'Did you beat them up and rob them? Did you kill them? Accidentally, maybe?'

'No! No, on my life!' Celsus looked frantically at Aquilinus and then back at Petrus.

'It may well turn out to be on your life soldier! This is a report of what you did and how you raped the girls. Sign or make your mark.' Petrus said pushing the tablet across the table.

As Celsus signed the tablet, Aquilinus hissed, 'I'll tell you what I told Vester. If their father turns up asking for compensation, it'll come out of your wages.'

Celsus nodded. Petrus took him outside to stand alongside Vester. 'Don't speak a word!'

Petrus interviewed the other two men; small, bald, fierce-looking brothers, Janus and Justus, who both gave the same story about that night. Petrus made them sign the tablet detailing their movements and Aquilinus told them their wages would be docked.

Petrus had a sudden thought and stormed outside to where the four men were waiting to be dismissed. 'Have you got anything in the pouches on your belts? Money? Anything?' he asked. 'Or anywhere on your body?'

They all shook their heads.

'I'm going to check,' he stepped forward and placed his hand on Vester's chest.

'I'll do it!' Aquilinus pushed him aside and ran his hands quickly over Vester's chest and back. He put his hand around the leather pouch at the young soldier's belt, squeezing it with his fingers. He yanked it hard, sharply breaking the thong holding it in place. Aquilinus tipped an aureus into his palm. He struck Vester hard across the face. Petrus flinched.

'My father gave it to me, f…for emergencies. So that I could always get home,' mumbled Vester.

Aquilinus gave the man his money back and turned on the other three men whose hands shook as they held out their pouches. The brothers' were empty, but Celsus had two denarii in his. Aquilinus quickly searched the three men's bodies.

'Take us to your room!' ordered Petrus.

Petrus and Aquilinus followed the men to the barracks. The room where they slept was clean and tidy, with fresh straw on the floor.

'Which are your chests? Pull them out and open them up! Which are your beds?' Petrus snapped.

Vester pointed to the four bottom bunks. Petrus quickly searched each bed, lifting the mattress and shaking the blankets. He didn't find anything. He went quickly through their chests but was frustrated to find only a few small coins amongst the clothing and trinkets. Annoyed he tossed the contents back into the chests and left the room. He could hear Aquilinus' low menacing voice berating the men behind him.

Eating the evening meal that Boga had prepared for him, he mulled over what he'd learned. He lay down to sleep but couldn't get the image out of his head of the two young girls being chased through the streets by the soldiers and then brutally raped. He knew Aurora and Mincona were sometimes still out of the house when it was growing dark. He couldn't bear the thought of them being attacked.

VII – Dies Saturni

'I'll read it later,' said Tatius pushing the report to the side of his table. 'Give me a summary now, and any conclusions you've come to.'

Petrus was soaking wet. During the morning parade the skies had opened, and rain had pelted the fort, soaking the men and the ground on which they stood, turning it to mud. Tatius had insisted on a meeting straight afterwards.

'It seems the dead men boasted that they had a lot of money. Each man claimed he carried around ten aurei in their pouches, kept inside their clothes, close to their chests. That's more than two years wages. Most of the men in the fort were probably aware they'd come into some cash. The women in the brothel heard them say something about money and a man, but they claim they don't have much Latin, so couldn't understand it. I don't believe them, so am going to try to get the information a different way.'

'Hold on,' Tatius interrupted, 'They told the whores something about money?'

'Not directly. They were talking about it in Latin, assuming the women wouldn't understand. I want to send someone else to the brothel to speak to them.'

Tatius nodded, 'Go on.'

'The witness said he thought the attackers may have been soldiers and gave a loose description which could match several men here at the fort and probably lots of men in the vicus. I've a list of men who were at the brothel that day and a list of soldiers who were out overnight, which is of interest if the attackers were indeed soldiers. Only three men are on both lists,

Maximus, and the brothers Nonus and Octavius. There were eleven men outside the walls at the time of the attack, including the dead men, myself, Germanus and the centurion.'

Tatius pursed his lips and Petrus hurried on, 'I was out late and came back with Germanus. I'd been visiting my family. As you may have heard my son, Titus, has an illness. He'd been ill again that evening and I needed to be there to help his mother. On my way back here, I found Faustus and Drusus fighting, separated them, and sent them back to the fort. I brought Germanus back with me. That was all in my report.'

'Go on,' nodded Tatius.

'Four of the men who stayed out late are from Aquilinus' century. I interviewed them in his presence. They all admitted to chasing two girls they came across as they left the tavern, just as it was getting dark. They caught them and took them to a copse where they raped them, repeatedly.' He emphasised the last few words.

Tatius waved his hand to silence him. 'Not bothered about that, this is a fort. These things happen.'

Petrus spoke through gritted teeth. 'They repeatedly raped them and then brought them back to the vicus. They did not pass back through the gate into the fort until the last hour of the night. So the girls endured many hours with them. Aquilinus has told them that if the girls' father comes to the fort for compensation, then it will be taken out of their wages.'

Tatius began inspecting his fingernails and picking at the cuticles. Petrus took a deep breath and continued.

'Nonus and Octavius, say they fell asleep in the brothel and were thrown out in the morning by the slave Riacus. That will be an easy thing for me to check.' He paused, 'All six of these men, the brothers, or the rapists, I mean, were out at the time of the fight seen by the witness. They could have killed the soldiers. But they would've needed help from local people to move the bodies.'

Tatius raised an eyebrow and opened his mouth to speak.

Petrus hurried on, 'There are no reports of anyone being absent from the fort on Solis or Lunes, so they couldn't have moved the bodies. We would all have heard if someone else was missing.'

Tatius closed his mouth and went back to picking his fingernails.

'I've yet to interview all the men who were at the brothel, but I have their names and workplaces for the next few days. They did not have the opportunity to attack the men themselves but could have been working with someone else. As I've said, it was no secret that the two men had money. It'll be harder to talk with any local men who were at the brothel. I'll see what I can do with my informant. In terms of where the two got the money, if robbery or revenge is the motive, Faustus and Drusus did normal work in the weeks leading up to their deaths, like guard duty, training and wall building,' he paused, 'I believe they accompanied you on a hunt?'

Tatius waved his hand and continued to pick at his fingernails, 'I usually leave the organisation of guards to Maximus, I don't get involved with the individual soldiers, so that may well be true. We can check with Maximus when he gets back, or with your librarius.'

Petrus nodded. He could see no reason why the men would lie about going hunting with the Prefect.

'The dead men didn't gamble much and the money they had was too much to result from normal gambling. No ordinary soldiers gamble with aurei. So, I am no further on with where they got the money from.'

'You seem to have ruled out all the soldiers in the fort, as they would have needed outside help, which is not very likely. Can't see soldiers working with locals like that.'

'Soldiers work alongside the barbarians all the time, they're local tribespeople. Look at Suasso and his men. It's not much of a stretch to think of soldiers working with other local people in the vicus.' Petrus eyed the prefect carefully. He was on dangerous ground answering him back like that.

Tatius scowled, 'That's a remote possibility I suppose. It still leads us back to the holy men as the killers, doesn't it?' He did not wait for a response, 'Anything else?'

'Er, yes. One of the two dead men, Drusus, left a will naming the two whores, Cara and Metta, as his beneficiaries. He had fifty-six denarii in his account. Do I…'

'That's quite a lot of money for the whores,' interrupted Tatius, 'There's a motive right there for killing them.'

'You're not serious, are you?' Petrus blurted out, before he could stop himself, 'I mean, I don't think local women would have the resources to undertake these murders.'

'No, I don't, not really, I'm just joking,' Tatius smiled.

Petrus didn't think it was a joking matter. 'Can I give the money and any belongings to the two women?'

'Yes, of course. A will is a legal document.'

'Can we keep this between us Sir? I don't want word getting out about it, the money is a significant amount.'

The Prefect nodded, he scribbled quickly on a tablet and pushed it across the table, 'These are the orders for you to collect the inheritance and take it to the beneficiaries. Go and get ready for the hunt. We'll take three of the barbarians with us, and one other soldier. We've taken more in the past, but Maximus felt it was unnecessary and I agreed with him. We'll meet you at the gate.'

'Is just one other soldier enough, Sir? Normally I would recommend more, at least four, maybe eight, in addition to me. Especially after the murders.' Petrus was reluctant to criticise the Prefect's decision, but hunting with so little protection was very risky.

'It's just a hunt, Petrus. What could happen? Do you think we'll be harmed by some dangerous deer? Surely, you could fight them off! Maximus agreed we didn't need so much protection.'

The Prefect stood up and ushered Petrus out of the office. He always followed Maximus' advice. Petrus put the orders in his office and then returned to his room. He undressed and rubbed himself down to dry off, trying to warm up his muscles.

He handed his wet clothes to Boga. 'See what you can do to dry those,' he pulled on dry tunic and trousers.

He grabbed a cloak and his sword and walked out into the wet street. The rain had stopped. The weak sun was fighting its way past the thick clouds but failed to provide any warmth as the chill wind cut across the fort. At the gate his horse had been readied for him; it snorted, blasting warm snot into his face. He wiped the back of his hand across his cheeks and climbed into the saddle. Three immaculately groomed horses stood waiting along with three scruffy mules for the slaves. Luci and two other barbarians were already mounted. One armed soldier, Atellus, waited on his horse with his sword in hand.

There was a sudden commotion behind them as Tatius strode along the street wearing a thick green cloak. He was followed by the two women in matching blue cloaks, their heads covered with hoods. Felix, the slave, hurried along behind them, his arms full of clothing. Behind him were two more slaves with bows, quivers of arrows and other hunting equipment.

A slave brought out a large chest and one of the mares was brought forward. Prima pulled down the hood of her cloak, took the slave's proffered hand and climbed onto the chest. From there it was just a step onto the horse's back. Fabia drew back her hood. Her face was pale and she looked sad. A slave helped her to mount the horse and she gasped as she settled into her saddle. Petrus rode to stand beside her.

'Are you quite well, my lady?' he asked, 'It may be a long ride today.'

She smiled, 'Thank you Petrus. I haven't felt well this morning, I couldn't keep down my food, but I'm sure I'll find the fresh air and hunting invigorating.'

She swung her horse around and moved it to stand alongside Prima. Tatius, who had been watching this exchange, gritted his teeth and insisted on mounting his horse from the ground. He jumped but was unable to swing his leg over the saddle, one of the slaves stepped forward and silently pushed him into place.

Red-faced, Tatius kicked out at the man, striking him in the chest.

'Get out of my way, in the name of all the Gods!' Tatius shouted.

The slave made no sound; he climbed onto the mule brought for him.

The gate opened and Petrus gave a signal for them to walk across the ditch and into the vicus. The market was quiet. The stallholders, who had been there since dawn, looked cold and wet, shuffling their feet to keep warm and running cloths over their stalls to try to dry their produce.

Outside the vicus they left the road, moved towards the east and headed across the hills towards a large forest. The barbarians moved away spreading out ahead of them. Petrus instructed Atellus to ride behind the group and to keep careful watch. All the tribes in the area were at peace with the Romans, but there were groups of bandits who roamed the countryside. Petrus led them across the hillside, wading through bracken fronds bent low by the weight of the earlier rain. The two women were talking and laughing loudly as they rode, paying little attention to their surroundings. Petrus was irritated and caught himself hoping one of them would fall off. That might shut them up. He knew he should not be thinking such things and tried to divert his thoughts, but once the idea was there, he couldn't get rid of it. Tatius rode in silence.

Suddenly a bird emerged from the undergrowth immediately in front of them, flapping its wings frantically as it rose into the air. It startled Tatius' horse; it whinnied and reared up on its hind legs.

'Steady, steady,' soothed Tatius as the horse dropped back down to the ground, stamping its feet. He stroked its neck and whispered to it. Petrus' horse spun round nervously.

'I'm a better horseman than you imagined, eh?' Tatius said.

Petrus was unsure how to respond, 'You've calmed him right back down now, Sir.'

'Oh, my husband, I feared for your safety!' cried Prima,

bringing her horse alongside him and reaching out a hand to squeeze his arm. 'You could've been injured if you'd fallen.'

Tatius shook her off, 'No harm done. You two are alright, aren't you?'

'We are indeed,' she replied and cast a knowing glance at her friend who smirked.

Luci cantered up towards them, 'I've found a small herd of deer, very fine does, a few are mothers with fawns. It's a distance away, over there,' he waved his hand in a southerly direction. 'Albiso has spotted a great stag in the place the local people call The Gladed Forest. I've told him to wait there.'

'I want to take down the stag,' said Prima firmly.

Petrus waited.

'There're always plenty of deer in the woods, so we'll take the stag, and then go and look for others.' Tatius said.

'Very well. Show us the way Luci,' said Petrus.

As they approached the forest, they saw Albiso loitering near the trees. He was short for a Carvetti man and had tattoos covering his hands and face. A thick scar ran across his forehead and disappeared underneath his hair which was pale like white clouds. He was standing on the ground as his horse grazed on the sparse grass. Seeing them approach, he saluted and leapt back onto the horse. Luci cantered away to collect the remaining scout. They would return and wait at the forest's edge.

'It's quite overgrown in there,' Albiso said, 'we should go in single file.'

The weak sun barely penetrated the trees whose fallen branches cracked beneath the horses' feet as they trailed behind Albiso. The smell of damp wood and earth rose around them. Cold droplets of water fell onto the riders' heads and dripped down their backs. They had to lie flat across their horses' necks to avoid low branches. Petrus leant forward and a thick branch struck him across the face, scratching him and forcing him backwards in the saddle. He turned and grasped the horse's rump with both hands, clinging on as the branch scraped across his back. Behind him the women had stopped; they laughed as they watched.

Petrus dismounted. His cheeks stung. 'I think it would be safer if we all walked beside our horses,' he said, embarrassed.

They began leading their horses. Occasionally Prima or Fabia would squeal if a thorn scraped her hand. With each squeal Petrus turned to check on them; they covered their mouths with their hands to stifle giggles.

'Over there,' whispered Albiso, pointing towards a break in the trees.

The sun reached down to the forest floor and the trees cast sharp shadows across the hard ground in a clearing where a stag grazed on clumps of grass.

'If we circle to the left, we'll get a clear shot. Better leave the horses here, to reduce the noise,' Albiso whispered.

They handed their horses' reins to one of the slaves. As they stumbled over exposed tree roots and stood on twigs, each step seemed to cause a thunderous crack to Petrus' ears, however the stag was undisturbed. It was a mature adult with a thick brown winter coat which was thinning in patches and the skin showed the scars of old battles fought. Albiso held up an arm to stop them when the animal was about fifty strides away and stepped aside to allow Tatius and the women to get a proper look.

Prima let her cloak fall to the ground. Felix scooped it up as she snatched the bow from his hand. He handed her an arrow. She turned towards the stag, loaded her bow, took aim, and released it in one fluid movement. The stag sank silently to its knees. Its head drooped, its nose hit the ground and it slumped on its side. Prima dropped the bow and ran forward, sinking to her knees she placed her hand on the stag's side.

'I can still feel its heart beating,' she grinned, 'Quick, give me a knife.'

Felix looked at Tatius.

'Go on, give her the knife!' ordered Tatius.

She slit the animal's throat. Blood pumped out of the wide gash and seeped into her tunic and trousers. Oblivious, Prima stabbed the knife into the animal's belly and ripped open the flesh from chest to tail. She pulled the flesh apart, plunged her hands inside the body and drew out the intestines, cut them free and tossed them aside. She carelessly wiped her fingers on her blood-spattered tunic and brushed a wisp of hair from her face with the back of her hand, smearing blood across her forehead. Petrus watched, aghast. How could such a beautiful, refined Roman lady behave so savagely?

'Get it tied up.' She said as she stood up, 'Now hand me a clean tunic.'

She reached for the hem of her garment. Fabia ran to help her. Petrus realised she was undressing and turned his back along with all the men except Tatius who scowled, his face turned red.

Prima laughed, 'You can turn around now.' She glanced down at her blood-spattered trousers.

'Carry the stag over to the mule,' Tatius ordered Felix.

'What about me?' pouted Fabia. She cast a sideways glance at Tatius, 'Don't I get to try and shoot one? And what about Tatius, the brave Prefect?' She stroked her hand down his arm. He flinched.

Petrus frowned, 'Let's go deeper into the forest. There will be more deer there.'

Felix tied the stag's legs together and slung it over the back of one of the mules, smearing blood across the mule's flanks; he tied it securely in place. The mule was reluctant to move, frightened by the stench of death. Felix beat it with a stick, and it stepped slowly forward. The dead stag's head wobbled as the mule moved and it spattered droplets of blood across Felix's tunic.

Albiso led the party forward with his head down as he followed an invisible deer trail, raising his hand occasionally to stop them as he looked in all directions and listened. They reached another clearing where cast deer antlers and twigs littered the bare earth; there were no deer hoof marks. Strange finger-sized plants with white stalks and brown tops shaped like the hoods of cloaks grew in clumps between some of the fallen twigs. The tribespeople called these toadstools and Petrus knew that some of them could be eaten, others were deadly poisonous.

'No grass, no deer,' Albiso breathed to himself and crossed the clearing trampling over the toadstools.

'I wonder if we'll ever find any deer,' complained Fabia in a loud voice.

'Not if you make so much noise!' snapped Tatius bending to avoid a low hanging branch.

Thorns tugged at Petrus' tunic and scratched his skin as they walked. His horse lowered its head to sniff the ground and he jerked the reins to make it bring its head up. They approached another clearing and Albiso brought them to a halt. Ahead in the weak sunlight, two does were feeding, their coats were stretched tight across skeletal bodies.

'Sir, do you want these two, they're a bit malnourished?' Albiso murmured.

'Let's take them. Fabia wants a shot,' Tatius replied.

'Then I suggest you take the bigger one on the left and the lady can take the other. If you fire at the same time, I think that's best.' Albiso whispered.

'I agree,' Tatius took the bow and arrow offered to him.

'Let me try,' Fabia snatched a bow and arrow from Felix.

She drew the bow taut and began positioning the arrow. The bow wobbled in her inexperienced hands. As she struggled to control it, the bow trembled, and the arrow pointed straight at Tatius. Petrus moved instinctively, knocking the bow downwards. The arrow fired into the ground.

'What?! What are you doing? How dare you!' Fabia lifted a hand to strike Petrus.

Tatius grabbed her wrist and twisted it behind her back. She squealed in pain.

'Never point the bow at a person!' Tatius hissed. 'You could've killed me, you stupid woman!'

She wriggled out of his grasp, rubbed her wrist, and pouted her lips, 'You weren't in any danger. He shouldn't have touched me.'

'He saved my life! You've scared the bloody deer away,' Tatius snapped, 'I've had enough of this. Let's go back to the fort before she kills someone.'

The men shuffled their feet unsure of what to do.

'You heard him,' said Petrus, 'let's go. Albiso, get to the front, we don't want to get lost.'

Albiso crossed the clearing and took the reins of his horse. They retraced their steps, careless about the noise they created.

'I'm getting cold now in the shade,' moaned Fabia after a while.

Tatius did not reply, and Petrus decided it was not his place to comment. They emerged into the winter sun where Luci and the other barbarian were waiting.

'Help me, husband,' Prima said.

Tatius picked her up and shoved her roughly onto the horse, pushing her so hard, she lost her balance and almost slid off the other side. She squealed and scrambled back upright.

'Petrus, can you help me?' Fabia whispered, placing her hands on the front of the saddle.

Petrus stepped forward and lifted her onto the saddle. She smiled down at him, tilted her head on one side and winked. He turned his back on her. Tatius managed to mount his horse unaided while Petrus and Atellus assisted the slaves with the mules before mounting their own horses. They began to walk, the horses pricked up their ears as they knew they were heading for home and the riders had to slow them down so that the awkward mules could keep up. As they made their way down a stony slope the mule carrying the stag slipped and unseated Felix who fell face-forward onto the ground. He staggered to his feet and touched his face which had been rubbed raw against the gravel. A bead of blood formed on his cheek and dribbled down onto his tunic. Dazed, he rubbed his head; his hair was matted with dirt. Fabia giggled as she watched him. The mule stood with its head hanging close to the ground, expecting a beating but Felix silently scrambled back onto it and kicked his heels against its sides to move it forward.

'At least we didn't lose the deer,' giggled Fabia, 'that would have been a waste of…' she stopped mid-sentence as Tatius glared at her.

Prima caught her friend's eye and gently shook her head. Fabia made her expression serious. Petrus wondered who would bear the brunt of the prefect's anger when they got back to the fort. Tatius would not hit Fabia, she was another man's wife. Petrus had walked past the Prefect's house one night some weeks previously and heard screams as he beat Prima. Petrus had felt shocked and angry. Boga had told Maximus what he'd heard from the Prefect's slaves; Prima had bruises across her face and shoulders and her eye was swollen shut, so that even makeup couldn't hide the beating she'd had. Maximus had flown into a rage. He threw things round his room and threatened to beat Boga when he'd been slow to bring him some wine.

A day later, Petrus had seen Maximus standing near the praetorium's window whispering animatedly to someone inside the building. Now that Petrus knew that Maximus and Prima were from the same clan, he realised he'd probably been speaking to Prima. Perhaps he'd been trying to comfort her.

The sun grew warmer on their backs as they continued across the countryside. Fabia and Prima remained silent throughout the journey. They reached the road which was relatively quiet with only a few people walking towards the town. Merchants approached and past them as they moved out from the vicus laden with goods.

The vicus' streets were busy with women shopping and children playing. A grey-haired man in a torn tunic and ragged cloak sat begging near the water trough with his hand outstretched. Petrus led the party back through the fort gates. He saw Carantii walking towards him carrying a bucket of metalwork. The blacksmith was a frequent visitor to the fort, making metalwork for horses and their riders when the fort's blacksmith had too much work to do. Petrus and Carantii did not acknowledge each other as they passed.

The Prefect, Fabia, and Prima dismounted at the praetorium, and the two women wordlessly followed Tatius into the house. Felix began organising the other slaves to unload the mules and take the stag round to the kitchen. Petrus continued to the principia. He handed his horse to a soldier and made his way to his office, where he wrote a report about the morning's hunt, including how Fabia had nearly shot Tatius. A messenger ran into his office and thrust a tablet at him.

'Sir, Sir. I've come from Camboglanna. Maximus will be back tomorrow. He has the murderers!' The man exclaimed breathlessly.

Petrus read the message. Chief Gna's people had identified a holy man and his three followers as the murderers. Petrus dismissed the messenger and went to inform the Prefect. Tatius was seated behind the table watching the curtain to his robing area as it twitched.

'I trust you're rested after the expedition this morning, Sir?' he said.

Tatius glared at him.

Petrus quickly pushed the tablet across the table. 'A report has arrived from Maximus. He'll return tomorrow with four men who've been identified as the killers.'

Tatius smiled and clasped his hands together, resting his elbows on the table. 'There. It's done. We'll put their heads on stakes outside the east gate for all to see.'

'Their heads? What about a trial?' asked Petrus.

'A trial won't be necessary if they confess,' sighed Tatius

Petrus had no doubt that under torture, they would eventually admit to being the murderers, or die. He felt disappointed with the prefect.

'What about my findings?' he asked.

'We can make a decision about your investigation after we've spoken to Maximus. You can carry on for today. Tomorrow return to your normal duties.'

'Will you still speak with Maximus?' asked Petrus.

Tatius raised an eyebrow.

'About the brothel and being out overnight,' persisted Petrus.

'I said I would,' Tatius snapped and waved him away, 'The three of us will talk tomorrow.'

Petrus walked briskly into the vicus. He was running out of time. He still thought Maximus was wrong about the holy men. The sound of hammering reached him as he approached the forge. As Carantii supplied the fort with ironwork, Petrus reasoned it would not appear strange to the local population if a Roman soldier visited his workshop. Carantii looked up from his work as sweat ran down his forehead onto his cheeks.

'Greetings Aurelius Petrus.' Carantii said, his voice loud, so that anyone in the street near the forge would hear him.

'Greetings.'

Carantii struck the glowing metal rod and sparks flew, dying as they landed on his shiny leather apron which was streaked with black soot. He plunged the iron into a barrel of water. It hissed and steamed. Carantii leaned the tongs against the barrel and wiped his face with the back of his hand.

'How can I help the Imperial Army? Or is it a personal matter?' he winked.

Petrus liked the blacksmith. He had learned his skills from a young age at his father's side and taken over the forge the year before when the old man had suddenly become unable to speak or move one side of his body. Petrus knew Carantii and his sister cared for the old man in the rooms behind the forge. The blacksmith was well-respected in the community and at the fort, honest in business and a fine craftsman.

'Is your sister at home?' Petrus looked towards the open door leading out of the forge into the house beyond.

'Yes. Did you want to speak with her?'

Petrus shook his head, 'I have a matter to discuss with you.'

Carantii raised an eyebrow and then closed the door.

'Saturni. You visited the brothel that evening.' Petrus lowered his voice and began speaking in Latin instead of the local language, reasoning that people passing may not understand what he was saying and even if they did, using Latin they would think it was official army business and not pay any attention.

'What of it?' Carantii snapped.

'Did you see any soldiers from the fort?'

'I didn't take much notice. There were one or two who I guessed were your men, but they weren't dressed like soldiers, they were off duty. They spoke in Latin, as soldiers would, but not to me.'

'What did you notice about the soldiers' behaviour?'

'One or two were a bit drunk, but that's normal. I had my mind on other things.'

'Did you see Maximus, the centurion, there?'

'No, I would've recognised him. Is this about the murders?'

Petrus nodded. 'The two dead men were at the brothel that night, before moving on to the tavern. Sylva reluctantly gave me a list of the men who were at the brothel that day. I can interview all of those from the fort but will have difficulty with the local men.'

He began to reach into his tunic to bring out the tablet with the list of names but stopped as he realised Carantii probably couldn't read.

'I won't bother you with a list of their names. Will you make some enquiries around here – see if anyone noticed anything in the brothel or the tavern, apart from the man you've already told me about? Can you also go to the brothel and speak to two sisters, Cara and Metta? They were with the two dead men that evening. When I spoke to them, they said they heard the soldiers talking about money and a man. They claim not to have understood very much more, as the men were speaking Latin, which they say they don't understand.'

'They'll speak Latin well enough,' Carantii said, 'especially if they've been there a while. They all pretend not to speak it so that they can learn stuff about the army and pass it on to Sylva. That's how she gets her information.'

'I thought so. Will you be able to do that?'

'With pleasure,' smirked Carantii, 'Are you going to give me some money? I'll need some for the brothel and some for the tavern if you want me to ask around.'

Petrus nodded and reached into his pouch.

'Drusus made a will, he left his property to the two girls from Sylva's place, Cara and Metta. After you've got as much information from them as possible, you could drop into the conversation that when you were at the fort you heard that he'd left them some money. The money could change their lives. Tell them you think that the best way for them to get the money would be to see me at the fort, or I could come and see them, if they get a message to me. You could even offer to be their messenger. Anyway, can I leave it to you?'

Petrus gave him some coins and glanced quickly over his shoulder. He could not see anyone in the street outside, 'If anyone asks why I've been here today, tell them I need a new sword and we were discussing it. If you have urgent news, come to the fort about the sword, otherwise use the ivy as a signal.'

Carantii nodded.

'Will you tell me the identity of the man who witnessed the murder, so that I can speak with him?'

Carantii shook his head, 'There was only the two of us there when he told me. He would know it was me who gave you the information.'

Disappointed, Petrus switched back to the local language. 'Stay well.'

'Go well, Petrus.'

Petrus walked quickly to his house. The door was unlatched. Aurora looked up and smiled as he entered the warm kitchen. She put down her sewing and moved to embrace him. He hugged her quickly and then held both her hands. He looked intently at her.

'What is it?' she breathed, a slight frown on her face as she looked up at him.

'Last week four soldiers raped some young girls who were in the street just as it was getting dark. I had to come to warn you. You must make sure that you and Mincona are always home well before it starts to grow dark. It can be so dangerous when the streets are deserted. I couldn't bear it if…' His words were cut off as Aurora kissed him.

'Thank you for the warning. But don't worry, we're always back in plenty of time.'

'I can't help it. When I found out about it, I couldn't stop imagining that you…' he couldn't finish.

'Hush,' she placed a finger on his lips, 'We're fine. We will be safe.'

He felt warmth surge through his body and his heart beat faster. He gently pushed her away. 'I can't stay. They're probably going to make me stop the investigation when Maximus returns tomorrow. Some people have been identified as the murderers.'

Aurora raised an eyebrow. 'Really?'

'They were identified by Chief Gna. It would've been a good way for him to get rid of some people he disagreed with. I need to get as much information as I can today. I just wanted to…' he paused, awkwardly. 'I love you.'

'I love you Petrus. Now go! Focus on finding the murderers.' She led him to the door.

Back in the street, Petrus went to the brothel. The young girl in the empty salon welcomed him with a cup of wine and went immediately to fetch Sylva. He relaxed against the couch. The familiar thick aroma of perfumed oil rose around him; he found it comforting.

Sylva entered the room. 'Petrus, again! You're becoming a regular. Aren't you worn out? Do you want the same two again?'

'I've a quick question for you, that's all. The night that the two dead men Faustus and Drusus were here, did two soldiers stay here overnight? I mean, did they fall asleep?'

Sylva laughed. 'Yes, yes, they were here, two brothers. Out cold. Too much wine, I think. We worked round them until the early hours and then around dawn Riacus asked them to leave, so that the girls could get some sleep.'

'You didn't think to mention that to me?'

She smiled. 'Is that all, Petrus?'

She got up and moved towards the hallway. She looked over her shoulder, 'I need my tablet back, the one with the list on. I can't keep letting people take tablets, I only have a few of them. I need to keep some records so that I can pay you people taxes. Bring it back next time. Go well.'

Petrus walked back to the fort. He spent the rest of the afternoon in his office interviewing the soldiers who'd been at the brothel. They all admitted they'd been there, but no-one had taken much notice of the customers or their fellow soldiers, although they all admitted knowing that Faustus and Drusus had a lot of money. It was well known inside the fort. Petrus was surprised that he and Maximus had not been aware of it. He made notes detailing all his findings and scratched his conclusions into the wax, still convinced that the four men who had attacked Drusus and Faustus were not holy men. He had no proof, but robbery was a strong motive. He locked his notes in the chest in his office, knowing that the Prefect and Maximus wouldn't like his conclusions. He felt frustrated, as he was still no nearer identifying the culprits.

Outside, the pale moon cast a faint light across the fort. In the dark shadow of the praetorium he turned to walk towards his room. Rats scurried past him; one ran over his foot. He kicked out at the animal, but it was too fast. Lamplight escaped from the window shutters in the Prefect's house and illuminated the street ahead of him. A sudden shriek made him stop.

'It was an accident, she's inexperienced. Can she just stay a few more days? I beg you. I am so lonely without her.' He recognised Prima's voice.

He could not hear any response. He stepped closer to the building, ensuring he stayed in the shadows. Eavesdropping on the Prefect would get him severe punishment, but he couldn't help himself.

'Hunting is one of the few pleasures I have,' Prima sobbed.

Again, he was unable to hear Tatius' reply. A door closed. All he could hear was crying.

Then another voice, Fabia, he thought. 'Did he hurt you?' There was a pause, 'I'm so sorry. I was careless. I didn't realise he beat you.'

'Only when he gets angry. Often, it's my fault. I provoke him or do something stupid. Today it's because of the hunt.'

'That's my fault, I'm so sorry. Here, let me look.' There was a pause. 'Always in places where it won't show.'

'He once hit my face and I couldn't hide the injuries from the slaves. He learned from that.'

Hot anger surged through Petrus, knowing that the prefect beat his wife so frequently.

'He knows how much we love each other and how much we welcome our time together. There are so few distractions in this miserable country, this desolate place, amongst these barbaric people. I miss Rome,' Fabia sulked, 'Sending me back to Septimus is a mean punishment. I can't stand him; he is always at me.'

'You should give him some children, an heir,' Prima sobbed, 'then he won't bother you so much. Tatius hardly even looks at me now that he has two sons and a daughter, as well as his choice of slaves.'

A noise in the darkness ahead of him made Petrus pull back further into the shadows, he hugged the side of the building. In the distance a light wobbled and moved down the street. Someone from the barracks was going to use the latrines. Petrus walked back towards his room.

As he entered, Boga produced a hot bowl of stew comprising of a few lumps of fatty meat lying amongst the turnips and leeks.

Petrus asked, 'Are we short of meat?'

Boga looked at the floor and muttered, 'Yes Sir, we've run out.'

Petrus grabbed a tablet from his table and scrawled instructions. He pressed his ring into the wax as extra identification.

'Here, take this to stores tomorrow and bring the meat back here. Maximus will be angry if we're out of food when he gets back. You should've told me, you idiot!' he growled.

Boga took the tablet and stood with his head bowed, expecting a beating.

'Just get out of my sight!'

Boga fled from the room.

Carantii

Carantii pulled a blanket over his father's thin body. The old man smiled weakly. He lay on his side. Each breath was a shallow rasp, drool escaped from his lips and dampened the mattress. Carantii placed a hand on his father's head, stroking the thin grey hair.

'Until the morning,' he whispered.

In the kitchen Eburacia was bent over a pot scrubbing it clean. She looked up; her chapped hands rested on the pot's rim. She had the same green eyes, brown hair and thin, sharp features as Carantii. Her blue smock was stained and tattered around the hem. Her thick woollen jumper had holes in the sleeves. He had been meaning to buy her material for new clothes, and wool for her to weave, but it had slipped his mind. He could easily afford to purchase plenty of cloth from the weavers in the vicus; he just kept getting side-tracked, a bit like tonight.

'I must go out,' Carantii said, 'I've work to do for Petrus.'

'Connected to the murders?'

Carantii nodded and stepped outside. He walked down the street towards the brothel's welcoming light. Behind him he heard Eburacia open the door and the splash of water hitting the earth as she threw the dregs from the pot into the alleyway.

A man mumbled something as he passed Carantii, who pushed open the brothel's door and stepped into the corridor, squeezing past Riacus. The relaxing scent of fragrant oils drifted around him as he moved into the unusually empty salon and greeted the girl who was sitting there. He'd not seen her there before. She looked about ten years old, her breasts were just beginning to form. As he looked at her pretty face and dark eyes, he wondered how long it would be before she was working in the rooms behind.

'Please take a seat,' she said, 'Did you want any particular girl tonight?'

'I haven't been with Cara or Metta, and I have heard they're very good, especially together,' he replied sinking onto one of the couches.

The girl looked at him for a moment and then said, 'Do you have enough money for two?'

Carantii raised an eyebrow and took out his money pouch which bulged full of coins. The girl's eyes widened in surprise. She shot to her feet and dashed out of the salon. He smiled to himself; 'you can't judge a goat by its hairy coat' he thought.

The girl came back. 'Sylva says money first,' she held out her hand and he placed a couple of coins on it. 'Down there, door right at the end,' she pointed.

Carantii walked in the direction she'd indicated. He'd not been in this part of the brothel before, normally he was in the cheaper side with its dingy corridor, faded rooms and tired women, who were often slaves. In the hallway a small girl was replacing the spent candles with new ones and gasped as hot wax dripped onto her hand. As he approached, she pressed herself against the wall, avoiding even the slightest touch. He pushed open the door. The walls were painted blood red and two burning torches lit up the room. Two pretty women were sprawled across the enormous bed. One was plaiting her own straw-coloured hair, the other played with the hem of her tunic. They looked up and smiled, reaching their hands out towards him. He allowed them to guide him to the bed. One of them knelt on the floor and began to remove his boots, while the other massaged his shoulders. He leant forward and took the soft hands of the woman kneeling before him. The smell of spices rose from her skin, tickling his nostrils and the back of his throat.

'Can we talk?' he said, pulling her up gently and moving her to sit beside him on the bed. 'I've already paid and that can be for just talking. I can also give you some more money here and now if you tell me what I want to know. That's money for you, not for Sylva. How does that sound?'

He drew some coins out of his pouch, opened his hand and closed it again so that they caught a brief glimpse of the money.

'Tell me about the two soldiers, the ones who were killed,' he began, 'and you,' he beckoned to the other woman, 'come and sit here,' he patted the bed beside him. 'Don't be afraid. When I was at the tavern, I heard that the two dead men had had a lot of money, flashed it about a bit. I'd like to know how they got it. To see if I could get some from the same source. Thought maybe they'd talked about it while they were here. Start by telling me your names.'

'I'm Metta,' she paused. 'They spoke in Latin. They all think we don't know their language. They said they got money from a man. One of them, the one with red hair said he saw the man that afternoon and there would be lots more money to come. They were planning to buy themselves out of the army and get married, perhaps to us, they said.'

'Did you want to marry them?'

She shook her head again. 'They were just stupid men. This is our life; we won't marry Roman soldiers. They don't want whores like us as wives. And they usually have women in the vicus as well, they probably tell those women that they'll marry them too.'

'Did the soldiers see the man here that afternoon?' Carantii asked.

Metta shrugged.

'We assumed that he did, as they both got very agitated,' said Cara.

'Agitated?'

'A bit frightened maybe, or excited,' Cara said.

'Did they say why the man was giving them money, or who he was?'

Cara shook her head.

'Why would they think you didn't know any Latin?' asked Carantii.

'Men don't really see us, as people, I mean. Sylva makes all of us learn Latin, even the slaves. That way we can listen into conversations and learn things which are useful to her.' Metta said.

'And what did you tell her about these men?' Carantii asked.

'Just what we've told you,' Metta said.

'Did she think they saw the man here at the brothel?' Carantii persisted.

Metta shrugged, 'She didn't say.'

'Have you told anyone else about this?' Carantii asked.

They shook their heads.

'I heard a Roman soldier came to see you afterwards. Did you tell him?'

Again, they shook their heads.

'Why not?'

'Sylva says we must listen to soldiers, but not tell them anything.' Cara said.

Carranti placed the coins on the table, 'Thank you. Is there anything else you can tell me? I really want to know how they got their money from that man.'

They shook their heads.

'Now just let me lie here for a while,' he lay back on the bed and closed his eyes. 'Just lie next to me, that is all I ask,' he patted the bed.

He felt the two women move and lay down next to him, one each side. Cara placed her hand on his chest and began to slide it down his body. He covered her hand with his own and stopped her movement.

'Just lie still and listen to what I have to tell you,' he murmured.

They snuggled into him, and he felt their breathing slow as they relaxed against him. He put his arms around them and tried to ignore the feeling of their breasts against his body.

'I'm a blacksmith. I sometimes work at the fort. When I was

there, I heard that one of the dead men, Drusus, made a will. That's a legal record of where he wanted his property to go if he died while serving in the army. Drusus named the two of you as the people he wanted to have his property. I didn't hear exactly what he left you, a few bits and pieces and some money.'

Cara raised herself on one elbow, her eyes widened. 'Money? And property? Why would he do that?'

Carantii smiled. 'Maybe he really did want to marry one of you.' He paused. 'You should claim your inheritance, I mean, the money and property that he left you. You never know, it might be quite a big amount. It could change your lives. I think you should contact the Roman who came to see you, the one asking questions. He is well-known in the vicus. He has been investigating the deaths. His name is Aurelius Petrus. You could get a message to him to come and see you. As I said, I go to the fort to work, I could give him a message, if you like.'

Cara lay back down and put her arm across his chest. 'Thank you, my sister and I will talk about our good fortune and decide what to do,' she whispered.

He hoped they would take the money and leave Sylva's brothel. He closed his eyes.

The rocking motion of the mattress woke him. He opened his eyes. Cara and Metta stood at the foot of the bed, watching him. He pushed himself upright and brushed his hand through his unruly hair.

'I'd better get going,' he murmured, wondering how long he'd been asleep.

Cara took his hand, 'Sir, the inher, the money, we'd like you to get a message to the Roman soldier please.' She looked at her sister and they both smiled. 'It was kind of the dead soldier to think of us.'

Carantii grinned. Perhaps they could start new lives with the money. 'I'll get a message to him, hopefully he can come to see you.'

'Why would he come to see us? He's an important man?'

Metta asked.

'The will. It's a legal requirement. He must get the money and err, the things to you.'

They nodded.

'Thank you,' Cara said.

He left them and walked back towards the salon.

'I trust you were satisfied?' asked Sylva as he grabbed his cloak and moved towards the door.

'Mm, yes, I'll come back again to see them I expect.'

He left the brothel.

He'd established himself as a regular drinker at the tavern, so that no one would find it strange to see him there chatting with the other customers. Petrus was paying for his drinks and sometimes he got some blacksmithing work out of it. As he entered, he was hit by a wave of heat and the odour of unwashed bodies. One of the torches had gone out and parts of the room were in dark shadow. He squeezed onto a bench and the taverner slapped a cup of ale in front of him, splashing it onto the table, already wet from previous spillages. He nodded his thanks and slurped a mouthful as he looked around. The stall holders must've had a good day's trading, as they were knocking back the drinks. The man next to him nudged his elbow.

He slurred, 'Carantii, my man. Have you had a good day? I was just saying, some people do good business with the Romans. You do quite well out of the fort, don't you? You're always in there helping them with this and that bit of ironwork.'

'They pay in cash and are regular customers, yes. You trade with them too, Netacius. Your woven cloth is on the backs of many soldiers and officers beyond that wall,' Carantii nodded his head in the general direction of the fort.

'Someone didn't like their custom though, did they? Went and killed two soldiers. They say the centurion has captured the murderers and he's bringing them back here from somewhere near Camboglanna fort. Seems unlikely to me, that he could've got the right people, I mean,' slurred the man.

Netacius slammed his drink down on the table, ale splashed across the wood and onto Carantii's sleeves. He didn't seem to notice as he leaned his elbows on the table and rested his chin on his palms. He turned towards Carantii and breathed hot stale beer into his face.

'I was at the brothel the night the soldiers were taken. We all were, us weavers, sort of celebrating a contract with the fort.' He waved his hand towards the other merchants. 'They'd placed a big order for cloth. After the murders, the fort threatened to stop the order, said they'd get the cloth from somewhere else if we didn't give up the men who killed the soldiers. We all saw the two soldiers flush with all their money, but we wouldn't have killed them, would we? Couldn't have moved the bodies all that way either or taken them alive. Look at me, I'm not as young as I was.' His fingers tapped his greying beard. 'I couldn't have overcome two young fit soldiers, could I?'

He shook his head and his chin slipped out of his hands. He struggled to stop himself from banging his face on the table and pushed himself upright.

'We couldn't give anyone up. We didn't know who did it. They asked about holy men. There are no holy men around here and even if there were, they couldn't transport the bodies either. I suppose they'll honour their order for cloth now they've got someone for it.' He belched, 'You were there too, weren't you, in the brothel? I remember seeing you there, I'm sure.'

'I was there. I saw you with some of the others. They weren't all weavers celebrating though, were they?' asked Carantii.

'No, there were a couple of other traders. Everyone else was soldiers. You can spot a soldier even out of uniform, can't you? Their arrogance and the way they speak Latin to make you feel inferior.' He spat on the floor. "Can tell when they've just been paid too, getting drunk and going whoring.'

'No harm in that,' murmured Carantii, watching him carefully.

Netacius looked around and whispered, 'You're not a spy, are you? Feeding information back to the Romans?'

'What do you think?' Carantii winked, trying to hide his alarm.

Netacius threw his head back and laughed. 'Not bright enough for that, are you? Must've got some of that iron of yours in your skull, I reckon. Spies don't go to brothels and drink like you do.' His elbows slipped off the table and he lurched forward again.

'Let me get you another drink.' Carantii felt relieved as he waved to the girl who was serving.

He gave her some coins and pointed at the two cups on the table. She poured the ale. Netacius put his arm around her waist and pulled her closer. He licked her neck and nuzzled his head against her breasts. She tried to push him away, but he pulled her tighter and started making sucking noises as he buried his head in her cleavage. Carantii grabbed him by the shoulders and pulled him away from the girl.

'Leave her alone,' Carantii said.

Netacius put his head on the table. 'I just wanted a cuddle,' he slurred. 'Not much to ask, is it?'

Carantii drained his drink. He held the cup out at arm's length for the girl to refill without getting too close to Netacius. She grabbed the coin from his outstretched hand and turned away.

Netacius began to snore. Carantii continued drinking slowly. Hiding behind his ale, he strained to listen to the conversations going on around him. A fight broke out at the next table as two men wrestled each other to the floor. The other drinkers shouted and cheered as the men landed blows on each other's bodies. Carantii got to his feet.

He gasped as the cold night air forced its way into his lungs. The street was deserted.

The kitchen was warm as the heat of the forge's fire warmed the bricks. He unrolled his mattress and placed it on the floor. Lying down, he pulled a blanket over himself and drifted off to sleep.

VIII – Dies Solis

Tatius waved Petrus away when he tried to update him after parade. 'Do you have proof that the holy men didn't kill our soldiers?'

'No Sir, I don't. But there are other men who had the opportunity to commit the murders.'

'When Maximus returns, we'll talk about everything.' Tatius got up from his table to move Petrus towards the door. Petrus opened his mouth to speak but Tatius shook his head and held up his hand. 'I'll ask him what he was doing outside the fort the night the men went missing. Now get back to your duties. I've given you enough time on this,' he snapped.

Disappointed, but not surprised by the prefect's attitude, Petrus left the room and walked to the area where the archers were practising. He was dismayed that only a few of the men seemed able to hit their targets. One eager young man ran to collect his arrows before the rest had finished their volley of shots. He collapsed to the ground as an arrow struck him, piercing his right shoulder. Horrified, the archers lowered their bows and placed them at their feet. The training officer ran forward and pulled out the arrow, throwing it to one side. The injured man winced and grasped his wounded shoulder. Blood seeped between his fingers as he got shakily to his knees and was pulled to his feet by the instructor.

'Bloody idiot!' grunted the officer. 'You two! Help him to the infirmary,' he barked, pointing at the nearest archers. 'Now!' he screamed as the men hesitated.

They stepped forward and supported the man away towards the fort.

'That's what happens when you don't follow procedures. He could've been killed!' he snarled at the remaining men, who stood still. 'That may be the end of his career as an archer, or even a soldier. Now pick up all your equipment, take down the targets and get out of my sight!'

'Rome pays these useless sacks of shit!' muttered the man as he walked with Petrus back to the fort. Petrus nodded.

At the barracks, Maximus' door was ajar.

'You stupid fool!' he heard the centurion shout, 'Get that cleaned up!'

Petrus went to his own room, hoping to avoid Maximus, who was clearly enraged. He scooped a cup of water from the pail in the corner of his room, replaced the cover, sat down wearily on his bed and gulped down the drink. Boga entered the room with some wine. Behind him the door flew open, crashing against the wall as Maximus burst in.

'Are you ready to see Tatius? I've brought back the murderers. Their heads will be put on stakes near the gate, I'm sure. That'll show the populace what happens when you kill Romans,' snarled Maximus.

'What about a trial?' mumbled Petrus, his mouth full of wine.

'You can't try dead men.'

Petrus tried to hide his shock. They went outside and walked across the fort. Beside the headquarters a slave held the reins of a mule with a bulging blood-soaked sack dangling from its saddle.

'Their heads are in there,' Maximus pointed to the sack as he strode past the mule.

Petrus quickened his pace to keep up with the centurion who opened the door to the Prefect's office without knocking.

'Maximus!' Tatius smiled. 'Pull up a stool, both of you.'

He waved towards a slave who stepped forward and poured two cups of wine. Petrus was surprised by the prefect's informal attitude.

'So, Maximus?' said Tatius.

'The barbarians went into the area around here and there were no recent reports of priests. Even after a couple of farms were burned, no-one came forward with information,' Maximus began, 'We went out towards Camboglanna and initially encountered resistance, but after some persuasion, we received a message from Chief Gna, telling us where to find the holy man and his three followers.'

'How do you know they were the culprits?' asked Tatius.

'They denied it at first. We got a bit physical with them and they confessed.'

'Why did Chief Gna hand them over to you and not to Petrus the other day?' Tatius asked.

Petrus thought that was a good question.

Maximus shrugged, 'I have a reputation. He wants to keep on my good side.'

'Why didn't you bring them back alive for a trial?' Tatius asked.

'They attacked one of the slaves and attempted to escape. We had to kill them. So, I took their heads, and we buried their bodies.'

Petrus was surprised that Maximus had buried the bodies. It would've been more normal to leave them as a warning to anyone thinking of challenging Rome.

Maximus was still speaking, 'I thought it best to bury their bodies. That way any other followers have no remains to venerate. I took their heads. We've avoided a trial. Shall I put the heads outside the east gate? I've already instructed the men to raise four stakes.'

Tatius nodded. 'Good thinking. You're right about any other followers making them into martyrs.' He looked at Petrus. 'Petrus has information he wishes to share. He's not convinced it was holy men who killed the soldiers. Thinks you've got the wrong men.' He smiled indulgently at Petrus.

Petrus related his ideas about the motive being robbery as the two dead men seemed to have a lot of money and were overheard talking about it by the two whores, Cara and Metta. When he got to his interviews with the dead men's contubernia, Maximus interrupted.

'I know what they said. I interviewed them.'

'I am sorry, Sir,' Petrus stammered, 'I was unable to locate your report.'

Petrus did not dare to look at Maximus as he said this and hurried on. Out of the corner of his eye, he could see Maximus place his clenched fists on the table. 'According to their roommates, the dead men had not done anything unusual in the last few weeks, just normal duties like training, workshops, guard duties for the Treasury and the praetorium. However, they had escorted Silvius Tatius and his wife on a hunting trip.'

Maximus interrupted again, 'That was a normal trip, nothing unusual happened.'

Petrus continued, 'I have interviewed all the soldiers who were at the brothel. They all admitted that they knew the dead men had money. Apparently, the whole fort knew about it, although I was not aware.' He looked at Maximus.

'There are some things which the senior officers don't get to hear about. I'm sure when you were in the lower ranks there were things which your centurion didn't know about,' muttered Maximus.

Petrus nodded. 'It is possible that any soldier who visited the brothel could have decided to take the opportunity to relieve the men of their money. However, they would have had to work with local people to move the bodies, especially all the way to the Temple of Mercury. No-one was reported missing from the fort in the days after the two men went missing.'

'And we all know it's unlikely that soldiers would work with local people in the vicus like that,' muttered Tatius. He held his hand up to silence Petrus, 'Suasso and his men are different.'

'I have someone in the vicus looking into things for me, as I can't really interview all the local men who frequent the brothel.'

'One of your spies?' asked Maximus.

Petrus nodded.

'Who are your spies? How reliable are they?' asked Maximus.

'I'd rather not say who they are, Sir,' Petrus paused. In reality, he had only one informant, Carantii. 'They have provided accurate information in the past. There were six men outside the fort during the early hours of the morning apart from myself, Germanus, the dead men and yourself, Julius Maximus.'

He paused, but Tatius said nothing.

'Last Saturni, I was visiting my family. My son has a falling down illness, the boy was not well, and I stayed later than I'd anticipated. You're aware of how I found the dead men fighting. Of the remaining men, two brothers fell asleep in the brothel that night. I've had that confirmed with the owner. And four roommates from Aquilinus' century got very drunk and then chased two young women through the vicus before raping them. All six of these men could have attacked Faustus and Drusus, but as with the others, they would've needed help to move the bodies to where they were found. The eyewitness said one of the attackers was big and one had white hair. That's not much of a description and could describe some men from the fort as well as some from the community.'

Petrus paused again. No one spoke.

'I… err,' he glanced at Maximus and tried to keep his voice steady, 'I had wondered what you were doing outside the fort that night, Sir.' He held his breath, expecting Maximus to explode.

Maximus looked surprised but answered calmly, 'I went to the brothel, but it was very busy, so I didn't stay. I went to my woman in the vicus. I fell asleep in her bed.' He paused and said slowly. 'That can all be checked.'

Petrus waited.

Tatius smiled tightly. 'So, that leaves us with the holy men as the murderers. Maximus was correct. The motive seems to be robbery. I say case closed, don't you? Put the heads outside the fort's east gates. We'll leave them there for two days. It'll soon spread through the vicus that they were the murderers.'

Maximus turned to leave the room. Petrus opened his mouth to speak.

'That's the end of it.' Tatius said firmly, 'And Petrus, you are to resume your normal duties immediately. You'll take my wife's friend Fabia back to Camboglanna in the morning.'

Petrus nodded. 'Yes Sir.'

'And Petrus? Have you given the whores their inheritance?' Tatius asked.

Maximus stopped, his hand on the door. He turned to look at Petrus.

'No Sir, I have yet to do that. I must get it released from the Treasury.'

'See that it is done,' muttered Tatius. 'It's an important matter.'

'Take Suasso with you to Camboglanna. I'll instruct him to set off first thing and meet you along the journey,' said Maximus, walking out of the room.

Petrus felt defeated.

He now had orders to follow. Maximus wouldn't hesitate to demote him if he felt he wasn't obeying commands. He left the building just behind Maximus who took the reins of the mule and began to lead it towards the gates, bellowing orders at men as he passed. At the gate, a small crowd of people had gathered on the opposite side of the ditch. Word had spread quickly through the community that Maximus had returned with the murderers and people were curious. Petrus was surprised to see Carantii lurking amongst them.

Maximus grabbed the sack from the mule's back and spilled out the contents. The people gasped as four heads rolled across the ground. Petrus grimaced and forced himself to look at them. One had the skull bashed in, a thick grey substance had oozed from the wound, dried and congealed in the man's black hair.

'That's the holy man,' declared Maximus, poking it with his foot.

Maximus picked up the man's head by the hair, carried it over to one of the stakes and pressed it onto the wood. It squelched as he pushed it down and the rank odour of rotting flesh and blood rose around them. Petrus turned away as his stomach heaved and he fought to control himself; he did not want to vomit in front of the locals. Maximus pointed to the remaining heads, indicating that Petrus should help him. Reluctantly Petrus picked up one of them by the hair. The man's dead eyes stared accusingly at him, and the open mouth breathed gaseous stink into his face. He forced the head down onto one of the posts releasing more putrid smells as leaking fluid dripped onto his boots. He grimaced and wiped his boots on the grass. He was relieved to see that Maximus had placed the other two heads on the remaining stakes.

'You would've taken forever,' muttered Maximus. He thrust the empty sack at the slave and the man silently carried it away, holding it at arm's length. Maximus strode away. Death clung to Petrus' skin; he tried to wipe his hands on his tunic but the odour stayed with him. He passed back through the gate.

'Aurelius Petrus?' Carantii came up behind him. He was carrying a sheathed sword.

'Blacksmith?' Petrus felt a surge of warm excitement rush through his body. Carantii had some news! He tried to look stern and uninterested.

'Your order for a sword, I just wanted to show you this one, to see if it was the kind of thing you had in mind. Perhaps there's somewhere that you could try it for weight?' Carantii handed the sword to Petrus.

'Mmm, yes.' Petrus took the weapon with both hands, judging the weight. He ran his hand along the leather sheath, conscious that some of the soldiers had paused to watch their encounter and the gatekeepers were leaning over the walls listening to their conversation. 'Let's go to the drill hall. I can swing it around there.'

Carantii followed him into the hall, closing the door behind them. Chilly air had drifted in through the high shutterless windows and sunk down to the floor, like a blanket of cold. Petrus shivered. It was gloomy inside; the afternoon light barely penetrated the dark corners, and he hadn't thought about bringing a torch. He took the sword out of its sheath and began to swing it at waist height and make stabbing motions towards an invisible enemy. The weapon felt good in his hands, just the right weight. He began to breathe heavily as he exercised.

'Do you have some information for me?' he gasped as he lunged forward.

'I've spoken with the women at the brothel. The two dead soldiers spoke about getting money from a man who they had seen that afternoon and that there would be more money in the future. They said they would like to marry the girls, but the girls didn't believe them. As you suggested they understood everything the men said in Latin and reported it back to Sylva. I told them about the inheritance, and they must've chatted about it while I was asleep, as they said they would like you to take the money to them.'

Petrus stopped swinging the sword, 'You fell asleep?' he gasped with a grin on his face.

Carantii blushed.

'I'll get the money and take it to them this afternoon. It's a substantial amount. I imagine they'll want to leave the brothel and may need help arranging that. Sylva won't be pleased if they leave. Keep an eye on them, would you?' Petrus put the sword back in its sheath and put his hand on the door.

'Hold on!'

Petrus stopped.

'I went to the tavern yesterday to ask around and spoke with Netacius. He says the traders were in the brothel that night celebrating various contracts made with the fort and they all saw the two soldiers flashing their money around. They, the traders that is, have heard that Maximus has caught the murderers, but they don't believe that he has the right men. They don't think local people or holy men would be able to get very far away with a hostage, dead or alive. He also said that the traders wouldn't kill soldiers, as they would lose all their custom with the fort. And that makes sense, doesn't it? Why bite the hand that feeds you?'

'Why indeed?' murmured Petrus.

'Netacius asked me if I was a spy and then said I was too stupid to be one,' Carantii laughed.

Petrus didn't laugh. Carantii became serious.

'How's all that for information?'

'Very helpful. But be careful. If people realise that you're an informant, it could be dangerous,' Petrus pressed some coins into Carantii's hand and returned the sword to him.

They stepped outside and as Petrus closed the door he said, 'A sword just like that would be fine.'

Carantii walked quickly away. Petrus made his way to the dead men's room. He didn't have the written orders from the Prefect with him, but he hoped that if he was officious, he'd be able to bluff his way through without having to go to his office to get the written orders. The soldiers had just finished work for the day. Two of them were preparing the food, while the other four were busy cleaning their weaponry.

'Argentus?' Petrus said.

The immune raised his head and laid down the chain mail which he was cleaning. He walked to the door, 'Aurelius Petrus?'

'Bring me Drusus' chest.'

Argentus did as he was told. Petrus opened it, moved aside the sack lying on top and checked that everything was still there from his previous visit.

'I'm taking these items to the beneficiaries of Drusus' will. I have authorisation from the Prefect to do so, do you need to see the orders?' He began to reach into his tunic.

Argentus shook his head, 'That isn't necessary.'

Petrus was relieved. He placed the chest's contents inside the sack, including the few coins and returned the chest to the immune.

'What about Faustus' stuff?' asked Argentus.

'Faustus didn't leave a will, so you can distribute his belongings between you. Do it fairly, mind. I don't want to hear complaints.'

'I'll see to it.'

Petrus carried the sack to the Records office. He hoped he could bluff his way through with the librarius as well but was worried as he was a stickler for rules. Manius was bent over his records and scratching into a wax tablet; he looked annoyed to see Petrus return.

'Greetings, Aurelius Petrus, what can I do for you?' Manius sighed.

'I'd like to withdraw the fifty-six denarii that Drusus left in his will. I am taking it to the beneficiaries. I have written authorisation from the Prefect,' again he reached into his tunic for an imaginary tablet.

Manius waved his hand, 'I've already spoken with the Prefect about the will and the whores.' He emphasised this last word.

Petrus raised his eyebrows. So much for keeping this confidential! He glanced across the office and caught the eye of Adrianus, the librarius from Aquilinus' century. The man looked away quickly. Petrus felt deflated, he had obviously been listening and the will was not a secret.

'I'd also like you to come with me to the Treasury as a witness.' Petrus said.

Manius did not respond, he fiddled with his records for a while and then drew up a tablet for Petrus to sign detailing the amount to be withdrawn and the reasons for it. He rose slowly from his chair and stretched his arms out above his head, arching his back. His bones creaked. He followed Petrus out of the office, trailing along behind him, taking tiny careful steps like an old man in pain. Petrus was relieved that the treasury was not far away, as both men knew that Petrus couldn't reprimand the librarius, who was under the centurion's direct command.

Inside the treasury, soldiers in full armour stood in front of the iron door to the vault. The Signifer, Ecdicius, sat nearby, pretending to study his records while he sipped wine. Petrus presented the tablet. Ecdicius looked surprised but began counting the denarii.

'Stop!' Petrus said, 'I want two aurei and six denarii.'

Ecdicius paused, pursed his lips and sucked his teeth. 'There's not many places will accept that kind of money, they've not got enough coins to give you change, even at the brothel,' he smirked.

'Just do as I ask,' snarled Petrus, thinking that the girls could easily hide two aurei and six denarii coins amongst their clothes. He signed his name and Manius scribbled his signature.

Manius headed back to his office at a rapid pace, showing none of the frailty he'd had just moments before. Petrus returned to his room. He took the money from Drusus' sack and placed it with the coins in his pouch, conscious of their weight hanging from his belt, half a year's salary for a basic soldier. He'd decided to leave the belt and crockery in his room as he didn't want to attract attention by carrying a sack to the brothel. He could take them separately if the girls wanted them. He grabbed an empty tablet and tucked it inside his tunic.

An icy wind whipped through the street and across the ditch. It rustled the hair on the dead men's heads and pushed their stench into the fort. Petrus covered his nose with his hand as he approached the gate. The guards had reluctantly climbed the steps back to their lookouts and stood with cloaks covering their faces. Petrus strode out of the gate. Staying alert, he glanced behind him and all around, however, he could not see anyone paying him any attention.

In the brothel, he threw himself onto the couch and took the cup of wine handed to him by the slave.

The young girl leapt up. 'Cara and Metta?' she asked.

He nodded and dropped some coins into her outstretched hand. He reached into his tunic and withdrew a blank tablet. 'Give this to your mistress. I'm returning her property.'

The girl nodded and ran her fingers across the tablet's smooth waxy surface, 'They're free right now. You know the way.' She waved a hand in the general direction of Cara and Metta's room.

Petrus gulped down his drink, handed the empty cup to the

slave and walked down the dimly lit corridor. Only two candles burned on the walls approaching the girls' room. He pushed the door open. Cara and Metta scrambled to their feet, smiles fixed to their faces, their arms outstretched, grasping his hands.

He allowed them to guide him to sit on the bed. Metta stroked his cheek with the back of her hand. Cara began to run her hand along his thigh. He covered her hand with his own, stopping the movement.

'I'm here to talk and to bring something for you,' he spoke in the local language.

Both women stopped moving.

'I know you've been told that one of the dead soldiers left you something in his will,' he looked from one to the other, they nodded. 'I have the money here for you,' he tipped the coins into his open palm.

They looked with wide eyes at the gold aurei. Cara picked one up and turned it over in her hand, she rubbed the surface with her fingers.

'This is a lot of money. It's six months' salary for a soldier,' he pointed at the coin in Cara's hand. 'Don't tell anyone about this. People might rob you if they know you have money.'

Cara nodded. Metta mouthed some words but made no sound as Petrus gave her the remaining coins. She closed her hand into a tight fist.

'There's a tiny bit of property too. Do you want me to bring that to you?'

Cara shook her head. 'No Sir, what are those things compared with this great treasure? Please do not bother yourself with them. Thank you for bringing this to us.'

Petrus smiled. 'Now can I just relax here for a while? I need to spend some time with you, otherwise people will wonder what we've been doing.' He lay back on the bed and shook his head as the two women moved towards him, 'No, I don't want you to do anything for me. I just want to lie here.'

He felt content as he closed his eyes. Perhaps the women would leave the brothel and return home. There was enough money for a dowry if they wanted to marry. The women were whispering to each other. He did not try to listen to them. He was tired. He needed to see Aurora.

After a while they fell silent, and he could hear them moving about the room. He opened his eyes and stood up. 'Remember, don't tell anyone.'

He left the room, strode through the salon and left the brothel. He turned towards his home. In the gathering darkness he was surprised to see a couple of women rushing down the street. Even after the recent rapes, some women still had to move about the vicus at night.

The door to his house was unlatched, and he let himself into the kitchen. Mincona looked up from where she was sitting at the fire stirring a pot. The smell of sweet porridge filled the room. He nodded a greeting to her, she smiled briefly and then returned her gaze to the food. Aurora entered the kitchen and squealed in surprise when she saw him. Mincona got up quietly and left the room. Aurora moved towards Petrus and planted a kiss on his cheek. Then she held him at arms' length, a frown on her face.

'How long will those heads be outside the gates?' she asked. 'It's horrific and the smell makes everyone sick.'

Petrus mumbled, 'Until the day after tomorrow.'

'Those poor men. I heard you helped Maximus put the heads on those stakes.'

'I was following orders! They confessed to the murders and that's the end of it,' Petrus snapped, feeling overcome with tiredness.

'The deaths of these men and displaying their heads like that at the gate could stir up resentment.'

'It could, but the Roman Army must be seen to act.'

She gently pushed him away. 'They didn't really kill the soldiers, did they?'

Petrus shrugged, 'Tatius and Maximus are convinced.'

'But you aren't?'

He shook his head. 'I think the dead men were robbed and the killers made it look like priests using the old druidic practices and other holy rites from different religions. I've been ordered to stop looking into it.'

'Will you? Stop looking into it, I mean?'

Petrus took a deep breath and exhaled loudly. 'I've no choice. I've already challenged Maximus today and he's dangerous when he's crossed. Anyway, I have to go to Camboglanna tomorrow to take Foslius Septimus' silly wife back to her husband.'

Aurora began stirring the pot.

'How is Titus? I have prayed for him,' Petrus said.

Aurora smiled, 'He's fine. There've been no ill effects from that awful fit. I just worry, worry that one day he'll stop breathing.'

Aurora had given birth to three other children, all of them had died within days of their births.

'I know, I do too. I couldn't bear it if we lost him,' his voice faded. He sighed, 'We have to pray that he'll grow out of the fits. Where is he now?'

'Asleep. You can look in on him you know. Will you stay to eat with us?'

He shook his head, 'I'm glad he's well. I wish I could stay, but I must get back. I've reports to write, and I must prepare for the journey tomorrow.' He didn't add that he expected a dressing down from Maximus. He kissed Aurora and hugged her, briefly feeling her breath on his neck as he reluctantly pulled himself away from her and left the house.

He hurried through the dark streets, nodded to the gatekeepers when they accepted his password and made his way back to his room. The place smelled of spices and roasted meat. Boga had prepared a special meal to welcome Maximus, the hero who'd avenged the deaths of the soldiers; he needed to be celebrated in the slave's opinion. Petrus wouldn't argue about a good meal and he ate his fill. Maximus was quiet; he didn't respond to

Boga's eager questions about the dead men, merely grunting and eventually Boga fell silent. Maximus barely acknowledged Petrus' presence and so he decided to remain quiet.

Satiated, Petrus readied his weapons for the next day and wrote up his report which he placed in his locked chest. He collapsed on the bed and drifted into sleep.

IX – Dies Lunes

Tatius had addressed the men at parade that morning about the heads on stakes at the gate and praised Maximus for solving the murders. He then returned to his house to check that his wife's guest was ready to leave the fort.

Petrus tried to hide his frustration as he waited for Tatius to settle himself in his office. 'Fabia is ready now,' Tatius said. 'Maximus has already sent Suasso and a couple of other barbarians to check the route. They'll catch up with you as you go. Take six soldiers.'

'Yes Sir.'

'I expect you to return early tomorrow. Don't linger.'

'Yes Sir.'

Petrus waited. Tatius stared at him for what seemed like a long time.

'It's over Petrus,' Tatius said firmly. 'You're not to spend any longer on the murders. I don't want to hear any more about it.'

Infuriated, Petrus left the office. He returned to his room to collect his weapons and helmet. The stench of death and decay laid heavily across the fort. As Petrus approached the west gate, his stomach heaved, and he fought to stop himself throwing up. Fabia waited with one hand across her mouth and nose. With her other hand she pulled the dark cloak tighter round her. She had changed her hairstyle to that of a Greek goddess and looked very pale. Her slave girl was already inside the carriage. He took Fabia's hand and helped her inside, closed the door and pulled the curtain across.

'As you may remember Ma'am, I'm covering the window

so that others cannot see who is inside. It is for your own protection,' he said.

'I remember,' she said softly.

He thought she was crying.

He signalled to the men and led them through the streets and out into the open countryside. The sun strained to reach through the grey clouds, its faint warmth slowly lifted the dew from the grass. He instructed his foot soldiers to march close to the carriage with one man on horseback at the rear. Fabia's slave rode behind the carriage, with the mule obstinately refusing to keep up. Fabia made no attempt to draw back the curtain from the window.

The undulating hills limited Petrus' view and he relied heavily on the barbarians circling ahead and reporting back to warn him of any dangers. Following the well-worn track, they descended into a valley. Water trickled down the hillside between rocks and around tussocks of thick vegetation, washing soil down into the flowing water in the valley bottom. As they approached the stream, the thick dark mud sucked at the horses' feet and the carriage's wheels. Petrus' horse struggled and stumbled. Behind him, the mule slid to its knees and the slave fell off with a squeal. He staggered to his feet, a layer of wet earth clung to his tunic and trousers as he grabbed the mule's reins and yanked hard. The animal moaned and hobbled forward onto firmer ground while the soldiers watched and sniggered. The carriage's horse strained hard, but the mud was reluctant to let it move. Suddenly the carriage came loose and surged forward, rocking violently as it struck hidden rocks.

'Stop, please!' Fabia screamed.

The driver stopped the carriage. Petrus dismounted and rushed to the carriage. 'Madam?' he said and pulled aside the curtain over the window.

Fabia sat trembling, 'I need to get out!' she pushed the door against him and clambered out.

She bent over with her hands on her knees and vomited. Part-digested food and pale red wine splashed on the ground and spattered her cloak. She wailed and wiped her mouth on her sleeve. 'Water,' she whispered.

The slave girl handed her a flask.

'I thought you wouldn't stop, and I would vomit over myself,' Fabia breathed. Her eyes filled with tears as she gulped down the water. 'I will have the curtain drawn back, so that you can hear me if I need to stop again. My stomach is so…' she grimaced and rubbed her belly.

'Very well, Ma'am,' Petrus interrupted, not wishing to hear the details of how she felt.

'I've frequently been ill in the mornings, especially today before we left Banna. I hoped it would stop. I may have eaten something that didn't agree with me.'

'Maybe,' Petrus murmured as he helped her back into the carriage.

The slave slipped as he tried to remount the mule. The soldiers laughed and jeered at him as he fought to stay upright.

'Help him!' ordered Petrus.

One of the soldiers stepped forward and lifted the slave onto the mule's back. Thick mud smeared over the soldier's tunic and covered his hands. He frowned.

'Not laughing now, are you?' Petrus muttered.

Suasso appeared beside Petrus and brought his horse to a stop. 'Too much fine wine, was it?'

'I don't know, and I don't much care,' muttered Petrus, 'I just want to get her safely to Camboglanna where I can hand her over to her husband. Have you and your men anything to report?'

'My father, Chief Gna, has sent a message. He would like to meet with you.'

Petrus was annoyed by the Chief's arrogance in summoning him to a meeting. 'He wants a meeting, does he? What about? He saw Maximus just a couple of days ago.'

Suasso shrugged, 'Perhaps to see what the Romans will do now they have the murderers.'

'He should have asked Maximus that. He's the Centurion.

We're not making good time; we need to get to the fort before it gets dark. Tell him to come to the fort first thing in the morning.'

'You won't ride to see him?'

'What did I just say?' Suasso's attitude annoyed him; he wouldn't have asked Maximus that question. 'If he wants to see me, he'd better be there first thing. I'm not waiting.'

Suasso galloped away and Petrus waved everyone forward.

The icy wind raked across the hills and numbed Petrus' cheeks. His fingers grew stiff on the reins. The cold whispered in his ears and tugged at his hair. Each breath forced freezing air into his lungs and numbed his mind.

'Stop! Stop! Now!' called Fabia.

Petrus leapt off his horse, rushed to the carriage and flung the door open. He leant inside. Fabia leaned away from him, smiling.

'Steady, soldier,' she grinned. 'I'm not going to vomit again. I need my slave to give me a blanket to put over my knees. It's so cold in here,' she emphasised the words. 'She can't open the chest when the carriage is rocking so much.'

Petrus reddened with fury. He bit back the words he wanted to say, to tell her what he thought of her behaviour. The slave girl fumbled with the catches and searched through the chest, pulling out a red blanket which she placed across Fabia's knees.

'Will you help me tuck it in Petrus?' Fabia smiled and winked.

Petrus closed the door and moved back towards his horse. Fabia was still talking, but he ignored her. She leaned out of the window.

'The rocking of the carriage is likely to make me sick again, can we go a bit slower?' she whined.

Petrus spoke loudly, without turning to face her, deliberately rude, 'We have to keep up the pace, or it'll be dark before we get to Camboglanna. The road is full of bandits. You know what could happen to you if you're caught out on the road in the dark,' he said. 'Try to pick the best path, will you, and avoid holes in the track?' he instructed the carriage driver.

The sun had passed its peak and begun the fall towards night as Camboglanna came into view. Suasso and his men were loitering outside. Petrus identified himself at the gate. The guards were reluctant to open it until they saw Fabia at the carriage window. Petrus immediately heard running feet and the gate opened. He told the barbarians to return the next morning at dawn and then led the party down the road to the praetorium where Foslius Septimus stood on the steps; behind him a slave straightened her tunic and ran into the building.

'Petrus! I trust you have looked after my wife?' said the Prefect.

Petrus saluted. 'Hail, Foslius Septimus. Your wife has been unwell on the journey.' He opened the carriage door.

Septimus stepped forward and helped Fabia from the carriage. 'My dear, you look pale. I didn't expect you back so soon. I will send for the physician.' He led his wife up the steps and into the building.

Petrus did not hear her reply. The slaves quickly unloaded the chests and went into the building. A strong smell of horses suddenly enveloped him.

'You again,' Carius muttered. 'You know where my rooms are. The slave will prepare you some food. Your men can stay where they were last time. Give your horses to my men, they know what to do.' He strode away towards the drill hall.

Petrus walked slowly to the centurion's rooms and put his belongings in the same room he'd used before; it smelt of fresh straw which crackled beneath his feet. He sat on the bed, removed his boots and rubbed his toes. He was relieved that Carius was not around. He didn't like the centurion and found it hard to respect and cooperate with him. He looked up on hearing a knock at the door, followed by the slave entering and placing a plate of roasted meat on the table and pouring him some wine.

X – Dies Martes

Petrus woke feeling refreshed. He pulled on his boots and went out into the fort where the early morning sun was melting the thin layer of ice covering the ground. The soldiers were readying the horses. There was a commotion at the gate as Suasso strode past the gatekeepers.

'Chief Gna is coming. Will you meet him outside?' he was breathless as he stopped in front of Petrus.

Petrus nodded and led his horse out of the gate and across the ditch. The breeze blew the stink of animal flesh and urine from the tannery towards him. Chief Gna flanked by two armed warriors rode his horse steadily through the street. He wore his bear skin cloak with the bear's head looming above him. He dismounted and took off his cloak, laying it on his saddle; the bear's head balanced on the horse's back and stared down at them. Gna approached Petrus with his arms open wide and his palms facing upward, head bowed.

'Hail Aurelius Petrus,' Gna said.

'Hail Chief Gna.'

'What are the Romans going to do with the murderers?'

Petrus' eyes widened in surprise. Gna was very direct, not wasting time on pleasantries. 'The men you gave up as the killers were interrogated and they confessed. They were to be taken back to Banna, but they attacked one of the slaves and tried to escape. They were killed. Their heads are on posts outside the fort. I am sure you already know that; Suasso will have told you.'

'Is that the end of the matter?'

'The murders have been solved. Is there anything else?' Petrus heard Suasso's sharp intake of breath at his rudeness.

Gna looked belligerently at Petrus. 'The Romans burned some of my people's farms. Will there be any money for those who have lost their homes?'

Petrus frowned, so that was it. 'You know you must address the issue of compensation with Julius Maximus. You should've spoken with him when you gave up the men.'

Gna waited.

Petrus did not speak again. Gna knew the rules. Compensation was in the gift of the centurion.

Petrus waited.

'Go well, Roman,' Gna walked back to his horse. He rode away without looking back.

'There was no need for rudeness,' said Suasso.

'As you know yourself, as one who is frequently rude,' snapped Petrus. 'There was no need for him to come and see me. We've wasted enough time, let's move.'

'Aurelius Petrus!' A slave ran out of the gate towards them. 'The lady asks you to take this letter to Julia Prima.' He handed over two tablets held together with a wax seal.

Petrus nodded, mounted his horse and gave the order to move out.

Beyond the vicus, the wind blew across the hillside. Petrus inhaled deeply and enjoyed the sharp pain of the cold in his lungs. The horses' feet crunched on the melting frost.

Carantii

It was mid-afternoon and Carantii hadn't got a lot of urgent work that needed doing, so he decided to check on Cara and Metta. He pushed open the door to the brothel and ambled through to the salon. There was one other man lounging on the couch, waiting for a girl. The usual bowls of oils were not alight, and the room smelled musty. The girl sitting at the table smiled coyly.

'What brings you here again so soon, Carantii, and in the daytime?' she fluttered her eyelids and licked her lips.

He felt uncomfortable, she was just a child. How did he expect a child brought up in these surroundings to behave? He'd never concerned himself about such matters before and was surprised to find himself so disconcerted.

'I want Metta and Cara again. I'm free this afternoon and I couldn't wait to see them.' He slapped coins on her table.

'Have a seat and I'll see what we can do.' She got up and left the room.

He was sipping his wine when Sylva approached him.

'Carantii!' Sylva smiled. 'I'm afraid Cara and Metta aren't here. They've gone back to their parents for a while.'

'Gone? When? How long will they be away for?' He tried to feign surprise. 'I was looking forward to being with them again today.'

'They went yesterday morning around daybreak. Solis, in the afternoon, they suddenly asked me if they could go home. They're new and I have to look after them. I gave them some money to pay Gamigoni, the trader who brought them here, to take them home and then bring them back again in a few days' time. After all, they've earned it. They're some of my best workers, very popular. The men from the fort seem to like them a lot. That Aurelius Petrus has asked for them several times, then there was one of those local men that the army have working for them, the bald one with tattoos across his whole head. He was here the day before yesterday I think, same day as Petrus, and there've been others as well.' She stopped, put her head on one side and watched him carefully, 'Gamigoni told them to go to his place at daybreak, so that's what they did yesterday. Can I tempt you with another girl?'

Carantii was pleased. The sisters had clearly not told Sylva about the money.

'Carantii?'

He smiled. 'Bring 'em out, let me have a look.' He felt obliged to use one of the women, after all it was a brothel, and he didn't want to arouse suspicion. Sylva whispered something to the girl who disappeared down what he now thought of as the "expensive" corridor.

Six women arrived and paraded round the salon, each dressed in a fine tunic and wearing silver-coloured bangles on her arms. They did not look at him or smile as they swung their hips in front of him. They were all attractive, but he wasn't really concentrating.

'Well?' asked Sylva.

'Er…that one.' He pointed at a woman with dark brown hair plaited down her back.

'Troucissa, a good choice, very athletic,' Sylva purred, beckoning the woman over.

Troucissa took his hand and led him down the corridor into a room which was identical to Cara and Metta's. He pushed her roughly onto the bed, lifted her tunic and took her quickly, then lay back on the bed, breathless and closed his eyes. When he felt her move on the mattress next to him, he opened his eyes, pulled up his trousers, and left the room without looking back.

The girl in the salon smiled up at him.

He nodded and walked out of the brothel. As he reached Petrus' house, he had a quick look round. No one seemed to be paying him any attention, so he tied some ivy to the boot scraper by the door and then made his way to the tavern.

Petrus

The stench of death had spread through the vicus. The West gates swung open as they approached the fort, he dismounted and gave his horse to one of the men. He gave orders to his accompanying soldiers to get some rest. The barbarians melted away into the vicus, except for Suasso, who lingered at the gate. The stink of decaying flesh forced its way into Petrus' body, becoming part of him as he walked through the fort.

Petrus found the prefect at his desk in the Principia.

'What took you so long?' snapped Tatius.

'We were delayed, Chief Gna asked to meet with me, he came to the fort this morning.'

'Gna? What did he want? Maximus saw him a couple of days ago.'

'Reassurance that this matter has now ended and to ask for compensation for the farms that were burned. I said the murders were now solved and as for money, he'd have to address that with Maximus.'

Tatius nodded.

'I've a letter for your wife.' Petrus drew the sealed tablets from his tunic and offered them to Tatius. 'It's from Fabia.'

Tatius waved it away. 'Don't bother me with these foolish things. Take it over to the house. When you've done that, take down the heads.'

'And what of the death rituals?'

'Get the barbarians to deal with that. I don't care what happens to them.'

Petrus was shocked by Tatius' attitude. Everyone deserved a

ceremony to speed them into the afterlife, even the enemies of Rome. He returned his armour and weapons to his room. Boga thrust some bread and wine towards him.

'I expect you didn't get much food at Camboglanna,' commented the slave.

Petrus smiled and thanked him. Boga took great pride in looking after the Centurion and his second-in-command.

Petrus made his way to the Praetorium and was ushered into the salon by Felix. Prima lay on a couch listening to one of her slave girls singing. Gaius, her son, was playing with some wooden animals nearby. She sat up and smiled as he walked towards her.

'A message for you, from the lady at Camboglanna,' he said, handing over the tablets.

She broke the seals to the two pieces of wood and read the letter. 'She's pregnant!' she cried, leaping up and stepping towards Petrus. He thought she was going to embrace him and stepped back, feeling awkward. She stopped, her face flushed red, and she returned to her couch, where she took a moment to calm herself.

'The physician says that's why she was ill in the mornings. It's such wonderful news.'

Petrus wasn't interested in Fabia's health and didn't think he was expected to comment; he bowed and left the room. He made his way to the east gate where Suasso was now deep in conversation with a local man. Seeing Petrus, Suasso broke away from the man and moved towards him.

'Take the heads down and give them a burial, the kind your people need,' instructed Petrus. 'Take a cart from here.'

Suasso nodded. 'I know a place where we won't be disturbed.'

'Will you give them full funeral rites?'

'Everyone deserves full rites, and anyway…' he did not finish the sentence.

'And anyway what?' snapped Petrus, wondering if Suasso had been about to say that they may have been innocent.

Suasso shrugged. 'I'll get my men together.'

A small boy with long dark hair and a smock that was too big for him ran towards the fort. Breathless, he struggled to get out the words. 'Aurelius Petrus, your wife has sent me with a message for you.'

Petrus smiled and placed a hand on the boy's shoulder, 'Easy, easy lad. What's the message?'

'She asked that you come home right away.' The boy trembled in fear.

Petrus nodded and gave the boy a coin. He ran away, quickly disappearing into the backstreets of the vicus. Petrus crossed the ditch; he passed a crowd of people watching in horror as the heads were removed from the posts. Whatever Suasso and his men were doing to the heads, it was making the smell worse and they groaned and retched as they worked. The stench of death followed Petrus down the street.

Ivy was tangled round the boot scraper at his door. He pushed it open. Mincona smiled, she was seated at the table stitching Titus' tunic.

'She's playing with Titus,' she said.

Petrus nodded.

He opened the door to Titus' room where his wife and son lay curled up together on the bed. Aurora had her arm protectively around the boy who was asleep; she smiled as he walked in, eased herself off the bed and pushed him out of the door closing it behind her. She reached up to kiss him and led him back to the kitchen.

'Leave that, Mincona, sit with Titus please.'

Mincona left the room.

'How is Titus?' Petrus lowered himself to a stool.

'He's fine.'

'Then?'

'In the vicus, people know I'm your woman. People know you've been involved in the search for the murderers. A woman stopped me in the market. Her name is Tossodia, she has a young son. She is, I mean was, with Faustus, one of the dead soldiers. The boy is his. She's very distressed. She's got no money and is really struggling. Can you help her?'

Petrus shook his head sadly. 'That explains why he had a child's toy amongst his things. The army rules are clear, as he didn't leave a will, his money reverts to the army and I've already issued orders for his belongings to be shared between his roommates.' He stopped and took her hand. 'Those are the rules. I'm sorry. It's very difficult. Any woman with children could say she was his and entitled to his goods and money.' He felt ashamed as he said this, but it was the harsh truth.

Aurora looked away. 'And is that what would happen if you were killed? Our son is not officially yours as we're not married. He's lucky that he was born a Roman citizen, because his mother is. These other women, unofficial wives of soldiers, are not so fortunate. There would still be no assistance for me as we're not man and wife in the eyes of the army. After all,' she mimicked him, "any woman with children could say that they were your wife."

He squeezed her hand, but she did not look at him. 'I have made a will leaving everything to you. Even the Prefect knows I have family here in the vicus. If the Gods choose to take my life, you will be taken care of. You know we cannot formalise our marriage until I retire, and that is some years away.' He took a deep breath.

She turned towards him, tears in her eyes, 'It's not right. What will the woman do? That man's poor son. He's only a child.'

Petrus pulled her towards him and hugged her to his chest. 'I'm sorry,' he whispered.

Aurora leant in to him for a few moments. He breathed in the smell of her.

She sniffed and wiped the tears from her cheeks with her sleeve. 'Carantii, the blacksmith, wants to see you.'

'Carantii? How do you know that?' he was a little alarmed.

'I saw him carrying his ivy in the street. And then he wasn't.

It's around the boot scraper. He should be more careful. Feelings are running high in the community after the killing of those men by Maximus. Carantii won't fair well if people find out he's an informant. And neither will you.'

Petrus sucked his teeth. 'You're right. I'll warn him.'

He was very worried. If Aurora had seen Carantii with the ivy and figured out he was an informant, then other people might have too. In some towns, informants had been murdered. He didn't want the blacksmith's death on his conscience, and from a selfish point of view, he didn't want to lose a valuable source.

He hugged Aurora tighter, kissed her cool cheeks and then made his way through the darkening street to the tavern.

It was cool inside; all the torches were lit even though only two tables were occupied. Carantii was in a heated exchange with a small dark man. Petrus sat at an empty table.

'Good to see you, Sir,' the taverner said as he placed a cup of ale in front of him.

'I'm on my way back to the fort, I've just come to see which men are here who should be thinking about going back,' Petrus said raising his voice.

Two soldiers stood up, nodded to Petrus and left. He drank slowly and ordered more ale. Carantii's argument was growing louder, and Petrus wondered whether they would come to blows. The blacksmith did not look like he was going to leave any time soon. Petrus had several more drinks before deciding he had better leave.

The moon was weak, barely penetrating the darkness, as Petrus walked towards the forge. He looked around him and, confident he would not be observed, stepped into the dark alleyway next to the forge.

'Jupiter's sake!' he swore as his boot squelched and the smell of rotting vegetables rose around him.

He stepped further into the darkness before turning around.

He stood with his back pressed against the forge wall. The stone was warm and comforting. He thought he was probably against the furnace. He peered out into the street, keeping his face covered by the hood of his cloak. A dark figure approached. Petrus took a step back and reached for his sword. The man kept walking and stepped into the alleyway. Petrus took his sword from its sheath as the shadow of the man loomed above him.

'Hail Petrus,' whispered Carantii, 'won't you come in?' He opened the door to his home and stepped in without waiting for Petrus to reply.

Petrus scraped his boots and followed him. 'What about Eburacia?'

'Oh, she knows all about us, same as your Aurora knows. We've no secrets from our women, try as we might,' Carantii smiled. 'Take a seat,' he indicated a stool near the fire.

Petrus sat down and removed his cloak. The heat from the forge forced its way through the wall into the kitchen making it warm and cosy.

'Aurora saw you today carrying ivy. That's how she knows you do work for me. You were seen,' Petrus emphasised the words.

'Seen?' laughed Carantii, who was clearly quite drunk.

'Aurora figured out you put it there when she saw it on the boot scraper. You must take more care. Informants have been killed in some towns.'

Carantii opened his mouth to speak but closed it as Eburacia entered and nodded a greeting.

Carantii

He'd had a lot to drink by the time he found Petrus in the alleyway, so waved away Eburacia's offer of more ale. He was frightened by what Petrus had told him but didn't want to alarm his sister and motioned for her to join them at the table.

Carantii pressed his hands together, leaning his forearms on the table, 'I've heard what you said, Roman,' he said. 'I will take much more care.'

Petrus nodded. 'Good. You wanted to see me?'

'I went back to the brothel today. To check on the girls, like you said, to see if they needed any help. They're not there. Sylva said that Solis they suddenly asked if they could go home to their parents' place for a few days. Must've been after you gave them their inheritance. Sylva made arrangements with the trader Gamigoni to take them home the following day. He's the one who brought them to Sylva in the first place. He does a lot of trade with people in their father's area. They left yesterday morning around daybreak.'

Petrus reached into his pouch and placed some money on the table.

'One more thing,' continued Carantii, 'Sylva said they were very popular with men from the fort and one of the local men you employ had been with them two days ago, same day as you. The description she gave sounded like Luci.'

Petrus looked surprised. 'Luci?'

'Yes, Luci.'

Petrus scowled. 'I've been told not to continue my investigation.'

'And will you? Stop investigating, I mean?'

Petrus appeared to think for a while and then said, 'It must appear as if I have stopped.'

Eburacia rose from her seat and took the lid off a pot on the fire and stirred the contents. The aroma of rich stew filled the room. Petrus' stomach gurgled.

'Will you eat with us?' Carantii smiled, watching the soldier carefully.

'Yes. Thank you.'

Eburacia spooned out the stew into bowls and rejoined them at the table. The tasty goat stew filled their stomachs. Carantii chatted about hipposandals – the metal shoes he made for the Roman soldiers' horses and how they had to be made to fit each one individually. He told them that he also had an agreement with the fort to make some decorative metalwork for horses' bridles. Eburacia nodded and smiled as he spoke. Petrus was staring at the wall behind Carantii's head.

'I think it's for the Prefect,' Carantii said, 'the horses' bridle work, I mean.'

Petrus nodded his head absently.

'And then I thought I'd make a dagger and stab it right through your Roman heart,' Carantii said, watching Petrus closely. Petrus carried on eating.

Carantii put down his spoon. 'What's wrong with you, my…' He'd been about to say "my friend". 'I've just said I'm going to make a dagger to stab you with!'

Petrus smiled awkwardly. 'I'm thinking about what you've told me. About Cara, Metta, and Luci. Thank you.' He turned towards Eburacia, 'and thank you for the meal and hospitality. Now, I must return to the fort.' He rose and stepped into the night.

Carantii asked his sister, 'How is our father?'

'Much the same,' she replied. 'He doesn't have much longer. You should look in on him.'

Carantii walked into his father's room; the old man was

asleep. He watched him in the light of the candle burning near his bed. His chest rattled with each shallow breath, and he moaned softly in his sleep. The smell of urine and dirt hung around the room; they would have to try to clean him up in the morning. He closed the door. The kitchen was empty. Eburacia had cleared the pots away and unrolled his mattress. He lay down and closed his eyes.

Petrus

Petrus banged on the gate. There was no response.

He shouted, 'Wake up you bastards!'

He picked up some small pebbles and threw them over the parapet, hearing them rattle on the stone floor.

The spyhole opened. 'Aurum' hissed Petrus.

The bolts slid back, and the gate opened.

'Asleep again!' Petrus grabbed Rufus by the throat and pushed him up against the wall. 'You and that other idiot will report to Maximus in the morning! Quirinus will be there too!'

He released his grip and walked down the street towards his office. He lit a lamp and wrote his notes, detailing all the things which Carantii had told him, including that the two whores had left the brothel telling Sylva they were just visiting their parents, but he thought they'd left for good. In another report he wrote about the gatekeepers Rufus and Pius being asleep, and that it wasn't the first time. They were Quirinus' men, and he would have to tell Maximus. He locked his reports in the chest in his office, turned out the lamp and closed the door behind him.

Outside, he could hear raised voices coming from the Praetorium, so crept closer, keeping his back against the wall to stay in the shadow. He was ashamed of his desire to listen in to the Prefect's private life, but he couldn't help himself. The voices carried into the night from the shuttered window.

'Don't hit me again, please. She's my friend. This is her first baby. I want to share that joy with her. For just a few days. Please.'

'She's a grown woman, not a child. I'm not going to waste

valuable resources by having you escorted to Camboglanna. Septimus is probably sick of the sight of you, just like I'm sick of Fabia!' Tatius' voice was full of menace.

Petrus heard a door bang. Quiet sobbing reached out to him in the darkness. His heart went out to Prima.

He made his way to the barrack room where Quirinus slept. All the occupants were snoring loudly. Petrus bent down and grabbed Quirinus by the shoulder, shaking him violently. Quirinus' eyes flew open, he struggled against Petrus' grip and reached for a weapon beneath his mattress.

'Stop struggling, Quirinus!' Petrus hissed.

Men about them were stirring.

'It's me, Aurelius Petrus!' he snarled, 'Get up Quirinus! Rufus and Pius were asleep on the gate again!'

Quirinus stumbled upright and pulled on his boots. The other men scrambled out of their beds and stood to attention in their bare feet.

'Get out there and sort them out, Quirinus! See Maximus in the morning!' snapped Petrus.

Petrus turned on his heel and left the room. Moments later, he heard Quirinus running down the street towards the gate. Maximus was moving around when he entered their quarters. Boga was fast asleep by the table.

'What's all that noise, Petrus?' grumbled Maximus as he bent to take off his boots.

'Quirinus' two men, Rufus and Pius were asleep at the gate when I came back. I woke Quirinus up to get him to sort them out. I told 'em all to see us in the morning.'

Maximus nodded. 'I'll replace Quirinus after I've spoken to the prefect.'

XI - Dies Mercurii

Petrus waited in Maximus' office after parade. The centurion drummed his fingers on the table. When Quirinus, Rufus, and Pius entered the room Maximus burst out of his chair and stood with his nose almost touching Quirinus' face. Quirinus trembled as the centurion spoke.

'What were your men doing asleep on duty!' Maximus roared. Flecks of spittle spattered across the Tesserarius' cheeks.

Quirinus remained silent. Maximus moved to stand in front of Rufus and Pius, whose faces were pale. Their lips quivered, they stared straight ahead as Maximus shouted at them, repeating the same question over and over and calling them lazy bastards.

'This isn't the first time you've been caught asleep! You miserable sods! You're going to get a beating and have your pay docked! Get into the yard and take your tunics off!'

They lowered their heads and walked out of the office. Maximus handed his vinestaff to Quirinus. 'Giving these men a beating is probably your last act as Tesserarius.'

Quirinus followed the centurion out of the office. Petrus walked out of the yard. Behind him was the sound of the vinestaff striking the men's flesh. He felt sorry for Quirinus. A soldier ran towards him and saluted breathlessly.

'Aurelius Petrus! There is a man at the East gate demanding to see the Prefect, he says his daughters have been attacked. The Prefect said you would deal with it.'

Petrus groaned inwardly and made his way to the gate. A grey-haired man leaning heavily on a staff stood beside two women in heavy cloaks. The women did not have hoods to cover their tear-stained faces.

'I want to see the prefect,' the man yelled, waving the staff at Petrus. 'I demand to be heard!'

The men in the gate tower leant over the wall, staring. 'We don't speak local,' one of them sneered in Latin.

'That's enough!' snapped Petrus.

Red-faced, the two guards disappeared beneath the parapet. Petrus approached the man, motioning with his arms to try to calm him. He spoke in the local Carvetti language. 'What brings you here?'

'I demand to see the Prefect. My daughters were chased by four soldiers a few days ago. When they caught my girls, they used them, repeatedly taking it in turns. They were virgins. One of them is still bleeding, even now,' the old man said. He pulled one of the women towards him and opened her cloak. Her clothes were dirty and tattered. Blood leaked down her pale legs below the hem of her smock. Petrus grimaced. He felt ashamed, ashamed to be a Roman soldier, ashamed to be a man.

'May the gods bring death to the men who did this,' said the man. He shook his staff at Petrus and let go of the woman's cloak, she wrapped it around herself and stepped away.

'Careful, old man. Don't threaten Rome. Two soldiers were killed here this last week. Call on the gods to kill my men and I may think you had something to do with the deaths.' Petrus knew it was ludicrous to suggest that the old man might have been involved in the murders, but he couldn't allow him to make threats in public like that, without warning him of the consequences. He knew the gatekeepers were listening.

The man spat on the ground. 'That wasn't the work of the men you killed, nor was it me. I'm here about my daughters. Who will marry them now? Now they will be afraid of men. Soldiers can't just walk through the community and attack our women. I demand justice from the Prefect.'

'I am Optio Aurelius Petrus. The Prefect has authorised me

to speak with you and offer you some compensation.' He was trying to think what a suitable payment might be. 'If you wait here, I'll fetch some money for you.'

The man nodded his assent and Petrus passed through the gate and hurried to the Treasury where Ecdicius was busy with his accounts.

'How much do we normally compensate when a girl has been raped?' he demanded.

Ecdicius looked puzzled.

'Come on. It's probably a fairly frequent occurrence. There must be a set rate,' snapped Petrus.

'If she's a virgin, then twenty denarii,' Ecdicius sneered. 'They're always virgins.'

'Give me forty denarii. Write a receipt – payment for the rape of two girls.' He gave the names of the four men who'd admitted to the rapes. 'Put it against their wages. The Centurion Aquilinus has authorised it to be docked from their pay. I'll take the receipt to their librarius to deal with.'

He scribbled his name on the tablet, took the coins handed to him and walked to the Records office.

The librarius read the tablet. 'Has Aquilinus authorised this?'

'That's what it says, you can check with him if you like, you need to pass it on to him anyway.'

'They've had their pay docked for this before.'

'What do you mean?'

'I recognise the names,' muttered the librarius. 'Aquilinus wasn't happy about it then, I expect he's spitting boot nails now.'

Petrus was horrified. He wondered how many other women in the community had suffered the same fate at the hands of these men. At the gate, the guards were ignoring the old man, who huddled with his daughters against the wall, trying to shield them from the wind. Petrus dropped the coins into his outstretched hand.

'This is the end of it. I'll see to it that the men in question are punished.'

The man put the coins inside his cloak and hurried away with his daughters.

Petrus made his way to Aquilinus' office. He knocked on the door and entered to find the centurion busy writing.

'Ignatius Aquilinus?' Petrus said, 'I've paid the compensation to the father of the girls that Vester and his comrades raped. Were you aware it's not the first time they've behaved that way?'

'I'd forgotten that. But now you've said it, I do remember. Giving the army a bad name in the community, aren't they?'

Petrus was shocked that Aquilinus could have forgotten about the previous rapes. Was it such a frequent occurrence that it was insignificant to him? Perhaps the men in Aquilinus' century were an unruly lot and frequently undisciplined. He didn't know; he and Maximus were only responsible for the men in their century. Aquilinus pulled a new tablet towards him and began writing.

'I'm cancelling their leave to go into the community. They'll be confined to barracks for six months. These kinds of events upset the locals. That's not acceptable.'

Petrus didn't know what he'd expected from Aquilinus, but he felt disappointed. He nodded and left the room.

Carantii

Sparks flew as he struck the glowing metal, beating it into shape. A merchant had ordered hipposandals for his horse. 'The distances I cover, I want some of those things the Romans' horses have,' he'd said and slapped advanced payment on the table. The horse had been tethered outside while Carantii had measured its feet. This was the first time he'd been asked by a local man to make hipposandals, and he wondered if they would become a status symbol, just as the decorative metal work on horses' bridles had once been.

Beads of sweat formed on Carantii's forehead and began to trickle down towards his eyes. He wiped his forearm across his face. Behind him, the door creaked open and Eburacia entered, her cheeks were damp with tears. He finished the shoe and laid it on the ground. He stepped towards her and drew her into his arms, hugged her thin body, and stroked the back of her head with his hand.

'He's gone,' she muttered into his chest, dribbling tears onto his leather apron as she sobbed.

Carantii closed the door to the forge and locked it. He placed some charcoal in the furnace and covered it with ash, knowing it may not be used again for several days, he wanted to ensure it remained hot enough to relight. He followed his sister through the kitchen to the bedroom where the old man lay. He stroked his father's grey cheek with the back of his hand, the skin was cold, the lips were blue. The stink of stale urine rose about them. He pulled the blanket over his father's face. He felt sad but knew it was a release from his suffering.

'I'll go and get a cart. Bring his spear and his torc.'

Eburacia nodded. She would prepare the body for the journey back to their home place, several hours away in the countryside.

Carantii loaned a horse and cart from one of the merchants. They wrapped their father's body in its blanket and carried it on the mattress, laying it in the back of the cart. Carantii looked up at the thick grey clouds moving across the sky, buffeted by harsh winds. The sun shone fleetingly as the clouds passed, but it was unable to provide warmth to the cold streets. He hoped that it would not rain later in the morning.

'Bring some blankets to keep warm. It'll be a slow journey.'

Eburacia handed him a blanket and wrapped one round her shoulders as she took her place in the back of the cart alongside her father's body. She lay her hand on the dead man's chest. Carantii turned the cart and they walked out of the town against a steady flow of people moving along the road towards the vicus.

Carantii began to tremble as the icy wind bit into his face and his lips went numb. He pulled the blanket around him and covered his head to try to stay keep out the cold. It was a long sad journey, but eventually he slowed the rickety cart to a halt near their roundhouse enclosure.

Chickens scratched at the earth. A dog beside the house barked. Beyond the house a herd of black cattle grazed, and a flock of sheep munched on sparse grass. A small shepherd boy sat nearby, watching them. Their brother Amba emerged from the house, straightened up, pushed his dark hair away from his face and smiled in recognition. Eburacia rushed forward and clasped Amba's hand.

'It was his time,' she whispered.

Amba nodded. The two men lifted the mattress and carried it into the dark interior of the roundhouse where they laid it on the floor against one of the walls. Sunlight reached through the hole in the roof and into the shadows, it touched the shrouded body. Specks of dust shimmered in the light and danced around them. Carantii kicked out at the dog as it sniffed around his boots. He went outside to unharness the horse. It snuffled the ground looking for things of interest as he gave it some water and some hay, then went back into the house to sit near the fire.

'He has moved on to a place without suffering,' Amba said.

Amba's wife Atta handed them all a cup of ale and some porridge. Carantii gobbled the food down, surprised by how hungry he was.

Carantii and Amba dug a knee-deep pit a few paces from the river's edge and then walked into the nearby copse where bare branches littered the woodland floor and the smell of damp earth hung in the air. They gathered the fallen branches, building them into a tall pyre in the pit and put aside two more piles of wood. They carried the mattress with their father's body from the house and placed it on top of the pyre. Atta and Eburacia followed them, each carrying a burning torch. The men took the torches and lit the fire. Yellow flames crept through the wood as it crackled and spat. The straw mattress smoked and caught alight, the old man's clothes blackened and shrivelled. The body began to burn, white flames and grey smoke snaked into the air. The smell of burning wood and roasting meat hovered around them.

The men began to sing the ancient chants passed down to them from their ancestors. The women joined in singing the words of their mothers and grandmothers. Their melancholy songs blended with the men's voices and carried across the air to the roundhouse where Amba's daughter, Brigia, was playing in the yard. She had a small baby wrapped in a shawl tied to her back. She heard the singing and ran towards her parents. The baby gurgled complaints as his head joggled from side to side against her back as she ran. She reached the fire and grasped her mother's hand, her lips moved as she tried to join in the singing.

The sun began to sink lower as the night approached. Darkness enveloped them. They continued singing. Brigia began to sink down towards the ground. Her mother unwrapped the shawl, took the baby from her back and handed him to Eburacia. Atta picked Brigia up, placing her shawl around the girl's shoulders and carried her towards the house. Eburacia walked behind them with the baby asleep in her arms.

The men piled more wood onto the fire and then walked to the house. The children were asleep beneath sheep's wool blankets. The adults sat round the fire with two torches burning, filled their bellies with stew, drank ale and spoke about their father's life. It had been a good one. Carantii reassured his brother that he would not be coming back to the farm to claim any property.

'I am busy enough as a blacksmith,' he said.

Amba nodded. 'And what of you, Ebu? Will you stay here now, or go back to the town? When will you find a husband? What do you want from here?'

Eburacia smiled. 'When the time comes for marriage, I will have my share. People know I can be found at the forge, even prospective husbands.'

'And you, brother, will you take a wife?' Amba asked.

'In time,' Carantii smiled.

'Do you remember Lugraca, the daughter of our neighbour Gava?' Amba asked.

Carantii smiled, 'Yes, yes, I do. She was small and dark and played with Ebu when they were children.' He paused, 'climbing trees and chasing sheep as I remember. Why do you ask?'

'We, that is, I, thought she might make a good maid for you when I am gone. Married, I mean,' Eburacia spoke quietly.

'Mmm, I guess she might. Isn't she married? Why the sudden interest in maids for me?' Carantii asked.

'Oh, we've just been talking, Atta and I,' replied Eburacia.

Carantii wondered what else they'd been talking and planning.

Amba pulled some straw into a heap against the wall for Eburacia to use as a bed. Carantii curled up on a cow hide on the floor. The house's familiar smells of smoke, fermented milk and animals comforted him. His sleep was interrupted by the cries of the baby reaching him in the darkness. Loud suckling noises followed, and he drifted back into a dreamless sleep.

XII – Dies Iovis

Carantii

The vicus' muddy streets were busy as they arrived back at the forge. Carantii was soaked through to the skin and his limbs were numb with cold after the endless rain throughout their journey. Eburacia was shivering.

The cart rocked as Eburacia got out. Carantii climbed down, opened the forge's doors and murmured encouragement to the horse as he tried to push it backwards into the gap between the doors. Initially reluctant, the horse snorted and stamped its feet, but finally it slowly moved; the cart creaked in protest. He tied the horse to the post outside and put a log of wood under each of the cart's wheels to stop it rolling. They carried sacks of food into the kitchen and hung the cowhides and their cloaks in the forge to dry. Carantii led the horse and cart back to the merchant.

Carantii walked through to his father's bedroom, undressed and rubbed his arms and body vigorously with a cloth, trying to get warm. Dressed in dry clothes he took his wet things through to the kitchen where Eburacia was reviving the fire. She had stopped shaking. She cleared the ash away from the embers, placed some small twigs on top and blew on it. Smoke and small flames began to rise, and she added more fuel. As flames began to crackle, she hung their wet clothes nearby to dry. She sat down at the table opposite him and unwrapped the food which Atta had given her. The bread had survived the journey without getting wet and they both ate hungrily.

He moved into the forge and began stoking the furnace. Flames burst into life. The building filled with warm air. Steam rose from their cloaks and the animal skins as they dried. He worked on the hipposandals and by the end of the afternoon had a set of four ready for the merchant to collect. He hung them on the wall for other customers to see.

Later, he moved his mattress into his father's old room and covered it with blankets. It felt strange to be sleeping there, but he felt his father's spirit. It meant the old man was at peace in the other world. He lay in his bed and thought about Eburacia, hoping that a kind man would come to ask to take her as a wife. She would make a good match.

XIII - Dies Veneris

The sound of marching soldiers thundered across the morning silence. Birds resting among the new leaves on the trees rose in fright like black marks against the sky. At the training ground outside the fort, the men grumbled as they formed into lines, scuffing their cold feet against the hard ground as they tried to warm icy toes. Petrus had spent the whole of the previous day supervising the workshops and was glad to be back training and drilling soldiers. He put the men into pairs and began hand-to-hand combat training. He encouraged and berated the men in almost equal measure, irritated that some men still hadn't grasped the basics of attacking the enemy whilst still protecting themselves. The men were soon sweating and gasping for breath.

'You can rest for a while,' he said eventually.

The men paused. Many undid their flasks and sipped from them.

'If you've forgotten your water, then it serves you right,' he said watching some of the men asking their colleagues for a drink.

'Aurelius Petrus!' A young soldier approached. 'I've orders here for you. You're to return to the fort immediately. Fabius Ruga is coming to take over from you,' he handed a tablet to Petrus.

Petrus scanned the document; it was signed by Prefect Silvius Tatius. He could see a man walking towards them. The distinctive shape of his helmet and vinestaff marked him out as a centurion, but he couldn't make out the face.

'Is that him?' he asked the messenger.

'I expect so.'

Petrus turned to his men, 'I'm leaving now. That's centurion

Fabius Ruga coming to take over.'

Petrus walked towards the vicus. As Ruga reached him, the centurion stopped. 'Hail Petrus.'

'Hail Ruga.'

'Everything alright over there?'

'As well as can be expected with so many new recruits.'

'Well,' grinned Ruga, 'I'm sure you'll enjoy whatever the Prefect has lined up for you.'

'The Prefect? Where's Maximus?'

'Off on duties somewhere in Camboglanna direction, I think. Went a short time ago. He took some barbarians and a couple of soldiers.'

Petrus wondered why Maximus hadn't told him that he was going away, although Maximus would have said he was under no obligation to tell Petrus about his movements. Petrus took his time walking back to the fort, breathing in the fresh Spring air. The sound of metal striking metal emerged to meet him from the open door of the forge. In the marketplace, the traders shouted out their prices. Slaves and women moved through the streets, shopping, carrying water, scolding children.

The guards were clearly looking out for him, as the gate opened before he reached it, and they didn't ask for a password until he prompted them. It stank of stale water near the gate, Petrus wrinkled his nose and looked around. Foul water oozed up around the stones covering the waste channel near the bathhouse.

At the headquarters Tatius waved him to a seat. 'There's a problem with the latrines. The morning flush through with water hasn't worked. They're full up. We've got hundreds of men needing to use them. It's urgent, we don't want the men to start shitting anywhere they want. The bathhouse can't empty its water either and the waste is coming up in the streets in the vicus. It's a shitty job. Might be worth using the men on punishment duty to help you.' He pushed a tablet across the table. It had six names on it. 'They were shouting abuse at the local men as they marched back from the training ground yesterday. Challenged 'em to fight and called 'em cowards. They're not from your century.'

Six men stood outside the building. Petrus immediately recognised four of them as the rapists from centurion Aquilinus' century. He was disappointed.

'You lot!' Petrus growled, 'You've not learned from the other night then?'

The men did not respond and stared straight ahead as Petrus stood in front of them.

'When I've finished with you, I'm sure Aquilinus will have more to say. You're a bloody disgrace! Follow me!' He led them towards the latrine building.

The cold wind blew through the latrine building and carried the stench across the fort. It made Petrus gag. Twenty seating places ran along each side of the wall in the room. In the centre of the room was a pile of dried moss for the men to use to clean themselves. Romans preferred to use sponges, but in Britannia they were too difficult to get hold of, so moss was gathered for this purpose. He peered inside one of the seat holes. Faeces floated amid clumps of moss in the brown water just below the seat.

'There must be a blockage in the sewer,' he said. 'The bathhouse waste channel is blocked as well.'

They loaded up a horse and cart with digging tools, six large amphorae filled with water, in case they needed to flush the drains, and some large slates, as Petrus thought they might need them to control the sewage flow. They walked out of the gate. The track near the bathhouse was flooded. The stink of stale water and rotting vegetables filled the air. Petrus was grateful it wasn't a hot day.

The men grumbled about the smell as they trudged through the mud alongside the waste channel which ran parallel to the ditch around the fort. The covered stone channel had been built to flush away water from the bathhouse when it emptied its tanks every morning shortly after sunrise. The large flat cover stones were to reduce the smell and stop people throwing rubbish into it. All the cover stones on the channel were submerged in stinking grey water. The channel was blocked its entire length. The wide stone sewer channel leading from the fort's latrines passed out through a hole in the fort wall and joined the bathhouse sewer, eventually flowing into the river. The fort sewer was similarly covered with large slates.

All of the slates covering the fort's channel had grass growing across them; they looked like they had not been lifted in years. At the site of the outfall to the river, Petrus dug round the edge of one of the slates, freed it and lifted it free. The sewer was almost empty, only a few small lumps of drying excrement stuck to the stones. He put the slate back in place.

'The blockage must be further back,' Petrus told the men as he walked twenty strides distance back towards the fort. He lifted the slate from the dry ground. Beneath it the drying faeces waited to be pushed into the river. He walked forty paces towards the fort. The grass covering the slates was wet and it smelled faintly of decay. He dug up the muddy ground around a slate and lifted it. The sewer was full, like a thick bubbling stew of shit and moss. The stench turned his stomach. He tried to breathe through his mouth as he turned aside and retched, vomitting onto the grass. The aftertaste in his mouth mingled with the stench of faeces, he heaved in disgust and wiped his mouth on his sleeve. He dug round one of the slates ten strides closer to the river and one of the soldiers stepped forward to lift it. The soldier gagged as he stared into it, turned his head aside and vomited, splashing his boots. The others began digging up slates at intervals and lifting them.

'For the love of Hercules,' muttered Vester taking a step back.

Petrus walked towards him and peered into the sewer. He gasped in horror. The lower half of two human legs were visible in the sea of shit. The bloated grey skin had been scratched by the rough stonework and was streaked with excrement. Beneath the brown slime on the ankle, he could just make out a delicate tattoo of a sprig of holly.

The rank air filled his lungs and he felt as if the sewer had entered his body, drawn deep inside his belly. 'I think it's one of Sylva's girls.' He paused, and breathed out the fetid air, 'Lift ten slates going that way, so that we are well clear of where her head might be.'

The men stood motionless for a moment.

'Go on then! Move!' he barked.

They lifted ten slates higher up the channel and placed them on the ground. The men stared into the filth, unsure what to do next. Petrus' stomach churned. He turned aside and retched again, his empty belly heaved and twisted in pain. He forced himself upright and walked to the cart. He carried one of the slates from the cart up and forced it into the channel near the last lifted slate. The putrid mess squelched as he pushed the slate down and it slopped onto his boots. He swore and stepped back.

'Block the channel down there, where it's nearly empty. That's below the blockage. When we do get her loose, I don't want a huge torrent of shit washing down from the fort. We'll get covered in it and we might lose the body.'

The men nodded as they began to understand what he was trying to do. Janus lifted a slate and pushed it into the empty channel.

'You,' Petrus pointed at Justus, 'Get in the channel and start digging her out, carefully.'

Justus reluctantly removed his tunic, trousers, socks and boots. Shivering in the cold morning air, wearing just his underpants, he stepped carefully into the trench. He gagged as he began moving the sewage carefully with his shovel, placing it onto the grass beside the channel. The remaining men grimaced and retched as they watched. Justus uncovered more of the dead woman; she was wearing a red smock which had ridden up around her waist.

He glanced uneasily between her legs for a moment and then pulled the smock down to cover her. Petrus wondered whether this was to give her some dignity, or because he couldn't bear to look at the woman's swollen body lying in the filth, when he'd no doubt used her thoughtlessly at the brothel.

'Mercury save us!' cried Justus.

Two more grey feet had emerged from the excrement at the first body's shoulder. Petrus could just make out the holly tattoo on the ankle beneath the slime.

'Another girl from the brothel,' murmured Petrus. He pulled a tablet from his tunic and scribbled a note on it.

'You!' He pointed at one of the men who stood staring into the channel with a look of horror on his face, 'Take this back to the Prefect as quickly as you can. Then return here with four more soldiers and some blankets for carrying the bodies. Don't speak to anyone apart from the Prefect. Hurry!' He pushed the tablet into the man's hands and watched him run away.

Justus continued working. He had stepped out of the channel and was kneeling on the grass, leaning into the channel and gently removing the waste from around the first dead woman with his hands. Janus knelt down opposite his brother and plunged his hands into the shit, scooping it out onto the grass beside him. He turned his head aside as he gagged and moaned in pain. Petrus ordered Celsus to get into the trench to hold the ankles of the first dead woman. Celsus grimaced, removed his clothes and boots and stepped into the trench. He grabbed the swollen feet, his fingers sliding in the slime, he struggled to hold onto them. The body began to slide forward, and a wave of sewage flowed down the trench over Celsus' feet. He winced and groaned in disgust but managed to maintain his grip. A woman's face and the rest of her body rose through the filthy water. The soldiers gasped. The shit-smeared face was Cara's.

Janus reached down and lifted her torso clear of the trench. Celsus lifted her feet, and the two men carried the body clear of the sewer and laid her on the grass. The grey feet of the second woman started to move as the sewage shifted and began to flow down the channel. Justus stepped into the channel and grabbed the body by the knees as the sewage lapped at his feet. The second woman's face had emerged from the dirty water. It was Metta. She wore an identical red smock to her sister. Janus stepped into the sewer, pushed his hands into the fetid mess and grasped her underneath the shoulders. They lifted her out of the trench and laid her next to her sister.

Petrus looked down at the two bodies. Death had robbed the women of their beauty. The stinking channel of excrement had bloated them and scraped their delicate skin. Their fine yellow hair was streaked with shit and matted with moss. There were bruises around their necks. Petrus was filled with sadness. He'd spoken to them just a couple of days before and offered them hope of a new life.

The men around him were pale.

'Use the water to clean them,' instructed Petrus, lifting one of the amphorae and carrying it over to where the two bodies lay.

Justus and Janus knelt next to the girls and began to carefully pour water over their bodies, using grass to wipe away the excrement and dirt from their skin and clothes.

'Look Sir, there's something there,' Justus pointed to a slight bulge that pushed against the smock just underneath Metta's left breast.

'Let me!' Petrus pushed him out of the way. He fumbled with the sash she'd used as a belt. Unable to loosen the knot, he took out his dagger and sawed through the soaked material. He lifted the dress up above her waist and exposed her nakedness. A wave of sorrow washed over him as he looked down at her swollen stinking body, shit-streaked and scratched. A band of cloth was wrapped tightly round her torso beneath the small breasts. He poked the blade of his dagger beneath the fabric and lifted it up, sawing gently through it, careful not to mark her body. It fell away and a pocket of green cloth dropped to the ground. He picked it up and opened it. Two gold aurei and six denarii fell into his hand. His body turned cold, and he felt tears prickle his eyes. He turned away. Behind him, Justus pulled the smock down over the woman's body.

Petrus moved over to Cara's body. Janus had already cut the sash on her smock. Petrus pushed it up and exposed her distended belly and scarred flesh. She was not carrying anything concealed about her body. He pulled the smock down, covering her once more. He stepped back to allow the men to continue washing them.

They gently turned the girls over and poured water over their backs, then they laid them back down on fresh grass. The men rinsed their own hands, arms and feet. Vester lifted the slates which were blocking the channel. Stinking waste surged past. He rinsed the slates with water and put them in the back of the cart. The men began putting the slate covers back over the channel. The smell of sewage was all around. Petrus felt as if it was being absorbed by his skin. One of the soldiers had tears running down his face and his lips were moving, but he made no sound. Vester kept shifting his gaze to his three roommates and then back again to the bodies. Petrus found himself praying silently to Cocidius for help in finding the women's murderers and hoping that his prayers would be heard.

Vester picked up an empty amphora and loaded it onto the cart. 'We'll make space for the bodies on the cart, Sir,' he said without looking at Petrus.

As he returned for a second amphora, the other men were startled into action and began lifting the remaining vessels. They stacked them securely.

'Petrus! What in the name of all the gods is going on? I've told the physician to meet you at the brothel like you asked. You'd better not be making me look an idiot!' Tatius bellowed as he strode towards them with five soldiers marching behind him carrying blankets.

'It's the bodies of the two sisters from the brothel, Cara and Metta,' replied Petrus, 'That's what has caused the blockage.'

Tatius moved to stand beside him and looked down at the scratched faces of the dead women. He turned his head aside and vomited. Clearly embarrassed, he wiped his mouth with his hand, pulled a perfumed cloth from his sleeve and held it to his nose.

'The physician might be able to tell me how they died,' Petrus said.

'Very well. Get them taken back to the brothel. Then come and see me!' Tatius began walking back to the fort with two of the soldiers.

The men wrapped the bodies in blankets and placed them onto the back of the cart. They carried their tools. The man driving the cart moved it carefully and slowly out of respect for the dead women. They walked back along the path near the bathhouse channel, the water around the paved stones had subsided, the channel was now running freely. Local people watched in horror when they realised the Romans' cart was carrying bodies. As word spread, more people came into the streets as their macabre curiosity overcame their fear.

Petrus walked into the brothel, pushed past Riacus and strode into the salon. Three other men who had been waiting in the salon scurried past him and out of the building. Petrus didn't wait for the girl to greet him.

'Fetch Sylva!' Petrus said.

The girl wrinkled her nose and opened her mouth to speak.

'Now!' he roared.

The girl leapt up and ran down one of the corridors. Petrus paced around the salon, leaving grey stinking marks on the floor as he walked.

Sylva wafted in.

'Aurelius Petrus, welcome. How can..? What's that stink?' She put her hand to her nose.

'Come with me,' he moved to take her arm, but she shook him off. 'Come on!'

Sylva followed him towards the door mumbling complaints as she walked. 'I don't know what you want. I've a business to run. Look at the mess you've left on the floor.'

They emerged into the morning light. The soldiers had lifted the bodies down and laid them on the ground with their faces uncovered. The physician, Arsenios, had arrived and hovered nearby, nervously peering past the soldiers at the wrapped forms laying in the dirt.

'What's that smell?' Sylva covered her nose with a scarf. 'What are…?' the words died in her throat as she looked down at the scratched faces of Metta and Cara.

'We found them in the sewer,' said Petrus.

Sylva was trembling, tears filled her eyes, 'For the love of the Gods,' she whispered as tears coursed down her face. 'Bring them round to the back.'

She began walking away. Petrus beckoned to Arsenios and the soldiers to follow her. She showed them to a room with a small plain bed and no decorations on the walls.

'This is my personal slave's room. Put them on the floor. I'll get them cleaned up and contact their family.'

'Let our physician examine them first. I want to know how they died,' said Petrus. 'Give us a short time,' he moved towards her. She stepped back frowning as he ushered her out of the room and closed the door behind her. The stink of shit filled the room.

Arsenios did not seem to be bothered by the sight and smell of the bodies as he uncovered them. He observed them for a while and then he prised open Cara's eyelids. The blue of her eyes was surrounded by blood-red pools.

'You see those bruises round the neck,' Arsenios pointed, 'They look like finger marks. The red around her eyes proves she was strangled.' He lifted Metta's eyelids. 'Same with her. That's your cause of death. They were in the sewer a few of days, judging by the amount of swelling of the bellies,' he pointed at Metta's rounded stomach.

'Thank you.'

'Can I go now?'

'Yes.'

Arsenios opened the door and pushed past Sylva who entered the room.

'Now I'm two girls down. Maybe Gamigoni can get me some more,' she mumbled.

Petrus was surprised at her heartlessness.

Outside, he ordered the three men who had been standing in the sewer channel to visit the baths as soon as possible, saying they would be excused from duties for the rest of the day.

'I'll talk to Aquilinus about you four men,' Petrus said, pointing to the rapists. 'You were banned from coming to the vicus as a result of your appalling behaviour towards local women. And then you tried to provoke a fight with some local men! However, you have behaved honourably today and that will count in your favour. Aquilinus will decide what to do with you. You're to see him after parade tomorrow. And you three who are going to the baths, once you've finished, you're to return straight to the fort. Is that understood?' He looked at them carefully. They avoided eye contact with him. 'I'm going to post a guard outside the baths, and he'll escort you back to the fort. Don't be late for Aquilinus in the morning.'

He ordered one of the soldiers to station himself outside the baths while the three men were inside and sent another with a message to get a slave to bring them some clean clothes. Then he dismissed the rest of the men. He went back inside the brothel. Sylva had tears streaming down her cheeks as she supervised her slaves cleaning the bodies.

'Sylva, I need to ask you some questions,' he began.

'Can you at least clean yourself up a bit first?' She mumbled and pointed at his feet, 'You're treading shit through my establishment, and look at your hands!'

Petrus looked at his hands. They were stained with shit and his boots were splashed with vomit and only the gods knew what else. 'Mmm,' he mumbled, embarrassed.

'In the yard,' she pointed.

Petrus strode into the yard. A slave girl stood next to a steaming pot of water and a bucket of sand. She held a bowl of fragrant oil. Its thick aroma reached Petrus and he happily breathed it in, hoping to displace the rank stink of the sewer which filled his body. She poured the oil onto his outstretched hands. He rubbed them together and then dipped them in the bucket of sand. The coarse grains scratched at his skin as he massaged his hands and arms up to the elbows. He held his arms out and she scraped them with a metal scraper, then she scraped down his hands and each finger. The sand slid off in clumps and fell to the ground, leaving his skin pink and raw. He plunged his arms into the pot of hot water and felt the skin's pores open. A thin film of oil floated in the pot, a rainbow of colours in the winter sun. He shook his arms and water droplets fell about him. He hissed as the cold air sliced the tiny scratches on his hands. He dried himself with a cloth. She poured water over his boots and their soles as he lifted his feet. She let a few drops of scented oil fall onto his hands, and he massaged it into his skin. He breathed in the odour of spices; forcing the stench of sewers from inside his body.

He walked back into the brothel. A slave was cleaning the floor and another had lit more bowls of fragrant oil, to smother the smell of the bodies. Sylva had recovered her composure.

'What do you want to know? They were supposed to be going with Gamigoni back to their parents' place for a few days. I'd arranged it and even given them money to pay him. They left early the morning of Lunes, just before the daylight.'

'Did anyone see them leave?'

'Riacus sleeps by the back door. He would've had to let them out.'

'Send for him then.' He waited while she sent a slave to fetch Riacus. 'Do you know why they suddenly wanted to go back to their village? Did anything happen?'

She shook her head. 'They'd just been working as normal. They were very popular, especially with you men from the fort. Well, you've had them yourself, so you know what I mean.'

He nodded.

'Your centurion and even one of those local tribesmen you employ have all been with them in the last couple of weeks.'

'Can you give me a list of them all?'

She shrugged. 'You and your lists, I'm not one of your librarii. I only keep the records for a couple of days; I haven't got an endless supply of tablets and have to keep reusing them. I total up each week, so that I can correctly pay my taxes.' She shook her head, "I know what you're going to say, 'two girls have been murdered." There's usually the same men here over and over. But it was the first time that local man of yours had been here. You know the one I mean, tattoos right over his bald head?'

Petrus nodded. 'His name's Luci.'

'Yes, probably,'

'When did the two women leave?'

'Lunes, first thing, just before daylight.'

'I'll go and see Gamigoni. But first, can I see their rooms? The ones they slept in, I mean, not their working room.'

'There is only the one room. The girls live and work in their rooms. I'm not made of money. I'll get someone to take you.' Her voice faded. She moved towards the door, 'I must tell all the others.'

Riacus led Petrus through the building to the dead girls' room. Petrus pushed open the door and walked into the gloom. Riacus followed him and opened the shutters on the window. It was clean and tidy with a lingering smell of incense. The bed was made, and the scarves were scattered artfully across it. The cushions were arranged on the couch.

'They woke you up on Lunes when they left, didn't they? Did

they say anything, or do anything unusual?'

'No Sir, they were just in a hurry. They each had a bundle of belongings with them.'

Petrus wondered what had happened to their bundles. Riacus looked upset. Petrus wondered if he'd had feelings for one of the girls.

'Did you see anything when they left? Was anyone waiting outside for them?'

Riacus shook his head. 'It was only just getting light, and they walked quickly away. They were supposed to be going to Gamigoni's, it's just a few minutes' walk from here. Madam Sylva says she wants to accompany you to see Gamigoni when you've finished. That's their belongings, in that chest, over there.' Riacus pointed to a chest in the corner of the room.

Petrus lifted the lid. It was empty. They had taken everything with them, not intending to return. He walked through to the salon. It was full of weeping women. Some hugged each other. The young girl lay curled up on a couch. Her body shook as she wept. Petrus felt guilty and ashamed. The two women had left the brothel shortly after he'd given them their inheritance. Perhaps he should have offered to take them home himself. Fifty-six denarii was worth killing for.

'I've closed as a sign of respect,' murmured Sylva behind him. 'In any case, the girls are too upset to work.'

'I'll do everything I can to find out who did this. I'm going to start by visiting Gamigoni. Riacus said you wanted to come with me?'

'Yes. I want to know why he didn't take them to their parents' place.'

'Did they have any friends in the community? Or was there anyone who may have wished them harm?'

Sylva shook her head. 'They kept themselves to themselves, hardly even spoke with the others. They never really left the building. They're not from round here. This,' she waved her hand around, 'this is, was, their world. They didn't know anyone else, did they?' She looked around the room. The women all shook their heads.

'Let's go.' He strode towards the door.

They walked out of the brothel. The torch above the front door had been extinguished. As they passed the bathhouse, a slave from the fort saluted Petrus. He was carrying fresh tunics and other clothes for the three men who'd got covered in sewage. The soldier stationed outside the baths pulled himself into a lazy half-salute. Petrus did not have the energy to tell him off. He felt drained. They passed deeper into the narrow streets of the vicus and approached Gamigoni's shop. Petrus was relieved to see it was open.

'Greetings,' Petrus said to the man whose long brown hair and beard were speckled with grey.

'Greetings Aurelius Petrus, Madam Sylva,' Gamigoni put aside the cloth he had been folding. 'What brings a Roman soldier to my business?'

'It's about Cara and Metta,' Sylva said, before Petrus had a chance to speak. 'Why didn't you take them to their parents' home like we'd arranged?'

'Why? Because they never turned up, did they? You told me they would arrive at first light on Lunes. I waited and waited. I thought they must've gone with someone else, or changed their minds? What of it?'

'Their bodies were found this morning,' Sylva said.

Gamigoni went pale. 'What happened to them?'

'That's what I'm trying to find out,' Petrus said.

Gamigoni mumbled, 'I just assumed they'd changed their minds. After all it wouldn't have been easy for them to return to their village, being what they were,' he glanced at Sylva, 'I'll go and tell their parents.'

'Can you take their bodies home?' Petrus asked.

Gamigoni looked at Sylva.

'I'll pay you,' Sylva said. 'Bring your cart tomorrow. I'll have the bodies prepared.'

Gamigoni nodded, 'What shall I tell their parents?'

'That they were intending to come home to live for good.' Petrus ignored Sylva's questioning gaze. 'That they were murdered and that this is being looked into by the Roman Army. I'll send two tribesmen to accompany you. There are no belongings to take with you, they'd emptied their room.' Beside him, Sylva tutted, 'I'll send the tribesmen at first light.'

'You didn't tell me they'd taken all their belongings. I didn't know they were leaving for good,' Sylva remarked as they left.

'Would you have let them go?'

She was silent.

'Go well, Sylva.' Petrus walked back to the fort and to the Principia.

Tatius did not look up from his work as he entered the office, so Petrus waited.

'Well?' asked Tatius.

Petrus began, 'The slates covering the waste channel from the fort had not been lifted in years, they were overgrown with grass, so I think the two sisters were killed in the vicus and their bodies were put into the waste channel near the bathhouse. As you know, that channel goes straight to the river. It is joined part way down by the one from the fort. The bathhouse empties its tanks every morning shortly after sunrise and the killers would probably have known that; everyone in the vicus knows it. The killers would have assumed that the bodies would just get washed into the river. If they hadn't got stuck, no-one would ever have known.'

'That's a good theory.' Tatius was now looking directly at Petrus.

'They'd taken all their belongings with them, so I don't think they intended to return to the brothel. We didn't find any belongings with the bodies; they might have been washed away in the waste channel or stolen by the killers. I had given them their inheritance, fifty-six denarii the day before they left the brothel. I…'

'So, there's a motive for their murder,' interrupted Tatius, 'robbery.'

'One of them had the money strapped to her body,' he pointed to his chest, 'here, just below her breast, quite well hidden.' Petrus dropped the pouch of money on the Prefect's table.

Tatius pushed the money back towards Petrus. 'Take it to the family. It's not the army's money.'

'If the killers were intending to rob them, they might have missed it, or they might have been disturbed and had to get rid of the bodies quickly. Or maybe robbery wasn't the motive.'

Petrus waited for a rebuke from the Prefect. None came, so he continued, 'The barbarian, Luci, had visited the brothel the same day I gave them the money, after I had left. So did some other men associated with the fort including Maximus, I believe,' he paused.

'And a lot of local men. So?'

'The women had spent time with the two dead soldiers. Someone may have wanted to silence them.'

'Who?'

'The murderer of the two soldiers.'

Tatius banged his fists on the table and roared, 'The killers of Faustus and Drusus are dead! You helped Maximus stick their heads on posts outside the fort! Damn you! Why do you persist with questioning that? Robbery is the obvious motive for the whores' murders. You gave them the money. You put them in danger!' he pointed at Petrus.

Petrus went quiet. He'd been so distracted by the trip to Camboglanna and his other duties that he hadn't thought about how much danger the women could be in.

'So, you've got nothing to say about that?' Tatius' quiet voice had menace.

Petrus remained silent.

'I want you to find the killers of these whores, after all, you owe them that much. If you feel that's beyond you, then you can easily be replaced, both as Optio and as an investigator.'

Petrus tried to hold his voice steady. 'I can do it.' Then a thought occurred to him, 'I wonder if we could offer a reward to anyone with information about the deaths. I mean, information that leads directly to the culprits. I wouldn't want to pay everyone who might come forward.'

Tatius rubbed his chin with his hand. 'That might work. You might get a lot of people giving false information. Equally, you might get none at all if there is a lot of animosity towards the fort right now.'

'We'll just have to see.'

'Do it. Will you put a notice up in the vicus?'

'I will. I doubt many in the community can read Latin, but I'll put one up and spread the word via my informant.'

'Five denarii reward then. Anything else?'

'I'll also speak with Luci, see if he knows anything.'

Tatius nodded. 'This murder is a priority. They were only whores, but the populace will be unsettled by more murders. So will the men here. After all, many of them frequent the brothel.'

'At daybreak, I'd like to travel with Gamigoni to the dead women's family home. I'll give their parents the inheritance and also ask them about their daughters. They may know if they knew anyone else in the community, someone who might want to harm them. I'll tell their parents that I'm investigating and that the killers will be brought to justice.'

'Don't make promises you can't keep, Petrus,' Tatius returned his attention to his reports. 'That breeds resentment. Prioritise this investigation. What about the gatekeepers?'

'The gatekeepers?'

Tatius frowned, 'The bathhouse is within sight of the gatehouse. If the bodies were put into the waste channel as you suggest, then the gatekeepers should've seen it.' He spat, 'Do I have to conduct this investigation myself?'

Petrus stuttered, 'I… I… I hadn't thought of that, Sir. I'll ask them. Rest assured I can deal with this matter.' Struggling to keep his voice steady, he said, 'I'll also check the gate records and see if anyone from the fort was outside the walls when the women disappeared.'

The Prefect reached for another tablet. Petrus left the room and went to his office where he wrote the details of the reward on a tablet in clear Latin and went to find Suasso, who was in his usual place near the east gate.

'Maximus didn't take you with him then,' Petrus said.

Suasso looked down and pinched his left arm with his fingers, 'It would appear not.' Seeing Petrus' face, he became solemn and said 'He took Luci, Albiso and Maccis. What do you need?'

'You've heard about the two dead women from Sylva's place?'

Suasso nodded.

'You and two others are to accompany me to take their bodies home to their parents. Prefect's orders. We're going with Gamigoni in the morning.'

'Will they want them, the parents I mean?'

'We'll see, won't we? They'd only been here a few months and were planning to visit their parents when they were murdered. There must still have been a connection, or so they hoped.'

Suasso nodded. 'We'll be ready at first light.'

'Did you know Luci frequented the brothel?'

Suasso smirked, 'He's not the only one. We're men too, you know. I've even been known to go there myself.'

'The Roman army are offering a reward of five denarii for information leading to the identification of the murderers of the two women.' He gave the tablet to Suasso, 'Go and pin this up in the marketplace.'

Suasso peered at the tablet. 'Not many around here can read Latin.'

'That's not important. Word will get round. In fact, you can tell anyone who sees you putting it up what it's about. Do it now. Then I'll see you and the others at daybreak.'

Suasso walked off.

Petrus was hungry and returned to his quarters. He was relieved that Boga always had bread and cheese stored away in their rooms. He munched on a chunk of bread. Boga went to pour water into the amphora of wine, but Petrus stopped him, he needed a strong drink after what he'd seen that morning. He closed his eyes as he drank; all he could picture in his mind were the bloated bodies streaked with excrement. He blamed himself for the women's deaths.

He walked to Aquilinus' office and found the centurion working on his reports.

'Vester and the three rapists tried to pick a fight with some locals on their way back from the training ground yesterday,' Petrus said pushing his report across Aquilinus' table. 'The Prefect had them on punishment duty today when he asked me to sort the latrines out.'

'Yeah, I heard about that. Shovelling shit is about all they're good for. You found the bodies of those two whores, didn't you?'

'Yes, and your men behaved very well. I thought you'd want to know about their good behaviour as well as the bad. I've given them all the afternoon off, they're at the baths trying to wash off the stink. Well, three of them are. I told them to report to you after parade tomorrow.'

Aquilinus glowered. 'Leave it with me. I'm not sure what further punishment I can give that will have any effect on their behaviour.'

Petrus left him and made his way to Manius' office. Manius did not acknowledge him as he entered and continued working, scratching letters onto his tablet and moving records around. Petrus cleared his throat. Manius laid down his stylus, put his elbows on the table with his chin on his hands and smiled, as if noticing Petrus for the first time.

'Petrus, how can I help?'

'Overnight Solis to Lunes, who were the gatekeepers for the east gate this week? Can I see their records? Also details of anyone who was outside the fort during those hours.'

Manius cleared his throat and inspected his fingernails for a few moments. 'Give me a few minutes, they might be difficult to find.'

'I'll just wait here. It's something the Prefect wants to know.' Petrus moved a step closer to Manius' table.

The librarius got slowly to his feet and walked over to a stack of tablets. He took a few off the top and then returned to Petrus with one in his hand. He pushed it across the table along with a blank tablet and a spare stylus, 'You'll want to write down the list of their names, I expect.' He collapsed back onto his chair.

Petrus was not surprised to see the gatekeepers were Rufus and Pius. There were six men who'd been outside the fort overnight and returned at the last hour of darkness, or the first of the daylight. Maximus and Boga, his slave, had been out. That was interesting. Petrus grimaced as he read the remaining four names:- Vester, Celsus, Janus and Justus. He pushed the list back across the desk along with the blank tablet.

'Thank you Manius, I can remember those names. I expect the gatekeepers are in their barracks now as it is their rest day.'

Manius did not respond. He pulled some reports closer to him. Petrus left the office and made his way to the rooms where Rufus and Pius stayed. The two men were busy preparing food and didn't notice him as he walked in. He watched them for a moment. Rufus was chopping turnips and Pius was cutting carrots into large chunks.

'Rufus, Pius!' Petrus' voice sounded loud in the room.

The two men leapt to their feet and saluted. Petrus kept his distance; they were still holding their knives. Rufus had gone pale; his freckles appeared more prominent. Pius' eyes darted back and forth between Petrus and the floor, like a guilty child.

'You were on duty the night of Solis and Lunes morning, weren't you?'

'Yes Sir,' said Rufus. 'Is there a problem? All our records are with the librarius.' He looked at Pius, who nodded.

'You can clearly see the bathhouse from the gate, can't you?'

They both nodded.

'Tell me what you saw at the end of the night and the first hour of the morning near the bathhouse.'

'What we saw, Sir? We, we didn't see anything,' Pius said.

'Maybe you heard something?'

'Nothing Sir, nothing at all.'

Petrus watched them closely, 'Did you fall asleep while you were on duty, like you have in the past?'

The two men's eyes widened, they quickly glanced at each other and then back at Petrus.

'No Sir, we did not,' Pius replied.

'When the centurion Julius Maximus and his slave returned to the fort in the morning, did they have to wake you?'

'No Sir, absolutely not. We saw them coming and were right behind the gate when they knocked.'

'And what about the other four soldiers who were also out? Did they have to wake you?'

Pius did not reply immediately.

'I can check with them.'

'We…er…we didn't hear them knocking at first. It was just after daylight. They came before the centurion. Maybe they didn't knock so loudly,' mumbled Pius.

'Fides sake! You were asleep!' spat Petrus. 'Beatings haven't been enough then?! Why can't you bastards stay awake?'

There was no response, the men just shuffled their feet.

'Maximus will have your hides!' Petrus stormed out of the room.

Petrus hurried back to Aquilinus' office, wanting to catch him before he went to his rooms. He arrived gasping at the centurion's desk and realised he'd been holding his breath.

'Aquilinus, Sir! I would like to speak with Vester and his companions. They were outside the fort in the early part of Lunes which is when the dead whores disappeared. I think the women were killed and put in the bathhouse sewer. They might have…'

'Those four again? Can't you wait until the morning?' Aquilinus interrupted. 'Are you suggesting..?'

'No,' blurted Petrus, 'The gatekeepers should've been able to see anything that went on near the bathhouse that morning, but the bastards were asleep. So, I'm hoping…'

'That Vester and his comrades might have seen something?' Aquilinus cut in. 'Then you should go and talk to them. They'll be back in barracks by now. I don't need to be there; I'll be seeing them in the morning. They know they're in for a bollocking after the argument with the locals yesterday. That should mean they're keen to help you. Just let me know if you think they're being difficult.'

Petrus nodded and walked back to the barracks. The four men were just preparing their meal. Vester looked up as Petrus entered, he mumbled something to the others, who all straightened themselves up and adjusted their clothing.

'Did you want to see us, Aurelius Petrus?' Vester asked sheepishly.

'Yes. What were you doing on the night of Solis and Lunes?'

The men glanced quickly at each other. Petrus waited.

'Well?' he snapped.

Vester's eyes met his. 'We'd won some money gambling, and went out to the tavern to… to… well, to drink our winnings. We had enough money to be there for a long time and everyone else had left. The taverner didn't kick us out as we showed him that we still had money to pay for more and well, we sort of fell asleep. We must have, because he shook us awake. I had my head on the table and Celsus was asleep on the floor. It was daylight by then and he told us to clear off. We headed back.'

'What about the guards at the gates?'

'What…what about them?'

'Were they asleep when you got back?'

Vester did not reply.

'Answer me!'

'They didn't answer when we first knocked on the gate and shouted,' mumbled Vester, no longer able to look at Petrus. 'We had to throw stones up over the wall, quite big ones.' He paused. 'Yes, they were asleep. They… they're always asleep.' He looked at his colleagues, who stared at him aghast. Vester snapped, 'Well, they are! The whole fort knows it'll be difficult to get back in if they're on duty!'

Petrus raged, 'Why wasn't that reported?' He knew why. No-one wanted to tell tales on their comrades. 'That puts the whole fort at risk!' It would also be seen as Petrus' and Maximus' fault.

'And when you left the tavern, did you see anything going on near the brothel?' All the men shook their heads. 'What about when you were crossing over the ditch and waiting for the gates to open, did you notice anything at or near the bathhouse?'

There was no response.

Petrus sighed. 'So, nothing then?'

They shook their heads.

In his office, his report stated that he had not been aware that the two gatekeepers had a reputation for sleeping on duty and suggested that they be checked up on throughout the night. He groaned as he wrote that. It would be his responsibility to check up on them, along with the new Tesserarius. He wasn't sure whether Maximus had appointed one yet. The penalty for sleeping on guard duty could be death by stoning and he recommended that the two men be reminded of this, the ultimate sanction.

He made his way back to his room. Boga had prepared roasted meat for supper. Petrus knew he shouldn't really question Boga without his master being present.

'The night of Solis and Lunes,' he began. 'You and Maximus were outside the fort.'

'Yes, yes we were.' Boga didn't hesitate.

'And what were you doing until the early hours?'

Boga reddened. 'Maximus has a woman in the vicus, she and their children live in his house, the one he built near the parade ground. We were there. I was with his household's slaves. I fell asleep after dinner and Maximus had to wake me in the morning when it was time to leave.'

Petrus raised an eyebrow. It was unusual for Boga not to be up well before sunrise.

'Had you been drinking?'

'A little. It must've gone to my head. I was ashamed to be woken by my master. However, he didn't beat me. He was very kind.'

Petrus paused. Maximus didn't normally show any mercy or understanding towards his slave. 'And when you came back, was it after daybreak or before? What happened at the gatehouse?'

'It was just daylight. The guards must've seen us coming and been standing right behind the gate, as we didn't even get an opportunity to knock before they asked for the password and opened up.'

Petrus nodded.

After he had eaten his evening meal, he lay down in his bed. He fell asleep and dreamed that Cara and Metta were still alive; they danced in front of him. Then their bodies changed into the grey bloated forms from the sewer; still dancing.

XIV – dies Saturni

Shortly after daybreak Petrus and the three barbarians waited for Gamigoni to settle his horse into its harness and then they followed him to the brothel. Two of Sylva's slaves carried out the bodies wrapped in sheets and placed them in the back of Gamigoni's cart. The sheets were stained dark with oil and the thick scent of flowers rose from the tightly wrapped shrouds.

Sylva emerged and placed a blanket over the bodies. She pressed some coins into Gamigoni's palm. She nodded at Petrus as she passed him.

At the marketplace, Petrus slowed his horse. He could see his tablet still pinned to a post near the water trough. Outside the vicus he rode behind Gamigoni with Suasso at his side. The other two barbarians rode ahead. Birdsong drifted towards them from nearby trees as small brown birds flitted from branch to branch carrying twigs and leaves. Other birds hovered and dived as they danced their mating displays. A cool breeze wafted around them as they continued along the road. It was warmer than it had been for several days. The frozen puddles had melted, and the cart splashed dirty water behind it, forcing Petrus and Suasso to drop back so that they weren't repeatedly sprayed with mud.

As the sun approached its highest point in the sky, they reached two great oaks whose trunks were being strangled by ivy. Smoke snaked its way skyward from a nearby roundhouse surrounded by a low turf wall. A gap in the wall was blocked with cut brush. Inside the enclosure, a few scrawny geese pecked the ground and a pig snuffled through the rank waste in a pit. There were storage huts raised off the ground, one open and empty, the other had the door tied firmly closed. A short distance away was a field surrounded by a deep ditch, where brown sheep and thin black cows grazed. Gamigoni halted his cart. Petrus dismounted.

'Suasso, stay with me. You others go back to the road and wait,' instructed Petrus and watched as the two men rode away.

An old man with grey hair and a bent back hobbled out of the roundhouse and began clearing the brush from the gap in the wall. Gamigoni moved forward.

'Messi, I trust you are well?' Gamigoni began helping the man to clear the brush.

Messi spoke in a harsh whisper using a dialect which Petrus didn't recognise, and he looked to Suasso for assistance. The barbarian stepped forward and stood at his shoulder translating.

'What brings you here? And with this Roman as well? What's in your cart? I have nothing to trade right now. Come again in the early summer,' translated Suasso.

'I'm not here to trade,' Suasso continued as Gamigoni motioned for the old man to walk to the back of the cart.

'What?' mumbled the old man, looking at the shrouds and then back at Gamigoni.

'I am afraid it's Cara and Metta. They've passed,' Suasso translated.

Messi spoke quickly.

Suasso explained, 'He's asking if they were sick.'

Messi put his hand out to touch the shrouded bodies. He sniffed his fingers and rubbed them together as he spoke again.

'He's asking what the smell is and what's on the sheets,' Suasso said. 'Gamigoni is explaining about the oils Sylva put on their bodies.

Gamigoni spoke for a long time, but Suasso did not say anything.

Messi turned and moved slowly back to the roundhouse,

stooping low, but he did not enter. He spoke quickly to whoever was inside the house.

Suasso said, 'I can't make out the words.'

A woman emerged. She was immediately recognisable as the girls' mother, with the same round face, yellow hair and blue eyes. Behind her came a tall man with messy yellow hair framing his wind-chafed face, a brother, Petrus assumed. The woman wailed and ran to the cart. She clambered into the back and moved on hands and knees to the front. She pulled and tugged at the shroud, the end came loose, and she pulled the sheet clear of the dead woman's face.

'Cara!' she screamed stroking her daughter's face with the back of her hand. She touched the shroud of the other body whispering 'Metta!'

She turned towards Gamigoni and directed a torrent of words towards him.

'She's cursing Gamigoni,' Suasso said. 'She says her daughters would still be alive if it wasn't for him. They'd be alive, but poor. Shall we take the bodies off the cart?'

Petrus nodded.

Suasso spoke to the woman in low tones. Petrus assumed he was reassuring her and asking her to leave the cart, as she nodded and clambered out. Her son moved forward to stand next to her, placing his hand on her arm. Suasso climbed into the back of the cart. The brother stepped forward and took Cara's shrouded body by the feet. Suasso lifted the shoulders, and they carried the body forward with Suasso handing the body over to Gamigoni. The two men carried her to the house and followed the woman inside. Suasso and Petrus lifted Metta's body down and followed them. They laid her on the floor next to her sister.

A chicken began to peck at one of the shrouds. Messi's wife shrieked and kicked it out of the way. She knelt next to her daughters and placed one hand on each body, she was silent as the fire crackled. The smell of burning wood and smoke merged with the aroma of oils that hovered about them. Petrus felt he was intruding and he followed the other men outside.

'Translate these words exactly,' Petrus said. 'One of our soldiers died recently and he left his money to your two daughters in what we call a will. Your two daughters may have been killed because of the money, although it was not stolen from them.'

Petrus paused as Suasso translated.

'I have put the money in here.' He held out the pouch.

Messi was unmoved but his son stepped forward, took the money and spoke while Suasso translated.

'He's asking if the soldier was one of their customers at the brothel.'

Petrus nodded. 'Yes he was, but he must have cared about them to leave them his money.'

Suasso was silent. Petrus nudged him hard in the ribs. 'Translate, will you?'

Suasso spoke for some time and Petrus wondered what else he was saying. The young man then spoke in a local language that Petrus understood.

'What will happen now?'

'I will try to find out who killed your sisters and ensure they are punished,' Petrus replied. 'Perhaps you can help me. Did they know anyone else in the vicus, apart from those at the brothel?'

'No. They left all that they knew behind them when they went with him,' he nodded his head towards Gamigoni. 'They probably never left that place.'

Petrus said. 'Take care, people may be interested to know that you have come into some money. As I said, the money may have led to your sisters' deaths.'

The young man spoke in his language, but Suasso did not translate.

'What's he saying?' Petrus asked.

Suasso coughed and looked embarrassed. 'He's saying that

he's not a fool. You Romans should not take farmers for idiots.'

'I didn't mean to cause offence,' murmured Petrus and mounted his horse.

Gamigoni took his place on the cart and prepared to leave. The younger man took hold of the reins of the carthorse and spoke quickly to Gamigoni.

'He's thanking the merchant for bringing his sisters home. They'll be buried today. He's demanding justice,' translated Suasso.

Gamigoni nodded and the young man released the reins. The merchant swung the cart round and headed back towards the road. The barbarians fell in behind him. Petrus instructed them to remain with the merchant but set his own horse into canter and headed towards the vicus.

Petrus tied his horse to the post outside the forge. The heat hit him as he stepped inside. Carantii looked up from stoking the furnace. 'Greetings Roman.'

'Greetings Blacksmith,' Petrus smiled.

'I haven't been out much, my father died. We took him home. I don't have any news for you.'

'I'm sorry about your father. He was a good man who served the Roman Army well.'

Petrus paused briefly. 'Have you heard about Cara and Metta, the whores?' He didn't wait for Carantii to respond. 'They were murdered, and their bodies put into the sewer. They were supposed to be taken by Gamigoni to their parents' place, but they never arrived at his shop. I'd given them their inheritance, the money from Drusus, I mean. They may have been killed by robbers, although the money was still on their bodies. I've been tasked with finding the killers. I know few people read

Latin, but I had a tablet put up in the marketplace offering a reward for information leading to their capture. I'm sure word will have gone round. Can you see what you can find out?' He placed a handful of coins on the table.

The blacksmith nodded. 'Go well Roman.'

'Stay well.'

Petrus walked the horse to the tavern. He tied it up and walked inside. There were no customers. The windows were open and cold fresh air had driven out the stale smell of spilled ale. The soot smeared walls and stained tables did not appear so welcoming in the daylight. The taverner's wife was on her knees scrubbing the floor. She did not look up. 'He's in there,' she nodded to the back room.

Petrus walked through the door. The taverner was rolling a barrel of ale across the floor. He stood up and leaned back, stretching. 'Aurelius Petrus, what brings you here?'

Petrus spoke in the local language. 'Four days ago, the night of Solis and Lunes, I'm sorry, I don't remember your word for those days, were there four soldiers in here all night?'

The taverner paused. 'Yes there were the other night. I remember them, because they all fell asleep at the table, one under the table. They've been in here quite a bit recently. One has pale skin and white hair. Two of them are bald. They'd loads of money, so I let them stay. They fell asleep and I threw them out in the morning.'

'Was it daylight when you threw them out?'

'No, it was still dark. The birds started to sing soon after they left, so it must've been just before daybreak.'

Petrus frowned. Vester had said it was daylight when they left the tavern. He thanked the taverner and led his horse back to the fort. He made his way to the Principia. Maximus was giving his report to the Prefect as Petrus entered the office.

'The Prefect at Banna has written to the Governor asking to be relieved from his post within the next few weeks. He was due to go in the summer but wants to be in Rome for the birth of the baby and it's not wise for women to travel when heavily pregnant, he says, especially not with their first child. He's been advised it's a boy.' He shook his head, 'I'm not sure how they can tell these things. I left a letter from Fabia with your wife,' Maximus finished speaking and looked at Petrus.

Tatius said, 'Petrus believes the dead girls were put into the sewer near the bathhouse. Tell us what else you've found out, Petrus.'

Petrus slid his report from the day before across the table. 'The tablet offering the reward for information is up in the marketplace. I've also got a man in the vicus making enquiries, to see if there were any witnesses to the girls leaving the brothel. I did as you suggested, Sir, and interviewed the gatekeepers who were on duty the night and morning they were taken. It was Rufus and Pius, they said they didn't see any sort of activity near the bathhouse. When pressed, it seems they were asleep and had to be woken at daybreak by Vester and his comrades.'

Maximus gritted his teeth and scowled.

'Vester said they'd fallen asleep in the tavern and left there at around daybreak when the taverner woke them. They had difficulty rousing the gatekeepers who were, as I've said, asleep. Vester and his friends say they did not see anything at or near the bathhouse. However, I've questioned the taverner who says they left in the dark, so they have some time unaccounted for. I suggest Aquilinus should question them again, find out what they were up to.'

'I'll help him!' declared Maximus. 'We'll get the truth out of those bastards! They probably killed the whores! They have a bad reputation when it comes to women.'

Petrus hesitated and then said, 'It seems it's well known inside the fort that Pius and Rufus are often asleep on duty. I wasn't aware of their reputation.'

Maximus moved so quickly Petrus didn't have time to react. He came to stand against in Petrus' face, he could feel the centurion's hot breath on his cheek and in his nose.

'What do you mean, often asleep? That's a damned security risk,' he hissed.

'That's what Vester said. I've only been aware of this happening the couple of times which I told you about. It seems Quirinus, the Tesserarius, is not aware.'

'I've not decided on a suitable replacement for Quirinus.' Maximus turned to face the Prefect who was reading Petrus' report.

'Get him replaced immediately!' Tatius shouted, then more calmly, 'Petrus thinks that the two gatekeepers should be checked on during the night. That's a good suggestion. You'll also have to punish them. Clearly beatings are not enough. Remind them they could face the death penalty!'

Petrus could feel Maximus seething next to him. He tried to hold his voice steady, 'It'll take time for witnesses to come forward. Luci was with the two women the day they decided to go back to their parents' place. I'd like to speak with him, and also with Albiso as they're often together. Luci may have noticed if the women seemed spooked or if they were telling anyone about their inheritance.'

Maximus opened his mouth, but Tatius cut him off. 'That'll be fine, although I doubt the visit to the brothel is significant. The woman Sylva didn't say Albiso was there though, did she? He's fairly noticeable. Have you got a list of the other men who were with them just before they decided to go home?'

Petrus shook his head.

'Maybe because you were one of them?' Maximus asked. 'I heard you were also at the brothel the day before they asked to go to their parents' place. You didn't mention that did you?'

'I was there giving them the money from Drusus. That's in my report.' He pointed at the tablet. 'I have asked Sylva for a list of all the men who were with the dead girls in the few days before they left, but she says she doesn't keep records for more than a couple of days. Not enough tablets, she says. I find that difficult to believe; how else do we tax her business?' He looked directly at the prefect.

Tatius shrugged. 'I don't get bothered with the minutiae. I leave that to the librarii. You'd have to speak to them. If she can't demonstrate an income, then the Signifer would tax her a fixed amount. Where are Albiso and Luci?'

'Seeing to their horses, I expect. They've finished for the day,' replied Maximus.

'You should be able to find them then, Petrus. Write up your report, Maximus. Then go and speak with Aquilinus. I want the truth from Vester and his comrades about what they did when they left the tavern. Use as much force as necessary.' He turned towards Petrus, 'I'm disappointed in you, Petrus. You don't seem to have made any real progress on the murders. All you've got is 'ifs and maybes,' I told you I wanted a quick resolution to this matter. Now it's up to Maximus and Aquilinus to try and get the truth from those lads, as you've got nothing. Maximus and I will be looking to replace you as investigator. You'd better try harder to get somewhere. We may review your position as Optio as well, eh Maximus?' He paused. 'You both need to do something about the gatekeepers. That doesn't reflect well on either of you.'

Petrus hurried from the office towards the stables, anxious to get away from Maximus, who would be raging. Maccis was alone with the horses, talking to them as he groomed them and put away their tack. Petrus waited until he'd given them water and was locking the doors.

'Maccis, I am looking for Albiso and Luci, where are they?'

'I don't know, Sir. It's my turn to deal with the horses, so they've probably gone to the tavern or the brothel, or maybe just back to where they live, Sir, in the vicus I mean.'

Petrus was disappointed. He didn't want to go looking for them all around the vicus, so he walked slowly back towards the Principia.

'Petrus?' Maximus' voice drew him into the office.

'Sir?' he stood in the doorway, out of easy reach in case the centurion launched himself off his chair.

Maximus' voice was frighteningly calm. 'When are Rufus and Pius next on the gate?'

'In three days' time.'

'Then we shall take a night each and go and check on them a few times. If they're asleep then further punishments will follow. Tomorrow I'm going to tell them their pay will be docked. Beatings haven't made them change their ways. Quirinus' replacement will be Urban. I think he'll make a good Tesserarius. I'll sort all that in the morning. We don't look good here, Petrus.'

Petrus waited, but Maximus didn't say any more. His rage seemed to have dissipated.

Later that evening, as Petrus walked towards the east gate, blackness coated the fort and grey clouds covered the moon. He slowed as he passed an open window in the Praetorium and recognised Prima's voice.

'If the Governor releases him, they could be gone in a couple of weeks. I shall miss her so much. It's so lonely here.'

A door slammed and the sound of sobbing reached out to him through the darkness. It was a lonely life as a prefect's wife at a fort on the Wall. He picked up his pace, nodding at the guards who opened the gate as he approached. If he was replaced as Optio, he wouldn't have the freedom to visit home whenever he needed to, so he thought he had better make the most of what time he had left.

He watched Titus gobble down his supper, put him to bed and told him a story about a brave soldier who fought mythical fire breathing creatures and emerged unscathed to save his community. His son fell asleep with a smile on his face.

He told Aurora about his investigation into the women's deaths and how he had accompanied the bodies back to their home place.

'I've seen the tablet that you put up in the marketplace. It's been defaced now,' she said.

'I knew it would be, but not before word got round about the reward for information. There may be a witness who's prepared to come forward.'

Aurora shivered. 'Those poor women.'

'One of the dead soldiers left his property to them in his will. The money in his wages account was fifty-six denarii.'

Aurora gasped. 'That's a lot of money.'

'I took it to them at the brothel. They then decided they wanted to leave and return to their parents' home. It's possible that they told someone of their good fortune, or someone found out from gossip. I had tried to keep their inheritance a secret, but there is no such thing as a secret inside the fort. It's possible they were killed by someone trying to rob them. The killers didn't get the money though, one of them had it strapped under her breast. Here.' He leant forward and touched Aurora just below the left breast. 'It wasn't easy to see, so the killers may've missed it or been disturbed while looking for it.' He took a deep breath. 'It's my fault they're dead. I should've arranged for them to go home the next day with some sort of escort, or waited to give them the money just as they were leaving.'

Aurora took his hand. 'You couldn't have foreseen this. It's not your fault.'

'What did I think would happen to them when they came into a lot of money?' He shook his head.

Aurora stroked his face with the back of her hand. 'Not your fault,' she whispered. She squeezed his hands and leant forward to kiss him gently on the lips. He kissed her deeply and tore himself away so that he could head back to the fort.

Carantii

Carantii put his elbows on the damp table, grimacing as his sleeves soaked up spilled ale. He leaned across and waved his cup in the face of Vettius who sat opposite him.

'They were good girls, I mean nice, as well as good in bed. I know, I'd been there if you know what I mean,' Carantii slurred. 'Why would anyone want to kill them? They didn't deserve to die like that. No-one does.' He paused. 'Wonder if anyone will try to help the Romans. It's a big reward they've offered.' He put his cup down and watched Vettius. 'Lot of men knew 'em, maybe there was something else going on,' he mumbled, trying to provoke the other man.

'Vatto.' The man was barely audible. He swayed on his seat and grabbed the side of the table to steady himself. Carantii leaned a bit closer. 'He saw 'em. They should ask Vatto. See him over there, telling everyone what he saw.'

Carantii glanced to the corner table. A man with a shaved head and long red beard slammed his cup down on the table. The three men sitting with him jeered.

'He's in here most nights telling the tale. Only a question of time before the Romans hear about it and ask him a few questions,' Vettius paused. 'Now, are you going to get me another drink or not? We're supposed to be drinking to the memory of your father, aren't we? He was a good man. If you're half the blacksmith he was, you'll be doing well.'

Carantii waved the taverner over to get their cups refilled. He let Vettius relate tales of his father, some of them he already knew and others that he thought were untrue. Vettius slumped lower in his seat and his head drooped. His words became unintelligible, and he slipped forward with his head on the table. Carantii put some coins on the table and rose to his feet.

He stepped into the night and took a deep breath of the ice cold night air. He trudged along the empty street and reached inside his shirt taking out the ivy to leave as a sign outside Petrus' house.

Back at his own house, he entered his kitchen and the warmth hit him, he stumbled as the ale he'd drunk rushed to his head. He locked the door behind him and walked through to his bedroom, pulled off his boots and slid into bed, pulling the animal hides around him for warmth. He smiled as he felt his father's presence in the room.

XV - Dies Solis

Vester and his three comrades were summoned to Aquilinus' office after parade. Petrus could hear Maximus shouting at them as he moved through the fort. Maximus and Aquilinus had decided that they would beat the men and throw them in the detention cell if they weren't satisfied with their answers. Petrus hadn't wanted to witness the interrogation; Maximus could be brutal, and he had no doubt the young men would be in the cell by the end of the morning.

Petrus was annoyed. Luci and Albiso had not arrived at the fort that morning. Barbarians didn't have to be at the fort every day, but he had hoped that the message would have got back to them that he was looking for them. Perhaps they were avoiding him. It was drizzling as he set off through the vicus' deserted streets and he was grateful for his cloak which kept his body dry. He shook his head to clear the water dripping down his forehead.

He banged on the door at the back of the shop belonging to one of the grain merchants. He heard movement inside and took a step back as the door opened and Albiso's pale, haggard face peered out through the gap.

'Let me in, Albiso!'

The door began to close. Petrus put his shoulder against it and pushed hard, stepping in and putting his weight into the shove. The door gave way and he stumbled into the room, which smelled of stale alcohol and sex. Cold air rushed in behind him. Albiso shivered, he was wearing only his trousers. The opened door cast daylight onto the sparse furnishings and unmade bed near the smouldering fire. Smoke snaked upwards from the flickering yellow flame of an oil lamp. A woman wrapped in Albiso's cloak cowered in one corner.

'Get rid of her! I want to talk to you,' snarled Petrus.

Albiso grabbed the woman's smock from the floor and pushed it into her outstretched hand. She wrestled with it beneath the cloak as she tried to dress. She lost her grip on the cloak and it slid to the floor. Her dirty skin was stretched tight over her skeleton, the bones of her ribs and knees pushed hard against her flesh, as if trying to escape. Wordlessly she pulled the smock over her head and stumbled to her feet. She took a step forward. She gritted her teeth as her bare foot touched the earth floor; the toes were crooked and the nails were ripped. She took another slow step.

Albiso sighed heavily. He grabbed the woman by the shoulders. She whimpered. He picked her up and carried her from the room. Petrus assumed he had dumped her in the street, as he returned a moment later and pulled on his tunic.

'She's starving,' Petrus said, appalled at what he'd just seen.

'That's why she was so cheap,' retorted Albiso. 'Just wanted some food. What do you want?'

Petrus swallowed his disgust. 'I want to talk to you and Luci.'

Albiso's eyes flicked towards the interior door. 'Is he through there?'

Albiso nodded.

'Wait here. I'll be back.'

Petrus picked up the oil lamp and turned up the wick. He pulled open the door and stepped into a dark hall with a door on each side and one leading to the yard outside. He pushed open the door to his right and held the lamp above his head. A man with dark hair lay snoring in his bed. Petrus closed the door and flung open the other door, it crashed against the wall. He strode in and pulled open the shutters to the window, allowing the cold grey morning to enter the room.

'Wha… what?' grunted Luci.

He rolled out of bed, grabbed his sword, and staggered upright, readying for a fight.

'Easy. Easy. It's me, Petrus.' Petrus motioned for him to lower his weapon.

Luci looked around him, bewildered, and let the sword fall to the floor.

'Sit down, I want to talk to you,' said Petrus.

Luci lowered himself onto his bed.

'When were you last at the brothel?'

Luci shook his head as if trying to focus on the question. 'The Brothel? Why? Well, that would've been a few days ago, four or five maybe, I'm not sure. What's it to you?' he said belligerently.

'Which girl did you see?'

'I had two, those new girls, Cara and Metta. The ones you found in the sewer. Lucky I got in there when I did,' he smirked.

'Two? You must've had a lot of money to throw away. Why those two?'

Luci raised his head to look defiantly at Petrus. 'I'd heard they were good. I had some money to spare. What of it? You were there too. I saw you leaving. You'd had them as well.'

'Mind your tone,' snapped Petrus. 'What did you talk about?'

'I'm not much of a talker. Not when I… you know.' He looked away.

'Did they say they were leaving Sylva's, or going to visit their parents?'

Luci shook his head. 'Why would they tell me that?'

'Did you say anything that could've alarmed them?'

Luci looked at the floor. 'I wasn't there to talk.'

'Look at me, Luci!'

Luci raised his head and stared defiantly at Petrus.

'Did you say anything that could've alarmed them? Like anything about Drusus and Faustus?'

Luci's eyes were fixed on a point over Petrus' right shoulder. 'I don't know anything about Drusus and Faustus. Their murderers have been caught and killed. Their heads were on stakes outside the fort, as you know. You helped to put them there.'

'If I find out you've been lying…' Petrus didn't know how to finish the sentence. How could he threaten a man over whom he had no control? Petrus left him.

As Petrus entered the room, Albiso looked up from the hearth where he was breathing the fire back to life. The window had been opened and fresh damp air filled the room. Albiso had cleaned his face and combed his hair. The scar on his forehead seemed darker against his pale skin. Petrus guessed he was hungover from the night before.

'Have you been hanging out at the brothel recently? With Luci, or on your own?'

Albiso shook his head.

'Not spent time with those two sisters? Surely Luci told you how much fun they were?'

Albiso looked at the floor. 'He told me how good they were. But I didn't have any money and I didn't like hearing him go on about them, so I left him to it. That's why I end up with women like that.' He moved his head in the direction of the street.

'The desperate and the starving,' muttered Petrus as he left the room.

Carantii

Carantii opened his eyes as light sneaked into the room through the gaps in the window shutters and the comforting image of his father retreated into the morning. He pushed himself upright, pulled on his boots and walked slowly into the kitchen. His head throbbed.

'Long night?' Eburacia smiled up at him as she stirred a pot heating on the fire.

Carantii took the cloth off the pail in the corner of the room and scooped out a cupful of water, gulping it down. He refilled the cup and replaced the cloth.

'I didn't realise how much I'd drunk, Ebu. I was trying to get as much information as I could from various people and then it turned out that behind me, Vatto, was telling everyone that he'd seen the girls on the morning of their deaths. You know Vatto, right? The carpenter who drinks? He's been there most nights mouthing off about it apparently. I was so busy getting Vettius and others drunk that I didn't even see him come into the tavern.'

'It's hard work I'm sure,' she grinned. 'I hope Petrus is covering your costs.' She passed him a bowl of porridge. 'What would Vatto have been doing in the streets near the brothel before dawn? Not much for a carpenter to do at that time is there? He doesn't live near there.'

He shrugged. 'I guess the Romans will find out if they ask him.'

'I'm expecting a caller.' She did not look at him as she spoke.

'Oh?'

'Yes, a man has asked me to walk with him in the vicus,' she smiled shyly.

'Stay in the main areas, won't you? Do I know this man?'

'Maybe.'

She seemed reluctant to say any more, so he left her and walked through to the forge. He stoked the fire, and flames burst into life. He took another drink of water and then started work. As he began to sweat, the smell of stale alcohol seeped out of his body. He gritted his teeth in concentration as he handled the red-hot iron. His head felt as if it was about to explode. A horse whinnied in the street and a man lugged a sack of charcoal into the forge. Carantii placed the tongs and hammer on the ground and moved to join the man unloading the cart.

'I have the shoes ready,' Carantii said, when they had finished. 'Will you unhitch the horse from the cart?'

The animal was exhausted; it didn't even raise its head when he lifted its feet to file its hooves and nail on the shoes. When they had gone, he began working on the swords. Movement behind him made him turn. A red-haired man stood in the doorway. Carantii recognised him but he couldn't remember his name.

'I've come to see your sister, Eburacia,' the man said.

'I'll just see if she's there.' He opened the door to the kitchen and saw her sitting at the table sewing.

'You've got a visitor Ebu,' he grinned. 'Remember what I said.'

She smiled, laid down her sewing, picked up her cloak and walked past him into the forge. She nodded a greeting to the man and stepped into the street. Carantii went back to his work and began thinking about what he would do when she married. He needed someone to look after the home, either a wife or a maid. He smiled to himself. He was sure that Eburacia would have made that known locally as well.

'Greetings, Blacksmith,' Julius Maximus stood in the doorway. Beside him was a beautiful woman with long black hair and piercing grey eyes.

'Centurion,' said Carantii.

'This is Julia Prima, the Prefect's wife from the fort,' said Maximus, waving his hand in her direction.

The woman stepped forward and placed a necklace on the table.

'The links are damaged, is it something you can repair?' Her voice was soft and light, her eyes searched his face.

Carantii picked up the necklace, fumbling with it in his huge hands. It was made from shiny metal discs like bronze but not as heavy, the discs were inlaid with coloured stones and intricately carved patterns. The links between the discs were damaged in parts and the necklace was in five pieces. It was not expensive jewellery, and it surprised him that an important woman would wear such a piece.

'This is very delicate work for a man like me. There may be others better suited to working with fine jewellery,' Carantii said.

'The lady would like you to do the work as you're known at the fort as a fine craftsman,' Maximus said.

'Let me see if I have the tools to do it.'

Carantii put down the necklace and left the forge. In his bedroom he wiped the dusty lid of his father's ancient toolbox, he hadn't touched it since he took over the forge from his father. The hinge creaked as he opened it and took out the contents which were wrapped in cloth, placing them on the bed. He unwrapped them and ran his fingers over the well-maintained hammers, tongs and carving tools, marvelling at their delicacy. A shiver ran through his body as he felt his father's guiding hand as he touched the instruments. He inhaled his father's smell and relished the tingle of his breath on the back of his neck. He heard the old man mutter words of encouragement as he replaced the tools in the box. The image of his father faded as he carried the box into the kitchen.

The door to the forge was slightly ajar and he heard the centurion and the woman talking in Latin. He placed the box quietly on the table and listened.

'I can't bear the thought of losing her, Maximus. The Governor is due to visit next week and he'll be announcing his decision about Septimus' early return to Rome.'

'I know Prima, time is…' There were some words then which Carantii didn't recognise. 'They will confess and then…' the words were indistinguishable. He heard 'urgent,' more words, 'getting close,' and then after more inaudible words, 'a couple more days.'

Some more words he couldn't catch. 'Take care, Maximus.'

Carantii waited. They were silent. He coughed loudly as he picked up the box and pushed his way noisily through the door and placed it on the bench.

'I've got my father's tools and I think I'll be able to make the repair. When do you need it?' Carantii asked.

'We'll come back for it in two days' time,' Maximus said.

Maximus turned on his heel and went outside; the woman followed him. Carantii sat at the table and fingered the jewellery, examining the delicate clasps and joining rings. He laid them down and returned to the kitchen where he lit an oil lamp. Carrying it into the forge he placed it on the table and held the necklace close to the light. He peered at the clasps and used the tools to carefully force the links together. It only took a few minutes. He wrapped up the tools, put them back in the box and carried it back to his bedroom. He hung the necklace on a nail on the wall. Perhaps his other customers would see it, and he may get asked to repair similar items.

He sat down in the kitchen and gulped down more water. Thirst had dried his throat and tongue; the aftertaste of ale in his mouth was unpleasant. He felt the cool liquid seeping into his muscles, oozing out of his skin and dampening the pain in his head. He turned the encounter with the Romans over in his mind. Why had they brought the jewellery to him when there were plenty of skilled men at the fort who could have made the repair? Fine ladies from forts like Banna didn't normally walk in the vicus with centurions for company. They normally only passed through in their carriages or on horseback, although, he had seen her a few days previously when she had walked through the streets with her friend. Perhaps she had just wanted to venture out into the vicus without a crowd of soldiers around her. Perhaps she just liked to take risks.

Eburacia returned, smiling as she entered the kitchen.

'And?' he asked.

'Iliom is a kind man. It's not the first time we've walked out in the community.' She smiled at his evident surprise. 'You were always busy and didn't notice. He and I have spoken before, several times, when our father was still alive. I discussed it with him.'

Carantii nodded.

'I need a dowry.'

'I'll go back and speak with Amba. Are you in a hurry?' He looked at her belly.

'We're not in that kind of hurry.' She smoothed her dress down over her stomach and pulled it straight. 'I think Amba may be coming here anyway in a few days.'

'What makes you think that?'

She shrugged, 'I just think he will, probably tomorrow, or the next day. Let's wait and see, shall we?' She smiled shyly, 'And what about you, what will you do when I am married?'

He shrugged. 'I can get a slave, or a maid. I can afford it.'

He returned to the forge where he began working on a sword and fashioning a handle with inlaid stones. He'd made a very fine weapon and was pleased as he hung it on the wall of the forge.

'Greetings, Carantii.' Petrus' voice startled him.

'Aurelius Petrus,' he smiled and raised his voice, so that he could be heard by anyone passing the forge door. 'I haven't finished that sword of yours yet, I need more time I'm afraid. You're the second visitor from the fort today. My stock must be high right now.' He paused and lowered his voice. 'What can I do for you?'

Petrus moved closer to the table. 'Your message?'

He quickly told Petrus about Vatto's claim to have seen the dead women on the morning that they disappeared and that he was regularly in the tavern telling the story.

'Your centurion from the fort came in today, along with that fine lady, the prefect's wife,' he continued, 'She wanted me to repair that necklace.' He pointed to the one on the wall, 'when I told her I don't normally do that sort of work, she was insistent.'

Petrus took the necklace off the wall and turned it over in his hands before replacing it on the nail.

'I overheard them talking when I went to get my father's tools. There was some Latin that I didn't understand. They mentioned men confessing and something about getting close and urgency. What does all that mean?'

Petrus shrugged, 'Maximus is confident he can get confessions to the murders of the two women Cara and Metta.' He paused, not wanting to tell Carantii too much. 'And Vatto, where can I find him? What does he look like?'

'He's bald with a long red beard. In the evenings he's in the tavern. During the day, he shares a space with the cobbler, where he makes items to order, when he's sober, that is. He drinks to forget, I think. His wife and son died a couple of years ago from a strange disease, I can't remember the details, but he seems to want to join them in the afterlife. He's a very fine carpenter when he's not in drink.'

Petrus

Petrus walked through the vicus. His tablet offering a reward was still in the marketplace. The wax was scratched and chipped. It was impossible to make out the words. He reached up to take it down from the post, wiggling the tablet from side to side trying to loosen it from the nail holding it in place. The tablet gave slightly and then disintegrated in his hands. He cursed and tossed the remnants onto the ground.

He entered the shop. The cobbler was bent over a boot, working the leather with his fingers. To the rear of the shop a bald man with a red beard was rubbing his hands along a large flat piece of wood, caressing it. He looked up as Petrus approached, his eyes widened.

'Vatto?' asked Petrus.

'Aye' the man replied. 'What does the Roman army want with me?'

Behind him, Petrus heard the cobbler lay down his shoes and leave the shop. Vatto was unkempt, his clothes were dirty, and he had globules of porridge stuck in the bristles of his beard. He reeked of stale ale and his forehead was damp with sweat. He had dark circles under his eyes and his nose had the red vein marks of a heavy drinker. He trembled when he spoke; Petrus wondered if that was from fear or the effects of drink.

'I need to ask you some questions about the two whores whose bodies were found recently,' began Petrus.

Vatto nodded. 'What of it?'

'You saw them that morning, when they left the brothel.'

'Who told you that?'

'You've been telling anyone who'll listen in the tavern over the last few days, haven't you?'

Vatto did not respond.

'Did you know there's a reward for information leading to the capture of their murderers?'

Vatto nodded.

Petrus touched the pouch at his belt, letting the coins jingle. 'What did you see? What were you doing near the brothel so early in the morning?'

Vatto watched the pouch for a moment, then lifted his eyes to Petrus' face. 'I woke up in the alleyway near the brothel. Sylva doesn't like us peeing too close to her door, she says the smell puts off her customers. So, I always go a bit further down. Must've fallen over and just laid there asleep. I'm lucky to still be alive myself, I reckon. Could've died of cold during the night. I was woken by men passing by me, four of them. One of them caught me with his boot as he stepped over me. I heard them talking but I couldn't understand what they said. I was still drunk, I guess. I watched them. They waited near the brothel side door and when the girls stepped out, they followed them. I reckon they took 'em, don't you?'

'Can you describe the men?'

'One was bald, another had white hair, one wore a cloak, he looked like a big man. Didn't really see the fourth one. It was still quite dark and they only passed under the brothel's light for a moment.'

Petrus thought this vague description sounded a bit like Vester and his comrades, and probably like many of the men who lived and worked in the vicus, including some of the barbarians like Albiso and Luci.

'You didn't see their faces?'

'No, I told you, they passed by me and woke me as they went.'

'Why didn't you come forward, especially after we put up the notice about a reward?' Petrus jangled the coins.

'I err…I don't trust the Romans.' He glanced down, then looked up defiantly at Petrus, 'There, I've said it now.'

'Does that mean you don't want the money?'

Alarmed, Vatto looked around, checked that there was no one else in the shop. 'If it's available, I'll have it.'

Petrus handed him two denarii. Vatto raised an eyebrow and opened his mouth to speak. Petrus shook his head.

'You've given me the time, but your descriptions are vague and won't lead to their identification. You might not want to tell anyone that you took money from me today; the murderers won't know you didn't see their faces.'

Vatto took a sharp intake of breath and nodded. 'That's why I didn't come forward,'

'I thought it was because you didn't like Romans.'

Vatto did not respond. He placed the coins under the bench and turned back to his work. A thought suddenly occurred to Petrus. 'Another thing?' he said.

'What?'

'You're in the tavern most nights. See a lot of soldiers in there?'

Vatto nodded. 'You can spot 'em easily enough even though they're not in uniform; they're flash with their money.'

'You saw the two soldiers being attacked, the ones who were killed, didn't you? You would've passed the place where they were attacked on your way back here. You live behind this workshop don't you, so you saw them.'

Vatto's eyes darted towards the door at the back of the shop.

'Don't even think about trying to run!' Petrus warned him. 'You were afraid to come forward, weren't you?'

Vatto nodded.

'Tell me what you saw.' Petrus took out five denarii and held them out flat on his palm.

'Four men, one big, it looked like he was giving orders to the others, like, like a soldier. They spoke in a strange language.'

'Did you see their faces?'

Vatto shook his head.

Sudden inspiration came to Petrus. 'Is it possible that they were the same four men who followed the two girls from Sylva's place?'

Vatto's eyes widened in terror. 'I didn't see their faces; it was very dark. I, I couldn't say.'

Vatto was visibly shaking as Petrus handed him the money and left the workshop. Behind him he heard the carpenter moving around and locking the doors.

Petrus returned to the fort and his office where he wrote up his thoughts, including his feeling that Albiso and Luci were not telling the truth, but he wasn't sure why they would lie.

In the next room the light was on as the Prefect was working. A woman's voice sneaked out of there into the night and followed Petrus as he walked down the street towards the Praetorium. A dark figure emerged from the prefect's house, pulled his cloak tightly around his shoulders and moved towards the barrack blocks. Petrus recognised the broad stride of the centurion Julius Maximus. The sweet voice of a woman singing a song about the beauty of Rome floated out through the gaps in the Praetorium's windows. He was glad that Prima seemed happy.

Back at the barracks, Boga had made roasted pork with leeks and cabbage.

'Vester and his comrades are in the detention cell,' Maximus informed him as they ate. 'Couldn't explain why they lied to you about the time they got back to the fort or what they were doing in the time between being kicked out of the tavern and arriving at the fort gate. We got a bit physical with them and then threw them in detention. A few days in there might loosen their tongues.'

Petrus didn't know how to respond. Maximus' methods always produced a response.

'Would you like to hear my report this evening?' Petrus asked.

'No, no, I'm sure it can wait.' Maximus waved his hand, dismissing Petrus.

XVI – Dies Lunes

Petrus had been unable to speak with Maximus or Tatius after parade. The two men and the other centurions were locked away in Tatius' office with a soldier standing guard outside who turned away anyone wanting to speak with them, murmuring, 'My orders are they are not to be disturbed by anyone.' Petrus tried to insist that these orders did not apply to him, but the man showed him the tablet with the orders on it. Petrus read the words in disbelief, but the Prefect's ring seal was pressed firmly into the wax at the bottom of the orders. They clearly stated that officers were to carry on their duties as normal and had the authority to act in any way that they felt necessary. Petrus frowned; he knew this meant they could be reprimanded later if the Prefect felt that they had acted inappropriately.

He found Suasso in his usual place near the stables. He seemed to wait most days for instructions from the Romans but was unconcerned if there was no work for him to do, in which case he would wait outside the fort gates holding furtive discussions with local men. Petrus assumed this was how he found out what was going on in the area, guessing that money or favours changed hands. He asked Suasso to get Albiso and Luci to report to his office.

'If they can be found,' Suasso said.

Petrus didn't like his tone. 'You know how to find them, Suasso. Don't take me for a fool. I want them at my office. I have the authority of the Centurion today and I won't be afraid to use it.'

Suasso looked surprised and ambled off towards the gate.

Petrus spent the morning drilling the men in unarmed combat. He decided a demonstration was needed and picked a wiry looking man to fight with. The other men surrounded them and began cheering their comrade on. The young man's strength and skill surprised Petrus as he received some hard blows to the body and head. Petrus found himself sat on the ground; the young man knelt behind him on one knee with Petrus' head in an arm lock. Petrus struggled for breath, and he tried to twist his body while beating his fists on the man's arm. His heart beat faster and the blood roared in his ears as the man's grip tightened; he felt the world going dark around him. The cheering grew louder. His strength was ebbing away. In desperation, he reached behind him and grabbed the man's testicles, twisting and squeezing. The man screamed. Petrus twisted harder. The arm around his throat went slack. Petrus rotated his body, released his grip on the testicles and slipped out from under the man's arm. He gasped for breath. The soldier lay on the ground clutching himself. Petrus remained kneeling. The onlookers had gone quiet. Petrus felt the darkness lift, his breathing slowed, and his heart rate fell. Embarrassed and a little frightened at how easily he'd been overpowered, he got to his feet.

'Never get overconfident,' he warned as much to himself as the men he was training.

Later, after the men had practised some more, Petrus, who still felt embarrassed, dismissed them and made his way to his office. The prefect's door was still closed and guarded. Petrus flexed his aching muscles; the beating had left him feeling a lot worse than he'd expected. His office door opened, and Luci and Albiso entered the room looking sheepish.

'You wanted to see us, Aurelius Petrus?' Luci asked.

'I have the authority of the Centurion today to make further enquiries about the recent murders. Luci, I want to know where you were the morning after you'd been to the brothel and had Cara and Metta for the evening. What were you doing around sunrise?'

Luci remained silent.

'Don't make me fetch Maximus!' Petrus raised his voice. He hoped he could bluff his way through this. If they challenged him, he would be unable to fetch the centurion, who was still locked away with the Prefect. 'Well, where were you both?'

'You know where we were, Sir,' Luci smirked. 'We accompanied you to Camboglanna with Suasso. You were taking that woman back to the fort. We left just before daybreak, as we'd been instructed and met you along the route. Don't you remember?'

Petrus opened his mouth to speak, then closed it again. He felt stupid.

'And where were you the night the two soldiers were killed?'

The two men looked at each other.

'Home in bed with some women, I expect,' Albiso glared defiantly at Petrus. 'You've seen how easy it can be to get a shag for the night. Anyway, the murderers were captured and killed by Maximus, so why are you questioning us about them?'

'Get out of my sight!' Petrus spat, frustrated.

He still believed that four innocent men had been captured, tortured and killed by Maximus. Their only crime had been to get on the wrong side of Chief Gna. He sighed and began reviewing all of his notes to see if he had missed something.

He heard murmuring outside and recognised Maximus' voice. He locked away his tablets and left his office.

'Petrus, come in here, the Prefect and I have something to discuss with you.' Maximus' smile was cold.

Petrus followed him into the prefect's room.

'I understand one of the new recruits got the better of you this morning,' Tatius grinned.

Petrus felt himself redden. 'Yes. It was a close thing. I shouldn't have underestimated him.'

'News came today that the Governor, Ulpius Marcellus, will be visiting here in three days' time. That's what we've all been discussing.

I've sent an invitation to the prefect at Camboglanna and his wife to come here for a meal with the Governor and his entourage. They'll arrive tomorrow. Well, the Prefect will, he may leave his wife behind given her condition. I've decided that we'll go hunting the day after tomorrow for venison to eat at the feast. Maximus has a list of other things we need to do; you can help him.'

Petrus nodded and pain shot through his neck where the young recruit had held him with such force that morning. He frowned, 'Would you like to hear my latest report?'

Tatius smiled. 'I hope you've made progress.'

'A carpenter called Vatto, who lives in the vicus, saw four men following the two whores as they left the brothel. He'd fallen asleep drunk in the alleyway and was woken by four men stepping over him when one of them caught him with his boot. He saw them following Cara and Metta. His description is vague unfortunately, probably because he was still drunk. He said: "A bald man, one with white hair and a big man." That could fit the four men from Aquilinus' century, or Luci and Albiso, or a lot of men from the community.'

'As you know, the four roommates were kicked out of the tavern earlier than they said, I don't know what their motive would've been apart from robbery, but they have a low opinion of women.' He paused. 'As you know, they are rapists.'

Tatius nodded. 'Maximus?'

'We've hit them a few times, but they wouldn't say what they were doing in the time between being kicked out of the tavern and arriving at the gate just around daybreak. They're now in the detention cell. I'm going to leave them there for a couple of days, make 'em a bit hungry and cold, that'll jog their memories. In a day or so we should be able to either charge them with murder or release them. They won't be able to cope in the isolation cells.'

'I want it resolved before the Governor gets here,' the Prefect said and turned back towards Petrus. 'Continue, Petrus.'

'Luci was with the two dead girls the day they made the sudden decision to go to their parents' place. He could've frightened them.' He looked at Maximus. 'I was with them as well, giving them their inheritance. That's a matter of record.'

'I bet you didn't just give them their inheritance,' muttered Maximus.

'Vatto was also the man who witnessed the attack on Faustus and Drusus, the one who wouldn't come forward and give a statement,' said Petrus. 'He admitted that when I challenged him, and he looked terrified when I suggested it might have been the same men at both murders.'

'The murderers of the soldiers were found.' Maximus spoke slowly, his face was crimson red. 'How could it have been the same men?'

'Vatto, our only witness, clearly thinks they were,' Petrus persisted.

'Only because you suggested it to him! The soldiers' murderers were found!' Tatius banged his fist on the table. 'Any other ideas or lines of enquiry?'

Petrus shook his head and immediately regretted the action as pain ran down from his ears to his shoulders. 'Apart from the description being like Luci and Albiso.'

'Luci and Albiso went with you to Camboglanna. They set off before dawn. Anyway, the witness saw four men, who else do you think they could've been with? They're thick as thieves, those two,' Maximus spat.

Despondent, Petrus remained silent.

'I'm disappointed with you Petrus. You still cling on to the belief that Maximus got the wrong men for the original murders, and that's clouded your judgement. You don't appear to have any evidence and are questioning men who look vaguely like those described by a witness who's a known drunkard! I'm relieving you from the investigation. Maximus will continue looking into the deaths of the two whores, alongside his preparations for the Governor's visit.' Tatius held up his hand to silence Petrus' protests. 'Enough Petrus! I warned you! You'll focus on your normal duties and getting the men ready for the Governor's inspection. We'll take a view on your suitability as an Optio after the Governor's visit. Is that clear?'

Petrus was devastated. If he lost his position as Optio, he'd probably be transferred elsewhere and even if he wasn't, he would hardly ever be able to see his family as he would not be free to leave the fort whenever he needed to.

The Prefect stood up. 'Petrus, you're to come hunting with us the day after tomorrow. Perhaps you can use that as an opportunity to redeem yourself. Maximus is organising some new barbarians to track the deer; it'll be good training for them. We've discussed it; the two of you and two other soldiers should be sufficient as guards in the current climate. My wife is also coming with us.'

'Sir, is it wise to go out hunting at this time with only four soldiers including myself and Centurion Julius Maximus?' Petrus tried to hold his voice steady. It was his duty to point this out, even if he was to be stripped of the position of Optio. He took a deep breath, 'There've been four murders now. The last two,' he looked at Maximus, 'remain unsolved.'

'Unsolved by you! Are you suggesting we're inadequate protection for the Prefect and his wife?' scoffed Maximus.

'No, Sir. Just being cautious.'

Maximus waved him away. Petrus turned to leave. Behind him he heard Maximus telling Tatius that he would interview Vatto the carpenter, confident that he would get more information from him. Petrus felt exhausted as he walked towards the workshops.

Carantii

Carantii had been busy finishing a new plough that he'd promised to make for his brother Amba when they were at his place for their father's funeral.

'Well, if you're right and he's visiting today, or tomorrow, I'd better get it done, hadn't I?' he'd said to Eburacia at breakfast.

She would not be drawn on why she thought Amba would visit. Several hours later, he finished the plough and hung it on the wall. If Amba didn't turn up, then it was on display for other customers to see.

A cart drew up outside. The driver had his cloak pulled up over his head, but Carantii recognised the horse.

'Greetings, Amba.' He strode forward and grasped his brother by the hand before pulling him in to a brief embrace. 'Ebu said you were coming. What brings you to see us?'

Amba smiled and waved in the direction of the cart. 'I brought some hides and some grain for you. And,' he paused, 'I brought Lugraca to you.' He moved to the back of the cart and helped a young woman down to the ground.

Carantii reddened, he'd not noticed her. 'I didn't see you there. Come inside.'

He led them through the forge. Lugraca took down the hood from her brown cloak and shook out her dark hair as she looked about her. She ran her hand over some of the tools on display and paused to look at one of the swords with an engraved hilt.

Eburacia was mending some clothes in the kitchen. She looked up as they entered, put down her things and moved towards the other woman, grasping her hands.

'Lugraca! How wonderful, you're most welcome in our home,' Eburacia said.

Lugraca smiled. She had brown eyes and a small scar on her top lip. Her hands were rough from years of hard physical work and two fingers on her left hand were fused together.

Carantii felt tongue-tied and stammered. 'Yes, welcome. I haven't seen you since… since you were a child.'

Eburacia laughed. 'Atta and I discussed my marriage and she suggested Lugraca come to work for us. I thought it was a good idea. You'll need some help.'

'You planned it at the funeral?' he mumbled. 'Why didn't you discuss it with me?'

'These are not things for men to talk about,' said Amba. 'Let's leave them to get acquainted and you can show me that fine plough on the wall. Is it the one for me?' Amba walked towards the forge. Behind them they could hear the women whispering and giggling.

The men unloaded the cart, then Carantii took the plough down from the wall.

'It's got a good weight, a fine piece,' commented Amba as he held it.

'Tell me about Lugraca.'

'We all knew her as a child. She will make a good maid for you and who knows what else,' Amba smirked. 'She's a good, hard worker. And you know you would struggle alone. It's good that she wants to come here to work for you. But it will be a shock, this life, surrounded by so many people, and the dirt. She's never known anything apart from the countryside. You must take care of her, warn her of any dangers.'

Carantii nodded. 'I'm sure Ebu has enough time to explain things to her before she leaves.' His brother was right, and Lugraca was a good-looking woman, so who knew what might happen. He wondered what else his sister had planned. The two women passed by the cart on their way into the street, their heads bent close to each other as they exchanged secrets.

'That seems to be going well,' commented Amba. 'Ebu is deciding on her own dowry. Come and visit soon, brother,' he heaved himself back into the driver's seat and turned the cart around. 'Stay well.'

'Go well.' Carantii watched him leave and then returned to work. He hoped Eburacia would find a way of explaining his work for Petrus and that it must be kept secret.

Petrus

In the evening, Petrus reviewed all his reports again but couldn't see anything he'd missed. Frustrated and angry, he locked them away and went back to his room. Maximus was unusually chatty while he ate his supper.

Petrus went to bed despondent. He lay there and thought about his family. Soon he wouldn't be able to visit them regularly. How could he break that news to Aurora?

XVII – Dies Martes

Petrus was still angry at being told not to continue to investigate the murders of the two women, even though he had to admit to himself that he didn't know what he would have done next. Perhaps pressuring Vatto the carpenter might work. Vester and his comrades may have something to say after their beating. They'd spent time in the confinement cell, in the cold and probably in pain; that might have encouraged one of them to talk.

He spent most of the day putting the men through their drills on the training ground. The weather was dry, and the men worked very well. He was pleased and thought that they would put on a good show for the Governor. As he wrote up his training notes, he heard Maximus storm into the Principia. The centurion threw the door open, slamming it against the wall. The wood shuddered and tiny splinters flew across the room.

'Vatto has gone!' he shouted, 'The cobbler says he went soon after you'd spoken to him. I knew he hadn't told you everything.' He pointed at Petrus and emphasised his words, 'If, and it's a big 'if' right now, you remain as Optio, you'll need to learn how to interrogate people properly.'

Petrus didn't like the thought of learning about interrogation from Maximus. However, he did need to learn what questions to ask and how to apply pressure without resorting to torture. He thought that Vatto had run away after he had made the connection between the murders of the women and the soldiers. He was afraid of the murderers and the Romans who might come for him.

'And what about Vester and the others?' he asked Maximus.

'They're looking a bit sorry for themselves now. We're going to question them again today.'

'Do you need my help with the preparations for the Governor's visit?' Petrus tried to sound enthusiastic.

Maximus did not reply immediately. 'I'll let you know.'

Petrus walked through the fort, trying to see it as a visitor like the Governor might. It was dirty. The roads were full of filth where men had thrown away scraps of food and other rubbish. The odour of decay hovered all around him. The rats moved about unhurried, even in the daylight. He gave orders to the men to clean up the streets. There were murmurings of discontent amongst the men, but they began to work.

There was a sudden shout from the gate and the men about him stood to attention as the Prefect from Camboglanna and a carriage drove through, followed by a dozen marching soldiers. At the praetorium, Septimus dismounted, opened the carriage door and helped Fabia get out. She did not take down the hood of her green cloak as she walked cautiously up the steps alongside her husband. The house's door opened, and Prima reached out to embrace her friend who moved slowly towards her outstretched arms.

'Fabia, my dearest friend, you look so beautiful!' Prima cried pulling Fabia inside the house. Prima was wearing the engraved bronze-coloured necklace that he'd seen at Carantii's forge. He assumed Maximus must have collected it for her when he was looking for Vatto.

Petrus turned back towards his men, ordering them to continue with their work. The fort was beginning to look cleaner, and he thought that the smell was lessening.

Over their evening meal, Maximus told him that Vester and the others were still not talking.

'Perhaps they've nothing to say,' suggested Petrus.

'We'll see. I think you've identified the killers. We just need to get confessions.'

Someone shook him. He fought his way back to consciousness as Boga loomed over him with a lit torch, the light flickered as the slave's arm shook.

'You ordered me to waken you,' Boga whispered.

'Yes. Yes, I did,' grumbled Petrus as he pulled on his boots, grabbed the torch and strode outside. He made his way across the fort towards the east gate. He climbed slowly up the stone steps, careful to make as little noise as he could. He placed the torch in a holder on the wall. In the torchlight he could see that Rufus and Pius were side by side leaning on the parapet. They did not turn as he moved behind them. He cleared his throat and spat on the floor. There was still no reaction from the two men. They were asleep. He was disappointed but not surprised. He grabbed Rufus' shoulder and spun him round.

'Wha, wha..?' Rufus reached for his sword.

Petrus knocked Rufus' arm aside. Pius lurched towards him, clumsy with sleep.

'Don't move, soldier!' Petrus snarled and pushed him back against the wall.

The two men pulled themselves into salutes.

'You bastards were asleep again!' he hissed standing with his face right up against Rufus'. The frightened man's foul breath pushed into Petrus' nostrils. 'Stay awake! Damn you! Do you want to be stoned to death?!'

He roughly pushed them back into their places overlooking the wall.

'I'll be back!' he hissed, grabbed his torch and made his way back down the steps, crossed the fort, entered his room and fell into bed, exhausted.

XVIII – Dies Mercurii

Birdsong reached inside Petrus' room, dragging him into the day. He'd slept through the night; Boga had not woken him a second time. He pulled on his boots. In the next room, Boga was still asleep. Petrus resisted the urge to kick the man awake as he walked past and out into the fort. Grey clouds floated in the early morning sky. He jogged through the fort and began to climb slowly up the steps at the gate. Above him he could hear Rufus and Pius chatting quietly as they looked over the wall. He didn't disturb them. He turned on his heel and made his way back to the barracks.

Boga stood wide-eyed and trembling. 'I'm sorry I failed to wake you, Sir,' he whispered.

Petrus just nodded. Boga's hand shook as he passed a bowl of fermented porridge and a cup of water across the table. Petrus sat down and began eating. The water smelled stale and left an unpleasant aftertaste in his mouth.

'Boga, when did you last change the water? It tastes awful.'

The slave muttered something about regularly changing it but fell silent as Maximus strode into the room.

'I checked on the gatekeepers twice during the night,' mumbled Petrus. 'They were asleep the first time, but awake just before dawn when I went back.'

Boga was cowering in the corner of the room.

Maximus scowled and nodded. 'I'll sort them out after the hunt.' He didn't seem to notice his terrified slave.

Petrus made his way to the parade ground. His fingers grew

stiff in the chilly air, and he rubbed them together to warm them up. The two Prefects stood together surveying the troops who shuffled their feet in the cold. After the reports had been given, they sent the men to their duties and went to the Principia.

'Foslius Septimus is coming on the hunt today,' Tatius announced, 'along with Prima.'

Maximus turned to Petrus. 'Be ready.'

The Prefects' horses were smartly turned out with finely engraved metalwork on their bridles. The bay mare readied for Prima to ride was similarly attired. The men emerged from the house deep in conversation as Felix and another slave trotted behind their masters carrying spare clothes and equipment. As before, Prima mounted unaided, swinging her leg over the horse's back. She pulled her thick blue cloak tightly around her and covered her head with the hood. As she did so, Petrus caught a glimpse of the hunting knife she had attached to her belt. She was clearly planning to gut her own venison again that day. She watched with a wry smile as the two men were helped into their saddles. The slaves got onto their mules and the group turned towards the gate.

Suddenly the door to the house burst open and a slave ran down the steps.

'Master! Foslius Septimus, Prefect!' he shouted, and stumbled as he ran towards the horses who pricked up their ears in alarm. Septimus halted his horse and frowned.

'What is it?' he hissed.

'It's your wife! She's really ill. Vomiting and…and…the other…' he pointed to his bottom. 'Both ends,' he murmured.

'Ceres have mercy!' muttered Septimus. He dismounted and

looked towards Tatius. 'This could be serious. I think I'd better stay behind, just in case.'

Tatius nodded. 'Fetch help from the infirmary!' he ordered the slave who scurried away.

They made their way to the gate. Petrus was relieved when Flavius and Corvinus, whom he recognised from his own century, rode towards them fully armed. They weren't the best horsemen or fighters but would be enough to act as a deterrent. Maximus greeted the three barbarians waiting outside the gates. Petrus didn't know them. They were young and looked uneasy with their swords dangling from their saddles. One idly stroked his horse's neck, his hand was scarred, the nails torn and dirty.

'They're new recruits,' Maximus murmured, 'with a lot to learn. This should be a way to ease them into it.'

Petrus wasn't sure that ruining the Prefects' hunting trip was the best way to begin their training, but he didn't argue with the centurion, not with his own position as Optio in danger. They began walking through the streets where people were beginning to move around at the start of the day. Petrus' hands were numb with cold; barely feeling the reins in his fingers. He wiggled his toes inside his boots, trying to restore feeling in them.

Beyond the vicus, Maximus instructed the barbarians to ride in various directions to find deer and positioned the two soldiers at the rear of the party. It grew warmer, and Petrus relished the feel of the leather reins in his hands. The birds' raucous songs were all around them and their horse's ears moved back and forth, their eyes alert. Prima rode in silence alongside her husband at the front of the group; she did not look around as they moved through the countryside.

After a while one of the mules planted its feet and refused to walk forward despite the slave Felix's urging. He shouted and waved his arms to no avail. A soldier behind him dismounted from his horse and slapped the mule repeatedly on the rump, eventually he grabbed a fallen twig and beat it hard. The animal breyed in protest before finally moving forward behind the others.

One of the young barbarians cantered towards them, slowing his horse so suddenly that he was thrown forward in the saddle and struggled to regain his position.

Reddening, he said, 'Julius Maximus, we've seen a group of deer just behind that copse over there!' he pointed some distance away.

Maximus nodded and they began following him. Fallen branches littered the ground around the oak copse and each rider picked a route for their horse to minimise the noise of breaking twigs, hoping not to alert the deer. The land around them was partly cultivated and men were driving their cows forward as they ploughed the land, some stopped their work to watch the group of Romans riding past.

They walked all the way round the copse but did not see any deer. The young man looked crestfallen.

'Idiot!' muttered the Prefect.

'I'm sorry, Sir. They must've moved on,' mumbled the barbarian.

'Get going then!' shouted Maximus, 'Find some more!'

The man spun his horse around and cantered away. Maximus put his horse into a trot and they headed up a hillside through thick brown bracken heavy with dew. The water clung to the horses' legs.

'I don't know where the bloody barbarians are,' Maximus said, turning his horse to face Tatius. 'I suggest we go to The Gladed Forest. There're many spaces there where the deer feed and it should be good hunting. We went there the last time you hunted with your wife and her friend.'

'Lead the way,' Tatius scowled.

Maximus pushed his horse into a canter. The slaves gasped and squealed as one of the soldiers behind them leant down and whacked the mules on their rumps with the branch he carried. The mules surged forward, and the slaves held the mules' manes to keep in the saddle.

They slowed to a walk as they reached the forest. Behind them they heard a horse approaching. The soldiers turned to face the man moving towards them, relaxing when they recognised one of the young barbarians.

'Sorry Sir, I... I...' he gasped as Maximus held up a hand to silence him.

'You and your friends are a useless bunch of wasters! Find the other two and get back to the fort! Now!' Maximus yelled.

The man rode away.

Maximus spoke to the Prefect, 'I suggest we ride in as far as possible and then walk.'

They rode along a deer track between the trees until the low branches forced them to dismount and continue on foot, leading their horses. The silence of the forest settled around them, punctuated by the sharp crack of twigs beneath their feet. It smelled of damp earth and wet leaves.

Prima picked her way carefully along the track. Suddenly she tripped on a protruding tree root and fell beneath her horse. She screamed and covered her head with her hands. Petrus released his horse's reins and dashed forward, almost tripping himself.

'Julia Prima! Are you hurt?' he reached out a hand to help her up.

She brushed him aside and tried to crawl out from underneath the horse. As she moved, they heard the coarse sound of her cloak beginning to tear; the horse was standing on it. She fumbled with the clasp, let the cloak fall to the ground and crawled out from beneath the horse's belly. She stood up and brushed ineffectually at the soil and decayed leaves clinging to her green trousers. Petrus lifted the horse's foot and grabbed the cloak. He attempted to dust off the dirt. Prima snatched it and put it round her shoulders. She looked down at the tear and stroked it with her fingers.

'I might as well wear it until after the kill,' she said.

'Prima! Are you hurt?' Tatius had abandoned his horse and moved to stand beside her. He put his hand out to touch her, but she shook him off.

'I'm fine. Fortunately, the mare is well schooled,' she tossed her head and turned away from him.

'Shall I lead the lady's horse?' Petrus felt awkward.

'Yes,' Tatius turned away.

Petrus attached his horse's reins to the saddle of the mare and began leading them as Prima walked sulkily ahead of him.

Maximus raised his hand and the party stopped. He turned towards them and whispered, 'There ahead, two adult males. I think if you and your wife approach with me, you should both get a good shot.'

The slaves passed over the bows and arrows and the three of them began to creep forwards. In a clearing two fine-muscled stags grazed on the sparse grass which had forced its way through the clumps of moss and fallen twigs. Tatius and Prima separated from Maximus and moved carefully to stand near a huge oak tree. They raised their bows, paused and then in unison released the arrows.

The two deer groaned and slid to the ground. Prima dropped her bow and arrow. She rushed forward and knelt next to one of the deer, her hand on its neck and her eyes shining in excitement.

She reached inside her cloak, withdrew her knife, and slit the beast's throat. Blood gushed onto the earth and seeped into her trousers, tunic and cloak. The metallic smell of blood filled the air. She cast her cloak aside, leant forward and stabbed the deer in the chest. She cut down towards the tail, pulled the flesh apart and plunged her hands inside the belly. The innards spilled onto her knees. She cut them free and cast them aside. Blood dripped from her pale hands.

'Come husband, butcher your deer,' she grinned wildly.

Flavius and Corvinus were frozen in shock. Petrus hoped she

would not undress in front of them all as she had the time before. Tatius dropped his cloak to the ground and beckoned the slaves to follow him. One of them passed him a hunting knife. He knelt down next to the other deer and began to cut it open.

A sudden cry rent the air as three warriors wielding swords burst into the glade. They wore horned helmets and thin animal hide hung like veils across their faces, with holes cut out for their eyes. Petrus' heart began to beat faster; he heard his blood pounding in his ears as he rushed towards the leading man and slashed at him with his sword. The warrior parried the blow and lunged towards Petrus. Their swords clashed again and again. Petrus heard grunts and cries filling the air as Corvinus, Flavius, and Maximus fought somewhere nearby. The sound of metal striking metal rang across the glade as each man fought for his life.

Prima's scream tore through the glade. Petrus felt his insides tighten. Beneath an oak tree Crixus, the slave, lay dying. He clutched his neck, in a futile attempt to close the gaping wound across his throat and stop the river of blood flowing onto the ground.

Petrus thrust his sword high towards his enemy's head and then downwards as he slashed at the man's legs. The blade tore through the thin trousers and sliced open the flesh. Blood shot out of the warrior's leg; he stumbled and fell to the ground dropping his sword. He pressed a hand across the wound; blood forced its way through his fingers and his life seeped into the dark earth.

Tatius stood pale-faced and frightened, attempting to shield Prima from Maximus. He did his best to block the strikes as the centurion circled them, slashing towards them with his sword.

'Run Prima! Run!' Tatius gasped as he lunged towards Maximus.

Prima remained stock still, clutching the hunting knife, a smile frozen to her face. Maximus raised his sword and rushed at Tatius. Felix, the slave, threw Prima's cloak over Maximus, catching him up in the cloth. Maximus flailed his arms and swore as he battled his way past the cloak engulfing him and rushed towards Tatius, who was tiring.

Petrus watched as the lead warrior collapsed to the ground as he took his last breath.

Behind him Tatius screamed, 'Run Prima! Run!'

Petrus rushed towards Maximus with his sword high above his head, breathing hard and screaming.

Maximus knocked Petrus sideways. The two men circled each other, slashing and parrying over and over, as each man attacked and defended. Maximus knocked Petrus' arm aside and stabbed towards his body, striking his leather tunic. Petrus turned, slashed hard with his sword and Maximus blocked the strike as Tatius stepped forward and stabbed Maximus in the back. Maximus screamed. Petrus cut downwards slashing Maximus' belly, ripping it open. His guts spilled from the wound like fat pale snakes. Maximus gasped, dropped his weapons and fell to his knees, fumbling as he tried to push his entrails back inside his body. He leaked brown stinking shit and blood onto his trousers and the ground below him.

Petrus put his sword against Maximus' neck.

'Kill me!' Maximus whispered, his lips trembling, 'Do it!'

Tatius shouted, 'Finish him!'

Petrus raised his sword.

Tatius screamed.

Prima had stabbed her husband. He bent forward; his face twisted in pain as he tried to reach the hunting knife embedded in his back. Prima grabbed the knife, pulled it free and Tatius screamed as she raised her hand to stab him again. Felix, caught her wrist and wrenched it back, forcing her to drop the weapon. She twisted free from his grip and threw herself to the ground, grabbing the knife. She lunged towards Tatius. Felix stepped to the side and punched her in the face, knocking her out cold on the ground.

Petrus gasped for breath. He looked round. One of the warriors had been decapitated. Corvinus had removed the helmet. Petrus was horrified to see Luci's face staring at the sky, his mouth wide open as if screaming for his lost body. The other warrior had lost an arm and lay clutching his groin in a pool of piss and blood. Flavius stepped forward and brought his sword down on the man's neck, severing it from the body. The stink of urine merged with the smells of blood and shit filling the glade.

Petrus spoke to Felix and pointed at Prima, 'Tie her up! Quickly, before she wakes up. Then tie Maximus' hands. I don't care if he's dying, tie him up, tight.'

Petrus approached the Prefect, who was on his knees shaking and supporting his right elbow with his left hand. He was taking deep breaths as if it took all his strength not to collapse. Petrus peered at the wound on his back where the knife had pierced his shoulder, narrowly missing his neck. Tatius had been lucky. If Prima had struck slightly higher up, the Prefect would be dead. Blood trickled down Tatius' back seeping into his tunic. Petrus tore a piece of cloth from Prima's cloak and wrapped it around the wound, supporting Tatius' arm so that the weight was taken by the cloth. He helped him to his feet and moved him to sit on a fallen tree at the edge of the clearing. The Prefect's face was pale. He was whispering to himself. Petrus did not wait to try to understand what he was saying. Perhaps he was praying.

Felix dragged the mules towards the unconscious woman. He tied a rope to one of the saddles then knelt beside Prima. He lifted her hands, ran his fingers over her blood-stained palms and pressed them together, binding the wrists tightly. Prima began to stir as she fought her way back to consciousness.

'Wha, Wha?' she opened her eyes and began to struggle, swinging her tied hands, she tried to strike Felix and attempted to kick him.

'Untie me, you wretch! Untie me!' she screamed.

Felix slapped her face. Shocked, she stopped struggling. He

dragged her to her feet and tied her hands to the mule's saddle; she was left standing leant against the mule's rump.

'Let me go!' she pulled feebly against the rope.

'Stand still!' Felix hissed. He put the blade of her knife against her pale cheek and spat in her face, 'I'll cut you, you bitch. Just give me an excuse!'

Prima's eyes widened and she fell silent. Felix approached Maximus, who sat slumped forward. He waved his arm feebly towards the slave, trying to fight him off. Felix poked Maximus' belly with his foot. The intestines writhed and more of them slid onto Maximus' lap. Maximus groaned.

'Sit still soldier!' Felix muttered, 'Or I'll cut you.'

He tied Maximus' hands together and dragged the other reluctant mule across to stand over him. He raised the centurion's hands and tied them to the saddle. Maximus' lips were trembling as he rested his pale sweaty face against the mule's leg.

'Can you make him talk?' Tatius' voice reached across the glade.

Petrus took a deep breath and readied himself to torture his centurion. Corvinus moved quickly across the glade. He kicked Maximus' belly. Maximus screamed.

'Quick or slow, Centurion? Quick or slow? Choose how you die,' hissed Corvinus.

Maximus moaned; his eyelids flickered closed. Petrus let Corvinus continue.

'Wake up, you bastard! You've pissed and shat yourself, you miserable fuck!' Corvinus slapped Maximus' face. His eyes flew open, and drool ran down his chin.

'Why? Why attack us?' Petrus asked, his voice harsh above the dying man's erratic breathing.

'Last chance, last chance,' whispered Maximus, 'they were leaving. If the Governor gave his permission, Fabia would be gone. Last chance to kill…'

'Maximus!' hissed Prima behind them.

Felix slapped her hard across the cheek. 'Shut the fuck up!'

he said.

She squealed and buried her tear-stained face in the mule's side. Corvinus stabbed Maximus' thigh with his sword, burying the tip in the hard flesh of the centurion's thigh. Maximus opened his mouth.

'Or I could cut your cock off,' Corvinus twisted the sword in Maximus' flesh.

Maximus groaned and his eyelids closed.

'No! Stay awake!' Petrus desperately shook his shoulders. Maximus opened his eyes.

Sudden realisation hit Petrus hard like a blow in the chest. 'You killed the two soldiers!'

A weak smile spread over Maximus' face, he whispered, 'Had to…on duty at the Praetorium… overheard us planning. Prima, Prima and me. Started blackmailing.'

'So, the hunt for the holy man and executions, was just to cover that up?!' Petrus growled. Maximus nodded.

'And the women?' Petrus waited, but he already knew the answer.

Maximus was quiet. Corvinus poked his belly with the toe of his boot. Maximus moaned, and he licked his cracked lips.

'In case… in case the soldiers had told them. We'd planned a h… hunting accident. Prima or Fabia would accidentally shoot Tatius.' The words were barely audible. 'You… you had it all worked out, the rats, the curse tablets,' his voice was a whisper that gurgled in his chest. 'Knew… knew you wouldn't let it go. Had to get you demoted, but he, P… Prefect said you deserved another ch…chance, so had to kill you too.'

Petrus felt vindicated. A sudden movement behind him made him turn. Tatius was on his feet, lumbering towards them. Corvinus stepped aside as Tatius aimed a kick at the centurion's chest, rocking his body.

'How many barbarians are involved? What has it to do with my wife?' Tatius bent forward as he spoke; droplets of spittle sprayed onto Maximus' cheeks. Tatius stamped on Maximus' spilled intestines. They ruptured, and the stink of faeces filled the air. Maximus sighed.

'I made an oath, to protect her, my clan. She wants to return to Rome, to be with F… Fabia. These barbarians were… were,' the words were slow and laboured, 'unhappy. Helped me, with m… murders of soldiers and g… girls. They should've killed you all today.'

Maximus closed his eyes; his head fell forward onto his chest. His breathing seemed to stop. Flesh, blood and faeces clung to Tatius boot as he lifted his foot and stepped back. The centurion's death rattle followed him as he wiped his boot on a clump of grass, grimacing in disgust and moved to stand near the mules.

Prima stood facing her husband, defiant.

'I will torture you?' Tatius whispered raising his left hand.

Prima stared at him. Tatius slapped her hard across the face.

'Sir?' Petrus stepped behind him. 'We should take her back to the fort for questioning. We can do it in private, not in front of the soldiers and the slave.'

Tatius looked about him, as if seeing the soldiers for the first time. He stepped back. Petrus spoke to the two soldiers who looked shaken as they stood over the bodies of the dead warriors.

'You fought well, both of you. Go and catch all the horses, including the warriors'.'

The animals were wandering between the trees.

Petrus went over to the body of the lead warrior. He used his sword to flick away the mask from the man's face. He gasped as he stared down at Suasso, the son of Chief Gna, and leader of the barbarians. Petrus approached the severed head of the final warrior and lifted the veil with his sword. Albiso's pale face stared up at him. Hot anger surged through him. Their betrayal caused him almost physical pain.

Flavius and Corvinus returned leading the horses.

He asked them, 'When we were walking through the forest, did you hear or see anything, anything at all, to alert you to the fact that we were being followed?'

'No, Sir,' they both said in unison.

Petrus knew the Prefect was listening, he said, 'I wasn't aware either. That is my mistake.'

He pointed to the dead warriors, 'You recognise them, don't you?' The two men nodded.

'We'll take their heads and their weapons. Search their bodies, check if they've got money on them. Look inside their shirts, they may have money there,' Petrus patted his chest.

The two soldiers collected the barbarians' swords, shields and helmets, and tied them to the horses' saddles. They tore open the dead men's shirts.

'Look!' Flavius ripped a green pouch from Suasso's chest, it jingled as he handed it to Petrus. Petrus tipped the contents onto his palm; six aurei. He put it back in the pouch and slipped it beneath his tunic. The other two men were not carrying money.

Corvinus cut off Suasso's head. The two soldiers carried Albiso's and Suasso's heads by the hair and tied them to one of the saddles. Blood dribbled down the horse's body and ran down its legs. The horses' eyes grew wide in fear at the smell, the soldiers stroked their necks and muttered words of reassurance to calm them. Flavius had found the barbarian's spears amongst the trees. He picked up Luci's bald head and forced it down onto the tip of one of the spears. Flesh and grey fluid leaked from the head and slid down the spear's shaft into the grass. Luci's screaming face stared down at them.

'I'll carry that back,' Flavius muttered as he forced the shaft into the ground.

Petrus walked back to Felix. 'Pick up the deer and tie them to the back of the mules.'

Felix looked puzzled.

'We still need to feed the Governor.'

Felix nodded, 'What about Crixus?'

Petrus sighed, 'We can't take him back with us. I'm sorry, you both fought valiantly today. I'll send a party to bring him back to the fort or bury him here. The Roman army owes you both a debt of gratitude.'

'What about the animals? Crixus could be eaten by wolves or scavengers.'

Petrus looked about him, 'Cover the body with branches, that may stop them.'

Felix did not look reassured but did as he was told and piled branches over the corpse.

Petrus sliced through the rope tying Maximus to the mule; the body slid to the ground. Petrus brought his sword down on Maximus' neck, severing the head. He grabbed it by the hair and tied it to his horse's saddle, smearing blood across the leather. He took Maximus' armour and helmet and tied them alongside the head. His horse flared its nostrils in distress.

Felix lifted one of the deer onto the mule tied to Prima, blood dripped down the mule's rump. The dead stag's eyes stared accusingly at the woman. She tried to pull away in disgust, but Felix had bound her tightly to the saddle and she couldn't move. Felix put the other deer on his own mule.

'See if he's carrying any valuables,' Petrus ordered Flavius who stepped forward and ripped open Maximus' tunic with his knife. A bulging money pouch lay on the dead centurion's chest. Flavius slashed it off with the knife and threw it to Petrus who spilled fourteen aurei into his hand, before putting them back in the pouch and placing it alongside the other one in his tunic.

'Cover all the bodies with branches,' he told the soldiers.

The soldiers dragged the bodies of the barbarians over to Maximus' remains. They covered them with brushwood.

Petrus was still in shock, but he knew they had to get back to the fort quickly in case there were other barbarians in the forest waiting to attack. Tatius was clenching his fists and staring at his wife. His face had recovered some of the colour.

'Do you think you can ride, Silvius Tatius?' asked Petrus.

Tatius nodded and allowed Petrus to push him into the saddle.
'I'll put your wife on Maximus' horse and lead her.'

'I'll lead the bitch!'

'Can you manage?'

'Tie the horse to my saddle. She won't get away.'

Petrus lifted Prima up. She wriggled in his arms.

'Lie still, or I'll knock you out!' he snarled.

He pushed her onto the saddle and forced her to sit upright.
He tied her hands to the front of the saddle and tied another rope
under the horse's belly so that her ankles were linked together.

'If you fall off, you'll get trampled on.'

She looked terrified.

The two soldiers tied the dead warriors' horses together so that
Corvinus could lead them and then mounted their horses. Felix got
onto one of the mules and led the other while Petrus led Prima's
mare as they began to walk out of the forest. Flavius carried the
warriors' spears. Luci's head floated above them, screaming.

'Keep close, Silvius Tatius,' Petrus said.

They took a longer route out of the forest, allowing them
to remain on horseback. Prima sobbed quietly as they rode.
They emerged into the sunlight. Prima's horse slipped on some
gravel, she squealed and gripped the front of the saddle; her
fingertips turned white and she looked down in concentration.
Petrus turned round to check on her, but she remained upright.
Tatius did not look round, not caring if she fell.

As they reached the road, Petrus turned in his saddle.

'Put that cloak on her and cover her head and face. Let's
try not to cause a scene,' he ordered. He didn't want people to
know that Prima was now a prisoner.

Flavius moved up to Prima. She shrank from his touch. He
pulled her roughly towards him and put the torn cloak around
her shoulders. It covered her torso and hands, but her stained
trousers were visible below the torn edges. He put out his hand
to pull up her hood and she moved her head out of his way.

'Don't make me strike you!' he said, roughly pulling the hood up so that her face was obscured. She moved her arms and tossed her head so that the hood fell away. Flavius slapped her face. Her whole body rocked and she squealed, afraid she would fall from the horse. He grabbed her arm, pulled the hood back over her head and covered her hands with the cloak.

'Leave it!' he spat, 'You still look a sight, you bitch! If the hood falls again, I'll knock you out and tie you face down on the horse's back! Or cut your head off and add it to one of my spears!'

He pushed Luci's bald head against her face, the open mouth licked her cheeks. She screamed. He sneered.

Local people moving along the road stood aside in horror as the dead men's heads jiggled in a macabre dance as the horses walked. Some people ran away. Others stared, intrigued by the rider in the blood-stained cloak, with her fine clothes smeared with dark earth. The sun had dried the cloak and the metallic odour of blood clung to the riders.

Petrus was still struggling to understand what had happened. They reached the edge of the vicus and continued through the streets. As they passed the forge, Petrus saw Carantii at the door watching them. Beside him was a pretty young woman with long thick dark hair who looked terrified as she watched them. Carantii put his arm around her waist for reassurance. Petrus idly wondered whether the blacksmith had taken a wife.

As they reached the brothel, Sylva stood blinking in the sunlight and shouted towards him. 'Aurelius Petrus, when are you going to tell me what happened to my girls?'

He raised a hand and the horses behind him came to a halt. He walked his horse up to the brothel keeper and leant down towards her. Maximus' head was next to her face. She recoiled and took a step back.

'I'll come to see you soon,' Petrus said in a low voice, 'I think I'll be able to explain it all to you.'

She nodded and hurried back inside her building.

He gave the password and the fort's gates opened. Prima tossed her head and wriggled her wrists; the cloak fell away revealing her tied hands and tear-stained face.

'Get Fabius Ruga to meet me at the Principia,' Petrus ordered the gatekeepers.

One man ran to find the centurion while the other stood wide-eyed, watching the prefect's beautiful wife treated as a prisoner. Word spread quickly through the fort; soldiers and slaves rushed out of their barracks to watch, horrified to see the centurion's head tied to Petrus' saddle. As they drew level with the Praetorium, the visiting Prefect Foslius Septimus appeared on the steps looking alarmed, his hair tangled and unruly. His wife, Fabia, stepped up to stand behind him, her whole body shaking. When she saw Prima, she cried out and reached out a hand, groping the air. Septimus took hold of her wrist pulling it down and holding her tightly next to him. Her face twisted in pain. Felix stopped the mules, dismounted and led them to the rear of the building.

At the Principia, Petrus dismounted as a young soldier rushed over to take hold of his horse's bridle.

'You should go to the Infirmary, Sir,' Petrus said as the Prefect slid to the ground. 'I'll send a cart to the forest to collect the dead slave. Shall we bury the bodies of Maximus and the barbarians? Shall I get these heads put on stakes outside the fort?'

'Yes, yes. Bring back the slave's body but bury Maximus and the barbarians. Maximus has forfeited any funeral rites. Put the heads outside the gates.'

Petrus was relieved to note from Tatius' attitude that he seemed to have recovered on the journey back.

'Corvinus and Flavius!' Petrus ordered the two soldiers, 'Put these heads on stakes outside the east gate.'

Corvinus untied Maximus' hair and let it fall to the ground where it lay facing towards the sky. The watching soldiers gasped. Flavius cut through the hair securing Suasso and

Albiso's heads to the saddles. They fell and rolled along the ground, mud clung to their hair and skin. Flavius stopped Suasso's head with this foot. It stood upright as if it had been planted in the ground, the eyes open and staring. Corvinus grabbed the three heads by the hair and walked towards the gate. Flavius walked at his side with Luci's head bobbing on the spear as he pointed at men instructing them to bring stakes.

'I want to see her put in chains!' Tatius nodded towards his wife. 'Get her down!'

Petrus cut the rope tying Prima's feet and undid the knots binding her to the saddle. He pulled her hands sharply; she came off the horse and staggered against him. He forced her upright and began leading her to the rear of the Principia. She walked very slowly; he yanked the rope hard, and she cried out in pain.

'Keep up!' he snapped.

Tatius followed them.

Fabius Ruga rushed towards them. He was in full uniform and carrying his sword.

'What, what?' he began.

'The bitch and Maximus tried to kill me, er, us!' spat Tatius. 'They conspired with the three barbarians led by Suasso and attacked us in the Gladed Forest. One of my slaves was killed. I want her kept here in the cells. No one is to talk to her. The Governor can decide what to do with her.'

Ruga frowned. He opened his mouth to ask a question, but when Petrus shook his head, Ruga remained silent and followed them into the building. A soldier handed them the keys and stood aside.

Narrow windows let in thin shafts of light whose fingers did not poke into the corners of the cells. The rank smell of body fluids filled the air. Vester, Celsus, Janus, and Justus crouched on the floor on urine-soaked straw. Vester crawled towards them. His dirty hands gripped the bars as he pressed his bruised face against them.

'No more,' croaked Vester, 'No more.'

'Release them!' ordered Tatius. 'Take them to the infirmary.'

Ruga raised an eyebrow. He unlocked the gate. 'Get up. Follow me to the infirmary,' he snapped.

Three of the men dragged themselves to their feet and stumbled forward. Petrus took a sharp intake of breath; the men were cradling their injured arms and their faces were scarred and bruised. Their thick lips and bent noses were the results of brutal beatings. They hobbled out of the cell. Vester crawled behind them, clearly unable to stand.

'Help him!' snarled Petrus.

The soldier behind him stepped forward and carefully lifted Vester to his feet. Ruga moved to take his arm. Vester groaned at their touch. They lifted Vester and carried him out of the building. Petrus heard Ruga shouting to someone to go to the cells. A young soldier burst in and rushed towards them, gasping as he pulled a salute.

Petrus unlocked an empty cell. The floor was littered with mouldy straw, barely covering the stains from the previous occupants. Petrus dragged Prima over to the wall and clamped a chain round her ankle. She slumped to the floor as he undid the rope around her hands.

'Get some fresh straw for this cell and clean up that one. It stinks in here,' Petrus pointed at the empty cell. The soldier curled his lip as he reached for a broom and moved into Prima's cell. He began sweeping up the straw, casting furtive glances at the prefect's wife.

'Organise guards, Petrus,' Tatius ordered, 'No one is to speak to her apart from the Governor and myself. You will stand in as centurion for now.'

'Bitch!' Tatius said over his shoulder as he left the room.

Petrus gave the keys to the soldier.

'You heard what the Prefect said,' he muttered, and the soldier nodded.

Prima drew the cloak around her shoulders and leant her head against the wall, closing her eyes. Tears ran down her cheeks and dripped onto the floor.

'You killed him,' she whispered, 'He was helping me. He was my protector. I wanted to return to Rome.'

Petrus did not respond. He left the building, thinking she may get to go to Rome, but not in the manner she'd wished.

Fabius Ruga led three men towards the Principia. He stopped to speak with Petrus, telling the men to carry on to the cells and stand guard outside the building. Petrus quickly briefed him.

'Jupiter's sake!' said Ruga shaking his head, 'The barbarians I can believe, but Maximus? Why?'

'He said something about protecting Prima, she wants to return to Rome. He died before he could tell us anymore.'

Petrus did not add that they had tortured Maximus, he thought Ruga would work that out for himself. As pilus posterior, Ruga was now the most senior centurion in the fort. They went together to the gate to speak to Corvinus and Flavius. The heads of the barbarians had already been forced onto the stakes and stared accusingly at the two soldiers who were bickering over who should handle Maximus' head.

'For the love of the Gods!' shouted Petrus. He picked up Maximus' head, grimaced and forced it down onto the upright pole. Grey stinking liquid oozed out of the head and dripped onto the ground. The metallic tang of blood hit the back of Petrus' throat as he wiped his hands on his tunic. He felt angry and sad.

Corvinus spat on the ground, 'You can taste it, can't you?' he murmured.

Across the ditch, some local people stared, talking in low tones.

Petrus faced the two soldiers. 'You fought well today, both of you. The Prefect will no doubt give you both commendations. Corvinus, you got information from Maximus, that was good work. We'll find out the reasons why they did this. I imagine the Prefect will brief everyone tomorrow morning.'

Ruga selected a team of men to accompany Flavius to the forest to fetch Crixus' body.

'Bury Maximus and the barbarians,' Petrus ordered them, 'Treat Crixus with respect. I know he was only a slave, but he gave his life trying to protect the Prefect. Bring his body carefully back here.'

Petrus turned towards Corvinus, 'I want the three barbarians who went with us today. Find them and find out what they know. Were they part of it? Or were they genuinely as useless as they appeared? Use whatever methods you need to. Take four other men with you, Fabius Ruga will assign them to you. Come and report to me afterwards.'

Petrus made his way to the Treasury. He took the two pouches of money from inside his tunic and dropped them on the table in front of the Signifer.

'There's twenty Aurei there,' Petrus said, 'Give me a receipt stating that it is the money taken from the bodies of Maximus and Suasso.'

Ecdicius looked alarmed. 'Maximus? What's happened?'

Petrus sighed, 'You'll be told in due course. The Prefect will brief everyone.' He knew that word would spread quickly enough throughout the fort and the community. Flavius and Corvinus would already be sharing the details with other soldiers and Felix would have told the other slaves.

He made his way to his office. He felt suddenly weary and unable to concentrate on his report. Tatius walked into the office. He looked haggard. His injured arm was bound tightly to his chest and he moved stiffly.

'What's going on?' Tatius asked, his voice was weak.

'Soldiers have gone to retrieve the slave's body and bury the others. I've sent Corvinus to find and interrogate the three young barbarians who were with us at the start. We need to find out whether they were part of it.'

'The barbarian Suasso, he is, was, the son of that Chief, Gna, wasn't he?'

Petrus nodded.

'Then we must assume that the Chief supported this action. The Roman army must act against him.'

Petrus nodded. 'I can see to that.'

'No!' Tatius held up his hand, 'Let's get all the information we can first. If this was widespread, we may need to move against the barbarians. We, I, need to find out as much as possible from that bitch. Come with me!'

Petrus followed him to the cell. Prima lay slumped on the floor. Next to her was a plate with a crust of bread on it, an empty cup lay on its side. She did not stir when Tatius turned the key in the gate lock. The two men entered the cell. Tatius kicked her foot, she scampered away, as far as the ankle chain would allow and looked defiantly at her husband. He leant forward and punched her in the face. Her head shot back, cracking against the stone wall. She moaned. Tatius grabbed her hair and pulled her face towards him, twisting her head and pulling it upwards.

'Tell me why. I will torture you, just like your centurion!' he spat the words in her face and punched her again, breaking her nose.

Petrus winced as blood gushed from Prima's nose. She wiped her face with her sleeve. The blood continued to flow onto her cloak, merging with the dried stains from the deer's blood. She opened her mouth and gulped as she struggled to breathe. Tatius stamped on her foot. He ground his heel down onto her instep. Prima screamed, a gurgling sound like a drowning animal.

'Speak!' he hissed and reached to his belt to take his knife from the scabbard.

She gurgled, 'Fabia! Let me speak to Fabia. Let her come in here and sit with me for a short while. Then I'll tell you everything.'

He raised his hand to strike her again. She shrank back, hugging the wall, choking. He paused.

'Fabia, please,' she wailed.

Petrus realised Tatius wasn't sure what to do. He would normally have relied on Maximus' guidance and was struggling to make decisions while devastated by his wife's betrayal.

Tatius laughed harshly, 'Yes. You can say 'Goodbye' to your pathetic friend. Then I want everything.' He walked out of the cell.

'Is that wise, Sir?' Petrus said, keeping his voice low. 'They could have conspired together.'

Tatius looked at Prima as he spat, 'The Prefect of Camboglanna has a very beautiful wife, but she is not blessed with any intelligence. I can't believe that they would have involved her in this plot. She's too stupid.'

Petrus didn't think Fabia was stupid. She was calculating and manipulative. He coughed, 'What about searching them? Prima, I mean and also the Prefect's wife?'

'Not necessary. Look at her!' he pointed at Prima, 'And that pathetic pregnant creature? It's not necessary. Come to the office and I'll give you written orders to collect Fabia and bring her here.'

Petrus followed the prefect. Tatius furiously scribbled the orders on a fresh tablet. His face was drawn with worry. Petrus took the tablet and walked up to the Praetorium. Felix opened the door; he looked exhausted with unkempt hair, bloodshot eyes and grey-tinged skin. He had managed to find a clean tunic which hung loosely off his shoulders.

'The visiting prefect and his wife are in the salon,' Felix said.

Felix led him through the house, and they entered the salon; it was thick with the haze of scented oils. Fabia lay on a couch with her hands cupping her pregnant belly. She pushed herself upright as Petrus entered and opened her mouth, but she made no sound. The Prefect from Camboglanna sat at a table reading tablets as a slave girl stood behind him playing a lyre. The Prefect looked up.

'Petrus?'

'Er, I have orders here from Prefect Silvius Tatius,' he handed over the tablet, 'He has said that your wife should be allowed to visit the, the prisoner, in private. She, Julia Prima, has said she will give him all the details of the conspiracy if she can first see your wife.'

Septimus frowned as he read the tablet.

'That is if you are in agreement,' mumbled Petrus.

Fabia had risen from the couch and stood near the table. 'My darling, let me go to see her. There must be some confusion. The slave must be mistaken, she couldn't have stabbed Tatius.'

Petrus opened his mouth to say that he'd seen it with his own eyes, but Septimus spoke.

'Very well. If the Prefect wishes it. But you must take care, in your condition. You've made a remarkable recovery since this morning,' he smiled.

'I'll get my cloak,' she walked quickly out of the room.

Petrus felt awkward, unsure of what to do while he waited. The slave had begun a provocative dance in front of the Prefect, whose eyes followed her movements.

'A strange business this,' commented Septimus without taking his eyes off the slave, 'Julius Maximus had an exemplary service record from what I've heard. And the involvement of the barbarians? Makes me wonder about the allegiances of all of them, the barbarians, I mean.'

Petrus nodded. It wasn't his place to answer the prefect's questions. He wondered how much, if anything, that Tatius had told him and how much was conjecture.

'I see you're not going to tell me anything,' Septimus said, handing him the tablet with the orders on.

'I'm ready,' Fabia appeared in the doorway, pulling a thick cloak around her and tying the front of it tightly.

Petrus bowed to the Prefect and led the way out of the house. 'Watch your step as we go, Madam, some of the streets are slippery.'

'Then I shall grab onto you for support,' she smiled.

He did not return the gesture and walked slowly towards the Principia. A soldier blocked his way.

'No one is to approach the building, Sir, them's the orders,' the man explained looking embarrassed.

'I've signed orders here from the Prefect saying that this woman can visit the prisoner!' Petrus held out the tablet to the man who took it and turned it round and round in his hands, peering down at it.

'Mmm, I see,' he stepped aside and handed the tablet back.

Petrus shrugged; the man clearly couldn't read; he had held the tablet upside down. He led Fabia into the building where another man was leaning against the bars staring at the woman chained to the wall. She lay on her side with her eyes closed. Petrus waved the tablet in the soldier's direction.

'Orders from the Prefect. This woman is to be allowed in to see the prisoner. In private. Get Fabius Ruga and tell him to wait outside.'

The man nodded, handed Petrus the keys and left the building. Petrus unlocked the gate. Prima opened her eyes. Her red face was puffy and swollen, her nose was pushed sideways, and she still had blood dribbling down her chin. She gurgled as she fought to breathe through her mouth. Seeing Fabia, she scrambled into a sitting position and stretched out her arms.

Fabia rushed over, dropped to her knees and hugged her friend tightly. She held the injured woman's face in her hands and wiped some of the blood away with her cloak. Both women wept. Petrus locked the gate and left the building. He found Ruga hovering outside. He beckoned to him, and they walked quickly round the outside of the building and stood near one of the windows. Petrus tried to steady and quieten his breathing as he hugged the wall and listened to the sounds leaking out of the room. Ruga followed his lead and pressed his cheek to the wall near one of the window slits. The voices floated towards them.

'I hate Tatius! I hate him!' gurgled Prima, struggling to talk.

'I hate Septimus too,' Fabia wept, 'I think it's the lot of Prefect's wives, to hate their husbands.'

'Tatius is going to kill me. Even if I tell them everything, I will still die, at his hand or that of another. We shall never be together.'

There was sobbing.

'What happened?'

Prima's gurgling voice drifted out of the window towards Petrus, 'Tatius was supposed to die in a hunting accident. We'd even practiced it, that time you came hunting with us. After the accident, I would be able to return to Rome to my family, as a widow with my children. We had it planned. Two soldiers overheard Maximus and I talking. They blackmailed him. He had to kill them. He tried to frame some holy men for the murders. Tatius is stupid and he believed the holy men were the killers. It was only Petrus who insisted they had captured the wrong men.'

'The soldiers may have told two whores from the brothel, so they had to be silenced. They killed them that morning you went back to Camboglanna, just before daylight. The barbarians then rode ahead of your escort, pretending to scout ahead as normal and met the group later in the afternoon. Maximus underestimated that damned man Petrus. He realised that the people who killed the soldiers had also killed the whores. He'd found a witness.

Four soldiers vaguely matched the witness' description and had the opportunity to kill the girls, so Maximus tortured them, trying to get them to confess. They would've confessed eventually, to stop the pain, or died. That would've shut Petrus up. But they wouldn't die quickly, those four soldiers, and Petrus was beginning to suspect the barbarians. Even when he was taken off the investigation and threatened with demotion. He was relentless. And so close to the truth. He'd started questioning two of the barbarians. He was dangerous and had to be killed.'

There was a long pause and the sound of weeping.

'When you got pregnant, I was so happy for you. But then Septimus decided to ask the Governor for an early return to Rome. The Governor will be here tomorrow, making a decision about Septimus' request. Why would he refuse it? When my husband told Petrus to go on the hunt with him, it was an opportunity to kill them both, Tatius and Petrus. We planned to make it look like they were attacked by bandits. I love you. I couldn't be separated from you.'

Petrus strained to hear Fabia's reply.

'It was me. All of it. Maximus was doing it for me. We're from the same clan.'

'I can't bear it, being separated from you.'

'You must. You must face life without me. You'll have your baby to love, and the baby will love you. I'm going to die. Tatius will have me killed.'

They fell silent.

'I love you,' said Prima.

'I love you.'

'We will be together in the afterlife.'

There was silence.

Realisation hit Petrus like a blow to the chest.

He ran.

He flung open the door to the building and grabbed the bars as he fumbled with the keys in the lock.

'No! Stop!' Petrus shouted.

Ruga arrived at his shoulder. Fabia took her hands away from Prima's face. Prima was choking. There were bubbles of bloody foam at the corner of her mouth. She gasped for breath. Black snot dribbled from her nose. She clawed at her throat with her hands, scratching red marks on her white skin. Petrus rushed in, pushed Fabia roughly away and grabbed Prima. He forced her mouth open and stuck his fingers into the pink frothy mess desperately probing for what she had eaten. Prima bit him. He grunted and instinctively pulled his hand back; he felt her teeth scrape along his fingers.

'Bitch!' he muttered.

Prima began to shudder as he held her. Her body convulsed and she threw her head back, her eyes wide open. She went rigid in his hands. He shook her; her head fell sideways, her dead eyes stared at the wall. He let her body slide to the floor.

He pulled Fabia round to face him and shouted, 'What did you give her? What?'

She smiled and shook her head. Petrus grabbed her arm and pulled her to her feet. He was shaking with rage and fear. 'Tell me!'

She shrugged. Petrus clenched his fist, then pushed her aside and walked out of the cell, locking the barred gates behind him. 'Ruga, stay with her!' He thrust the keys into Ruga's hands.

Ruga was horrified, but he nodded.

Fabia knelt next to her friend's body, she stroked her hair, kissed her cheeks and whispered to her.

'She's dead!' Petrus blurted out as he walked into Tatius' office.

'What?!' Tatius leapt to his feet and charged out of the room.

Tatius walked up to the bars of the cell.

Fabia looked up at him. 'She's gone,' she smiled.

Tatius snatched the keys from Ruga's hand and unlocked the gate. He grabbed his wife's body and put his hand near her mouth and nose. He muttered to himself as he placed his hand over her eyes, drew her eyelids closed and let her body slide to the floor.

'What was it?' he shouted, at Fabia 'What did you give her?' He grabbed her by the shoulders and shook her, 'What?' He raised his hand to strike her.

'My baby!' she screamed.

Tatius froze. He lowered his hand and let go of her. She slid to the floor.

'Prima had it with her, inside her cloak. Look!' She pointed to the hood of Prima's cloak. Inside was a tiny pocket. It could have concealed a tablet or poison.

Tatius scowled, 'You stay in here. I blame you for this!' he waved his arm in the direction of Prima's body.

He locked the gate behind him. Fabia sat holding her friend's hand.

'Sir,' murmured Petrus, 'Should we search her? She may also have poison on her.'

'She's a pregnant woman. She wouldn't kill her unborn child. You must know that!'

Petrus didn't argue. The Prefect was in a volatile state.

'Silvius Tatius?' Fabia's voice behind them made them turn back to look at her, 'I loved your wife, and I would have done anything to be with her.'

Fabia's hand moved to her mouth. She took her hand away from her face and smiled. Blood red foam forced its way through her lips and onto her chin. Black snot ran from her nose. Petrus snatched the keys from Tatius, desperate to unlock the gate. He flung it open and ran forward. Tatius was at his side. Fabia threw her head back and laughed hysterically. Petrus grabbed her and tried to force her mouth open. She choked and her body spasmed. Her body went slack, she groaned and went still. Petrus laid her next to Prima. He felt a sob rise in his throat and turned aside to hide it with a cough.

'For fuck's sake!' shouted Tatius as he strode out of the cell, 'Don't speak about this to anyone,' he pointed at the two centurions, 'I mean it!' He stormed out of the building.

Petrus and Ruga looked at each other. Ruga shrugged. Petrus was reeling in shock. He was angry that Prima had escaped justice and felt sure that Fabia had been part of the conspiracy. He locked the gate and went outside with Ruga. He ordered the guards to remain where they were and not let anyone enter the room without the Prefect's permission. Petrus was disappointed. The Prefect's arrogance had allowed the two women to die rather than face justice. Tatius seemed incapable of making proper decisions without Maximus to guide him.

Petrus walked with Ruga to the stables and gathered together sixteen men from Ruga's century, telling them to get ready to ride out. 'Full weaponry and armour!' Ruga ordered.

'Aurelius Petrus!' Tatius' tired voice behind him made him turn. 'Walk with me.' Tatius began walking back to his house and Petrus hurried to catch up with him.

'I've told Septimus what happened. He's beside himself. This was my mistake, allowing them to be together in private. You suggested searching them, but I thought I knew better. You were listening outside the cell windows, weren't you? You and Ruga?' he sounded weary as he raised a hand to silence Petrus' protests, 'I'm not going to berate you for it. What did you hear?'

'Prima and Maximus conspired to kill you in a hunting accident. That trip we took the other day was a practice run. Prima saw how easy it would be when Fabia pointed her bow at you.' Petrus frowned as he said this. 'Prima wanted to return to her family in Rome as a widow so that she could be there with Fabia. They loved each other the way some women do. The two soldiers, Faustus and Drusus, were on duty outside your house when they overheard your wife and Maximus talking. They began blackmailing Maximus. The barbarians helped him kill them and then Maximus framed the holy men for the murders.

When I suggested that the two soldiers may have spoken to the whores at Sylva's place, they were also killed. They were planning to frame Vester and his roommates for those murders. Eventually Maximus would've got a confession from them or killed them trying. The plan, hers and Maximus' to kill you, was brought forward when Septimus requested an early return to Rome due to Fabia's pregnancy. They felt they had to kill me, as they thought I was too close to the truth and was too determined to solve the crimes, even when I was threatened with demotion.'

Tatius turned his face away from Petrus, red with embarrassment.

'With the Governor's arrival tomorrow, they had to move today. So they planned the ambush in the forest, aiming to kill you, me, and the soldiers and make it look like bandits.'

Tatius shook his head, 'That's why Maximus wanted you demoted and sent back to Fanum Cocidi,' he took a deep breath, 'I knew they loved each other intimately. But this! Was Fabia part of it, do you think?'

Uncomfortable, Petrus shrugged, 'I think she was part of it. Prima spoke as if she was telling Fabia something for the very first time. But I think Prima guessed we were listening and was trying to exonerate her. She probably didn't think Fabia would kill herself, as she was pregnant. It was Fabia who gave Prima the poison and then took her own life.'

Tatius' head snapped up. 'I should have let you search her. She showed us where she said Prima had stored the poison. I believed her,' he sighed. 'I also thought that Fabia wouldn't harm her unborn child. What do I know about women and the way they think, eh?' He paused, 'We've been saved the bother of what to do with Prima. I'll have her buried in the cemetery. I must think of what to tell her family, back in Rome. I don't know what Septimus' wishes are.'

'I want you to deal with the three young barbarians. You've sent men to find them, haven't you? Find out what they know. I want Ruga to take the sixteen men you're readying. He can go to Camboglanna tonight. In the morning he can find out what Chief Gna knows. I can't believe his son would have acted in this way without his father's blessing. Either way, Ruga will kill Gna or some of his people. It must be made clear that they can't challenge Rome in this way. Send Ruga to me and I'll give him those orders. I want you here when the Governor arrives tomorrow. Write up your reports. I assume you have all the previous days' tablets somewhere?'

Petrus nodded. They'd reached the Principia and Petrus moved to go to his office.

'And Petrus?'

'Yes, Sir?'

'Listen carefully, I will not be repeating myself. I should've listened to you in the first place. You were right at every step. You had worked it all out. I was wrong.'

Petrus nodded.

Tatius smiled wearily, 'And you did well today, in the forest.'

He walked away.

Petrus completed his notes and gathered them all together locking them in the chest in his office. He suddenly felt exhausted and made his way to his room where he lay back on his bed and closed his eyes.

A sharp knock at the door roused him from a deep sleep.

Boga entered the room. 'There's a soldier at the door to see you.'

Petrus rubbed his eyes and splashed water on his face before grabbing his cloak from the end of the bed and striding out into the afternoon sun. Corvinus was leaning against the wall with four other men. He pushed himself upright as Petrus walked over to them.

'Aurelius Petrus, we found the three barbarians at their house, near the tavern. They were reluctant to open the door to us, but I told them we'd break it down if they didn't. Marcus here was ready to kick it in.' He indicated one of his companions, a large man with bulging shoulders, thick arms, and legs like tree trunks.

'They were ashamed of their performance this morning, thinking we were going to beat them for not being able to track deer. Marcus got one of them up against the wall.' He grinned, 'I thought the barbarian was going to shit himself. They told us that Maximus approached them yesterday and instructed them to be at the fort at dawn for the hunt. They had no idea what would be required but didn't dare to say "no".

'They were recruited by Suasso from his home area about a month ago. They were surprised that he'd picked them in the first place, as they had never been interested in working for the Romans. They're not very bright to be honest. I'm confident they're telling the truth. Maximus would've had to keep this whole thing to himself and just a few others, just those three barbarians we killed, I reckon, don't you? The more people involved the harder it is to keep it secret.'

'Yes, I think you're right. Good job, all of you. Now go back to your duties.'

Corvinus nodded and they walked away. Petrus returned to his room and lay down.

Boga knocked at the door with his evening meal, poured him some wine and then hovered near Petrus' bed. Petrus looked at him and waited.

'Er, do you know what will happen to me? I mean now that Maximus is dead?' Boga asked.

Petrus hadn't thought about the impact on Boga. He had been Maximus' slave for a long time.

'I'm not sure, Boga,' he began, 'I'll make some enquiries. You should just carry on as normal for now.'

He wanted to reassure the slave, but he didn't want to give him unrealistic expectations. If there was no will, the slave would become part of Maximus' possessions and belong to the army. Anything might happen to him.

Boga nodded, 'Shall I wake you later?'

'Cocidius' sake!' He'd forgotten about checking on the gatekeepers, 'Thank you, yes, at the seventh hour.'

Boga left the room. Petrus lay down on his bed and tried to sleep.

Petrus was bathed in sweat even though the room was cold. He'd been dreaming about the fight in the forest, only it had been Petrus whose guts were spilled onto the forest floor. He flailed his arms as Boga shook him awake and he murmured something unintelligible as Boga handed him a lit torch. He pulled on his boots and made his way down the street in the silent darkness. An owl screeched and he grasped the hilt of his knife, mumbling a prayer to Cocidius, hoping the bird did not herald more death. He climbed the first two steps of the tower. The voices of Rufus and Pius reached down the steps. He paused to listen. They were talking about Maximus. He continued climbing, careless of the noise he made.

Rufus stood at the top of the steps. He saluted and took a step back, allowing Petrus to move alongside him. Pius turned.

'Just checking on you,' Petrus said, 'I'm glad to see you're awake.'

'Y… Yes Sir,' stammered Pius.

Petrus left them and returned to his barracks. He collapsed onto his bed and fell asleep. In his dreams, he pushed Maximus' head onto the stake, over and over.

XIX – Dies Iovis

Petrus rose just before daybreak. The sky drizzled cold rain onto all the men during parade. Tatius addressed them about the incidents from the day before. He blamed Maximus and the barbarians for the conspiracy to kill him, avoiding any mention of Prima. He praised the two soldiers and Petrus for their actions in the Gladed Forest.

After Tatius had dismissed the men, he asked Petrus to report to his office.

'I checked on the gatekeepers last night, Sir, at the seventh hour. I am pleased to report that they were awake and alert,' Petrus began.

'Fine. Keep doing it for at least two weeks. Maybe they've got the message. It's a nice little number gatekeeping, they don't have any other duties. You'd think they would want to keep their jobs. I didn't mention Prima or Septimus' wife this morning, as I don't think the men will know how they died.'

Petrus didn't say that the whole fort was already talking about it. He just nodded.

'I'll organise a quiet burial for Prima later this afternoon, and see what Septimus wants to do. He's beside himself at the loss of the unborn child. I told him she'd hidden the poison well.'

'I'll go with Aquilinus to check on the four men who were in the cells. I imagine they're still in the infirmary.'

'Mmm, yes. Maximus had convinced me they were guilty of the whores' murders. I gave him a free hand to get confessions. I'm sure they'll recover well in Arsenios' care. Then they can have light duties for a while. I'll leave you to liaise with Aquilinus about that.'

Petrus nodded. 'I also need to see whether Maximus had a will and go to the brothel to tell Sylva what happened.'

'Very well. Then familiarise yourself with the centurion's duties, you'll be acting centurion for now. I'm sending some of Aquilinus' men to hunt a boar for the Governor's feast. We'll have to move quickly to be prepared for his arrival.' Tatius waved him away.

Petrus hid a smile, the Prefect still wanted everything to be perfect for the Governor.

Petrus made his way to the brothel. In the empty salon, the girl was curled up asleep on one of the couches. Her smock had risen up, exposing the pale skin of her bare buttocks. He watched her for a few moments. She was smiling as she slept, and her lips were moving. He hoped her dreams were filled with pleasurable things away from her life in the brothel.

He spoke, 'Good morning.'

Her eyes flew open, she jerked upright and pulled her smock down over her knees, looking worried.

'I am sorry, Sir. Who can I get for you?' she asked.

'Get Sylva for me.' He threw himself down on a couch.

The girl ran from the room. He heard doors banging and raised voices.

Sylva strode into the room. She smelled of sleep and her clothes were crumpled.

'Petrus?'

'Sit down Sylva, and I'll tell you what happened to Cara and Metta.'

She did as he asked. He told her everything about why and how the women were killed, although he thought she'd probably already heard most of it and figured out the rest.

'Thank you for confirming things for me, Petrus.' She had tears in her eyes as she spoke.

Perhaps she really had cared about the two sisters.

'Those poor girls. I never trusted that Centurion, you know,' she said.

Petrus smiled to himself. Sylva, along with lots of others, wanted to distance herself from anything to do with Maximus.

'Will you get a message to her parents? Perhaps via Gamigoni? I want them to know the murder is solved and the perpetrators are all dead,' Petrus said.

'I will. It's the least I can do.'

He walked through the fort gate towards the Records room. Manius did not look up from his work.

'What can I do for you?' he asked.

'Here is the receipt for the money found on the bodies of Maximus and Suasso,' Petrus gave the tablet to Manius.

The librarius glanced at the receipt and then placed it on a pile behind him, 'I'll get to it later,' he muttered, 'Anything else?'

'Did Centurion Maximus leave a will?'

Manius rose to his feet. He moved some tablets around on a shelf and then returned to the table with one in his hand. He broke the seal and began reading it to himself.

He tapped the tablet with his fingernail. 'He gives Boga his freedom and leaves him eight hundred denarii. The rest of his account, his house, the one he built in the vicus, and all his belongings are left to a woman called Dagvaldia. It says here she's living there, in his house. They have three children. He calls her his wife. That's unofficial of course. She won't be entitled to his pension.' He turned the tablet round to show Petrus.

'That's a lot of money to leave Boga. I'll go and tell him. He also knows where the woman Dagvaldia lives, he's been there. What's the balance of Maximus' savings account?'

Manius began shuffling the tablets about, he picked one up, 'Currently, three thousand nine hundred denarii.'

Petrus whistled, 'She'll be a rich woman.'

'He's got some debts too,' continued Manius, 'I'll have to look those up, but I'm pretty sure, even after Boga has his money, there'll still be more than two thousand for the woman. Enough money to cost her her life, Petrus, just like those two poor girls.'

Petrus scowled. He didn't correct Manius, as the man had a point about the woman's safety. 'I might suggest to her that she leaves the money here and just takes what she needs as and when.'

Arsenios, the Physician, approached Petrus and Aquilinus as they entered the Infirmary.

'You bastards really worked them over, didn't you?' he snarled, 'They've got dislocated shoulders, broken ribs, and they're covered in bruises! That kid Vester's got a broken ankle and no toenails!' Arsenios pointed at the sleeping men, 'He's probably finished in the army. Did you enjoy pulling their teeth out?'

'Maximus was trying to beat confessions out of them,' muttered Aquilinus, 'He'd convinced me they were guilty.'

They approached the men's beds.

Celsus stirred, wincing as he struggled to sit up. 'Thank you for saving us,' his voice was weak. His face was swollen and black with bruises, several of his teeth were missing.

Ashamed Petrus said, 'Maximus was trying to get you to confess to the murders of the women from the brothel. We know you didn't do it.'

Celsus laughed bitterly, 'Covering up his own dirty work. I heard you killed him.'

Petrus nodded, 'What were you doing after you left the tavern that day and why wouldn't you tell me?'

Celsus took a deep breath, 'Women' he whispered. 'We were meeting some women.'

'For sex?' sighed Petrus.

Celsus shook his head and moaned, 'No. We… we've… we've been selling them food.'

'Food?' spluttered Aquilinus.

'We, er, we didn't want to get caught. We took a sack of grain when we were unloading it for the stores. We sell it or give it in exchange.'

Aquilinus opened his mouth, but Petrus put his hand on the man's arm to quieten him. 'Exchange for what?' he asked.

Celsus shrugged, 'Sex sometimes, that's what the argument with the local men was about, they knew we were having their women.'

'Idiots!' spat Aquilinus, clenching his fists by his sides, 'You've been stealing from stores and it nearly cost you your lives. Vester may be finished as a soldier if his ankle doesn't mend properly.'

Celsus didn't reply.

Aquilinus growled, 'I want all the details. How did you manage it? Where's the sack hidden? It's not in your room. Was the librarius involved?'

Aquilinus' voice followed Petrus out of the infirmary. He couldn't hear Celsus' mumbled replies. He was leaving Aquilinus to it, that investigation was not his responsibility.

Petrus went back to his quarters where he saw that Boga had washed his spare clothes and underwear, they were hung in front of the open window. The cool breeze tugged gently at his tunics. Boga was cleaning Petrus' weaponry.

Petrus smiled. 'Boga, put that down and listen to me for a moment.'

Alarmed, Boga dropped the shield he was holding, it clattered to the floor; a cloth hung limply in his hand.

'It's good news. Maximus left a will. He sets you free and names you as one of his heirs. You'll be a rich man. He's left you eight hundred denarii!' Realising he needed to explain how much that was, he said, 'That's eight years' salary for a soldier Boga, a lot of money. You're a free man!' He emphasised these last words.

Boga's lips trembled, 'A free man?' He picked up the shield and placed it on the table alongside the cloth. 'What do I do now?'

Petrus was surprised at the slave's reaction to the news. 'How long have you been a slave Boga?'

'Since Maximus became a centurion, and before then. He bought me from another Centurion, who was retiring to Rome. That was many years ago. I was little more than a boy when I was enslaved.'

'Where is your home area?'

'I am Dobunni. My father joined some rebels fighting against the Romans. All our family were sold into slavery, my brothers and sisters, my mother. There's nothing for me with the Dobunni.'

'There are other freed men in the vicus, men who've made their own way. Some have set up thriving businesses, perhaps you should go and talk to them.'

'Must I leave immediately?'

Petrus tried to sound reassuring, 'As far as I'm concerned you can stay here, carry on as you were, but, freeman or not,' he emphasised the words, 'I can't pay you. You can stay at least until Maximus is replaced. That'll be several days. I'll need you to take me to Dagvaldia's house. Maximus has left his property to her.'

'I will. When do you want to go there?'

'After the governor has arrived. Tomorrow.'

Boga nodded, picked up the shield and resumed his work.

There was a sudden commotion outside. Petrus ran to the gate where soldiers were crowding to watch as Septimus carried his wife's body and laid her in the back of a cart. Her face had been cleaned and pale powder had been smoothed across her cheeks. Septimus covered her with a funeral shroud. Two soldiers carried Prima's body wrapped in a sheet and placed it alongside Fabia. Tatius stood aside and watched them load spades and masonry equipment onto the cart.

Septimus mounted the horse which stood ready for him and signalled to the driver of the cart. Eight soldiers walked alongside the cart with Septimus riding at the rear.

'They're burning them and burying their ashes in the cemetery,' Tatius said. 'I've instructed the masonry immune to carve only her name and the date into Prima's headstone. Septimus wants him to make a fine memorial for Fabia and the baby, one that befits a Roman lady. He can't believe she was involved in the plot. We'll see what the Governor thinks.'

A group of men were approaching the gate.

'That'll be Ruga,' Petrus said.

Ruga dismounted and walked towards them. 'We burned the homes of Suasso, Albiso, and Luci. Their wives, children and wider families - brothers, sisters, cousins are now dependent on Chief Gna. He will have to find somewhere for them to live. Maybe he'll have them all in his compound. He offered his own life to stop us from destroying more homes. I'm confident that he had nothing to do with the plot. He said he knew Suasso had been restless and unhappy, but didn't know why.'

'Good job,' said Tatius, 'and you're back in time for the Governor's arrival. He's due to get here this afternoon. The slaves are already roasting a boar,' Tatius turned on his heel and left.

Petrus walked towards the Principia. He heard someone running behind him and was immediately on his guard, he grasped his pugio and turned to face any danger. Felix trotted towards him clutching a bundle of clothes and some tablets. He had a smile fixed to his face, but his eyes were wide, and he looked frightened.

'Felix! Where are you off to?' asked Petrus.

'Aurelius Petrus, I'm coming to see you, to ask you to come with me to the treasury. I'm a free man. Silvius Tatius has given me my freedom because I saved his life, and he's given me some money.' He handed the tablets to Petrus.

One of the tablets stated that Felix was to be given a thousand denarii. The other was a declaration stating that Felix was a freed slave. They were both signed by the Prefect and sealed with his ring. He handed the tablets back to Felix and wondered whether Tatius was trying to get rid of witnesses to the killings in the forest. Ever the politicians, both Tatius and Septimus would be rewriting the events of the last two days. The prefects' accounts would put them both in a good light.

Petrus smiled, 'Let's go.'

The Signifer raised an eyebrow when he saw Felix's tablet.

'Do you wish to take it all now?' he asked Felix. 'That's a lot of money, you could be robbed and killed for less.'

Felix hesitated.

'I'll take twenty-five denarii for now,' he said, 'I can come and get the money whenever I want now that I'm free, can't I?' He looked uncertain.

'Well yes, within reason,' murmured the Signifer as he counted out the coins and pushed them across the table towards Felix. 'Sign or make your mark.' He gave a tablet to Felix.

Felix peered at the tablet. His lips moved as he read. Petrus waited.

Felix nodded and made his mark in the wax, then handed it to Petrus, who confirmed the amounts were correct and scribbled his own signature as the witness. They walked outside.

'What are you going to do now Felix?' asked Petrus.

'I'm taking the name Aurelius Tatius Felix in honour of the Emperor and my former master. I've some ideas for business in the vicus and am going to make some enquiries roundabouts.'

'Maximus' slave, Boga, has also been granted his freedom. Perhaps you and he could work together. Either way, I wish you well.'

'Thank you, Aurelius Petrus. I shall look out for Boga around. I hope to see you again in the future. Perhaps we'll do business together,' Felix said as they walked outside the treasury.

'Perhaps we will. Go well Aurelius Tatius Felix.'

Felix set off at a fast pace heading for the east gate. He did not look back.

Acknowledgements

Without the help and support of my writing group 'Imaginary Friends' I would never have completed this novel. Their thoughtful comments and encouragement were invaluable.

My husband, Phil, has been a strong supporter of my work and allows me the space to write. Thanks go to all those at Northodox who have worked so hard to get it into print, in particular my Editor Amy and also James.

NORTHODOX PRESS

SUBMISSIONS

CONTEMPORARY
CRIME & THRILLER
FANTASY
LGBTQ+
ROMANCE
YOUNG ADULT
SCI-FI & HORROR
HISTORICAL
LITERARY

SUBMISSIONS@NORTHODOX.CO.UK

SUBMISSIONS

CALLING ALL NORTHERN AUTHORS!

DO YOU LIVE IN OR COME FROM NORTHERN ENGLAND?

DO YOU HAVE AN INTERESTING STORY TO TELL?

Email submissions@northodox.co.uk

- ☐ The first 3 chapters OR 5,000 words
- ☐ 1 page synopsis
- ☐ Author bio (tell us where you're based)

* No non-fiction, poetry, or memoirs

SUBMISSIONS@NORTHODOX.CO.UK

FIND US ON SOCIAL MEDIA

www.northodox.co.uk

f @northodoxpress

⊙ @northodoxpressofficial

𝕏 @northodoxpress

♪ @northodoxpress

● www.northodox.co.uk

A DEATH

ON THE HOME FRONT

THEY SURVIVED THE WAR - BUT ARE THEY
PREPARED FOR THE FIGHT AT HOME?

JENNY DENT

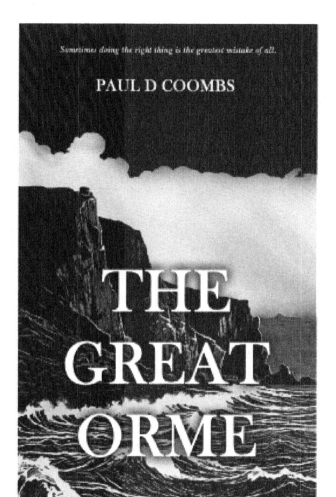

Sometimes doing the right thing is the greatest mistake of all.

PAUL D COOMBS

THE GREAT ORME

OUT OF
HUMAN
SIGHT

A HISTORICAL MYSTERY

SOPHIE PARKES

Printed in Great Britain
by Amazon